I0676508

Valentine and the Undead

Terry Hornby

Published by Terry Hornby, 2023.

This is a work of fiction. Similarities to real people, places, or events are entirely coincidental.

VALENTINE AND THE UNDEAD

First edition. October 2, 2023.

Copyright © 2023 Terry Hornby.

ISBN: 978-0645849141

Written by Terry Hornby.

Also by Terry Hornby

Valentine and the Devil
Valentine and the Undead
Sally's Got A Taser
Valentine and the Prince
Valentine and the Empire

To Glenda

My heart's companionMy best friendThe love of my life

Thank you for putting up with the zombies

Valentine and the Undead

Chapter 1

Last night my mates pulled me out of a drunken bar fight before random strangers kicked the living snot out of me. Again.

This morning my boss wants to see me, probably to get me to smarten up. Again.

I have skinned knuckles, assorted bruises, nausea and a bad attitude.

The hangover was not helped by shiny surfaces in the commander's office; my boss placed his scarred and weather beaten hands palm down on his desk. His shiny, clean desk. In his shiny, clean office.

No grime anywhere, I could even see the corners of the room. Whatever happened to good old dirt and bundles of rags?

Whatever happened to my life?

"Are you with us yet, Val? Starting to come good?" asked the captain, the man behind the desk.

"Yeah, I'm right," I lied. "Couldn't be better." Possibly a slight sway, hard to tell with the room spinning off and on.

"Enjoyed your time off then?" he asked. "Blew out a few of the cobwebs?"

"What do you want, Magic?" I asked, "I could do with a lie down very soon, and if you keep me talking it'll be on your floor. No promises, mind. Just thought I'd give you a bit of warning."

He took a blaster out of his desk drawer and placed it on the table, now we were getting somewhere. Nothing draws the eye like a big gun on a bare desk. This one was a big pistol, better than the gunpowder items we used in the old Watch; much, much better. I'd used one on an enemy quite recently – an ex-enemy. Very ex.

When someone sticks one under my nose I become fully focussed.

"Give it back to Teddy Boy, will you?" he instructed, pushing the weapon across the desk. "I can't keep returning it. The Man in Black is beginning to wonder where Ted gets all his firepower, I haven't been game enough to tell him it's the same weapon and I break regulations by giving it back. Tell Ted if it's confiscated again he'll lose it. For real this time."

No worries, I thought. Ted knows the rules, no blasters on board the spaceship; no projectile weapons at all. The internal walls were light construction and a blaster round could go through walls and even a deck or two. This made the Chief Trader a bit antsy in case a stray shot took out the dinner tray.

But Ted does love a shooty thing, so he would still walk around with a blaster and I couldn't care less. After saving my life at least once I could give the lovely man a bit of slack; not too much, and only when it suited me. I may be generous but I'm not an idiot.

"You're an idiot, Sergeant Valentine," commented my captain. "You did your party trick again last night. A bar on Deck 3."

That explained the black eye and split lip. "How'd I do?" I was curious about my survival.

"The usual - bloody useless," he replied. "Wallace and H'nuth dragged you out of the bar. Again." He sat back in his chair and looked at me. "Well, you've had your recreation, time to earn a living. Got a job for my favourite sergeant, I want you to lead a Security detail to escort some traders on a special little job."

He paused while I belched a little; there was a moment when we both wondered if anything would accompany the belch, a very pregnant pause. It passed, he took a breath and continued. "We're in orbit around a planet – now there's a phrase I never thought I'd say – anyway, this planet has some technology the Traders want. Apparently there is a better device for communication, better than sticking one of these Translator beads in your ear."

He held up a small, black jewel like object. When stuck in the ear they learned the audible language coming in and, eventually, translated it into something you could comprehend. The drawback was you still spoke with your own language so everybody in the conversation had to have a bead.

"When?" I croaked. Next week would be good, I thought.

He smiled an evil smile, "Two hours from now," the vile man. "Take a reliable corporal and a few of the NightWatch, you'll be babysitting a delegation of about twenty-odd other mixed species traders, technicians and whatnot. The shuttle has room for thirty so fill up the remaining seats anyway you wish."

Great, I get to go off into space again in another stupid little rocket thingy. Spaceships give me the heebie-jeebies; just thinking about being surrounded by lots of nothing causes my bowels to quiver, and now was not the time for quivering bowels.

"Who's leading the delegation? Who's boss?" Someone gentle and caring, I hoped, someone with compassion for a lonely guardsman down on his luck and feeling poorly.

He stood up and leaned across the desk, looking me square in my bloodshot eyes, "You are."

This gave me a start, "What! Get out of it! Me? Come on, Charles, get serious. I need someone to tell me what to do! I can't lead a delegation watchamacallit. If you'll cast your mind back a few months it wasn't too long ago I was just a humble footslogger in the Night Watch for a city with hot and cold open sewers in the middle of the street. Our idea of progress was if no one died on patrol. And I was just a flunky, not even a corporal, certainly not a thinker!"

He came around the desk and put an arm around my shoulder, I'm pretty sure he could feel me quivering and it wasn't just the alcohol I'd consumed. I can run and I can fight, I can shoot a bit and drink to world standards - but I did not want another independent command. Gamma 5 cured me of such aspirations, people who follow me tend to get dead.

Before I could marshal any further arguments, I realised his arm around the shoulder was not there for sympathy but to turn me around and prod me out of his office.

"Val," he said, opening the door, "You're hitting the grog a bit much; I understand why but you're no good to me, no good to anyone if you keep it up. Now, I need you to lay off the turps and learn about command. This exercise is a walk in the park, just babysitting; do you the world of good to be away from higher authority for a while."

I was outside his office, in the corridor but still hoping for a better resolution. I turned to him with a few good pearls on my lips but he cut me off. "To be quite honest, I am knee deep in this investigation about the murder of the last Chief Trader, it needs careful handling, baby steps. Subtlety. And you, Valentine, are not a subtle man. If I want this investigation to proceed I have to get you off this ship, otherwise you will come across a clue – because you are good at finding clues – and then kill someone in a fight – because you are very good at killing. Probably several someones and probably very messily. Subtle you ain't. Get to work, sergeant." He shut the door.

I stood in the corridor for a couple of beats and then lurched off to find some place to be sick. Better still, someone to be sick over. I am a mean, vindictive man.

****

My shoulder was continually being nudged, slowly awareness returned to my sleep starved brain, I became conscious I was sitting, leaning with my head on a window, mouth open, slobber and drool gently running down the glass plane. My bottom lip appeared to be stuck to the glass.

"Hnnh," I said, clarity above all. "Whassit? Wa'..." Eventually I managed to synchronise all my faculties. "What?" I demanded.

Beside me Right Honourable said, "We've landed, Fearless Leader." He got up from his seat and moved out of my vision, after a few more moments I clambered to my feet and followed him down the aisle and out the rear door of the shuttle. Mercifully I had slept through the flight; the nap plus a handful of painkillers had restored me to a semblance of normality.

Looking around I spotted Right Honourable marshalling the security guards he had chosen for the trip. I had found him lounging on a bunk after my interview with the captain and so had unerringly picked him to share my misery. "We'll take Teddy Boy, he needs a bit of time off the ship to let his weapons infractions die down. And bring Meataxe, in my present state he's the only one I can stand beside and feel clean and sober. You pick the rest, I'll be in the shuttle." I had then found a seat on the flying coffin, scoffed some water and the painkillers and dropped off to sleep. Right honourable did the work while I dozed - rank can be a bitch sometimes.

I was interested in who else he had ordered to be on this babysitting escapade – I spotted Wallace, H'nuth, Lonely and a couple of newbies. I wasn't sure I wanted to see Wallace and his mate just yet. Embarrassment mainly, never a good thought to know someone has seen you at your utter worst. Being pulled out of a stupid bar fight while drunk and filthy would certainly rate as a low point in my career. Maybe I was becoming a drunk, maybe Magic was right. He usually is, the bastard.

Lonely could be useful, he was born on the big spaceship and was more comfortable around technology than any NightWatch veteran from Earth.

Earth. Our planet had a name, our home, our lost home. Bloody Archbishop Dominic.

I strolled over and asked Right Honourable why he bought the two newbies. "To fetch and carry, of course, dear boy, to fetch and carry" he said before elegantly gliding across to chat up one of the female delegates. Made sense to me.

We were all ushered into a small room with raked seating, like a theatre. I sat at the back and told Right Honourable to set the guard roster, do the organising, see to the men and so on. He asked what I would be doing. "Bugger all, mate. I'm management," I replied, slumping into my seat.

After a few moments the light dimmed and a small spot illuminated the speaker's podium. Into the circle of light strode a very tall and cadaverous looking alien - I was sick of seeing new aliens by now – this character was about seven feet tall, pale white skin, big eyes and long, delicate hands and fingers. He was dressed from neck to feet in a long red robe trimmed with bands of yellow around the base and sleeves. Looked like a chorus member for a bad Greek play.

"Good afternoon, ladies and gentlemen," he said. "I know you can all understand me because you have your Translator beads inserted. May I ask you to please remove them?" He stopped and waited, we all looked at each other and eventually all eyes began drifting back to me, sitting high up, all alone in the back row. I wanted to look behind me, too, but realised it would not be the best message to send to the troops. After a couple of beats I reached up and took out the Translator bead, everyone else in my party – my party! – did the same.

Our tall and pale geek down the front said a few more words which I couldn't understand. No surprise there but some of the folks in front of me jumped a little and said something back to Stretch. I sat there watching them have a brief conversation thinking, great, so you can speak a few languages, so some of the folk don't need beads to talk with, so what.

Then Stretch repeated the exercise with a few other racial types from the ship; I was impressed when Lonely got in on the act but when H'nuth and our host had a gabfest I was seriously stunned. I can rattle on a bit in a few tongues but this guy was apparently fluent in a bucket load of languages.

His eyes rose to meet mine, he gabbled a bit and I responded by saying, "Sorry to disappoint, oh tall streak of misery, but I have no idea what you are saying." I smiled my best smile and sat back. He said a few more words after looking at Right Honourable who was far more courteous in his responses; he's a better diplomat than me.

This back and forth took a few more minutes and I could feel my eyelids start to close when I heard a strange voice say, "Can you understand me now, Earthman?"

I opened my bloodshot eyes to see Stretch looking back at me, wearing a toothy grin and waiting for me to respond. To him. He had just spoken in my own language.

"Hello, Sergeant Valentine," he said. "You may call me Slynkor."

What have you done to me, Magic, I thought.

Slynkor turned to his podium and wobbled hands over the surface, while doing so he ran through a bunch of phrases, one of which I understood as, "Please replace your Translator beads." We all dutifully stuck foreign objects back in our ears, I pondered the irony – normally I was pulling stuff like this out of my ears and flicking it into the street. Progress. A screen behind him lit up and we watched a little presentation. Right Honourable and Meataxe snuggled a little deeper into their chairs; they loved these sorts of entertainments and would sit for hours together chortling over any sort of show.

The presentation described the new technology, the one which would replace our Translator beads. The new technology was not a single device, not something you wore or carried. It was injected. They called them 'nanobots' and as far as I could work out they stuck a big pin in you and filled your arm with little beasties. The beasties travelled through your blood system – and let me tell you, I saw diagrams of the insides of more aliens than I ever want to see in my life again – and made their way to your brain. There they made a little home.

I was so not impressed. This was not going to happen to me, not a prayer would I let a bunch of little things crawl through my body. I mean, the itching would be a nightmare - and when they got to your brain they nested! And this was a good thing? Give me a break.

Where was the Archbishop when you needed him?

My mental interlude took a few moments and I missed a bit of the presentation but made it back in time for the lights to come up and see a toothy grin on Slynkor. He asked if we had any questions, a few hands went up from the rest of the delegation but I was more interested in the reactions of my comrades who had travelled with me all the way from our City. They were all looking at me with different expressions. Meataxe looked ill – with you on there, I thought; Teddy Boy was thoughtful – he probably understood some of what was happening; Right Honourable was beaming like a kid in a candy store – he couldn't have appreciated the seriousness of the situation.

I'm not good with space things, my sanity is only just hanging on by a thread. Emotionally I am still in a dirty alley carrying a halberd. I have tried to cope, really, really tried. But when it gets a bit much I have a drink. Right now I wanted several. It seems just when I was getting to a point where I could function on board a spaceship – how can it float in nothing? Space is nothing! Arghhh!!! – I was tossed something else new and horrible like wee beasties living in your brain. My life sucks.

Slynkor finished his answers and gave us all the next instruction. We were to leave the theatre, move into the next room where a technician would take a sample of our blood. Good, I was looking forward to meeting someone who tried that little stunt with me.

They'd be giving a fair bit of their own in exchange.

****

Chapter 2

I stood behind Teddy Boy as we entered the next room; before me the rest of the delegates were eagerly lined up, awaiting the extraction of blood. "What do they want some of our blood for?" I asked Ted.

He turned around to answer, "Tests," he said.

Great, I thought, getting information out of Ted can be like pulling teeth. "Tests for what?" I asked. "Come on, Ted, give me a break. Pretend I wasn't listening to the briefing."

He gave a look reserved for the marginally intelligent – I know, I've seen enough of it. "They have to tailor the nanobots to each species, only a few changes are needed but they're critical."

"What happens if we all get the same little beasties, the whaddyacallits, nanobots?" I asked.

"It varies" he replied. "Usually they just don't work."

I picked up on a key word, "Usually? What else could happen?"

He shrugged, "Dunno, nothing good, I'd bet. Bunch of weird shit inside your skull, could get freaky."

My choice was to have the apprentice vampire suck out some of my blood here and now or take a risk I wouldn't have any side effects when I got my own personal batch of bad fairies running around my body. I suppose I could always refuse to have any of them, the only problem was Magic. Bloody man wanted me to be a leader. Trusted me. Bugger.

By this time the line had moved along and it was my turn. A technician who looked exactly the same as Slynkor waited for me to do something, I noticed his neck to floor robe was bright blue with sprinkles of red. A roomful of these characters could really hurt the eyes if they all had the same colour range. I looked at him and he looked at me. He smiled. I didn't.

"Please roll up your sleeve, sir," he asked.

"Why?" I asked, perversely pleased with my pettiness.

He blinked in a strange way before saying, "I must take a sample of your blood, sir. To do the task I must put a needle into your arm."

I rolled up my sleeve, cracked my knuckles, made a big, scarred fist and placed it under his nose. Looking at my tall companion I said, "Now, we're not going to hurt each other, are we?"

We had a nice little tableau going before Right Honourable saw me. "It's just a needle, you big girl's blouse. Get a move on." Suitably motivated I allowed the sample to be taken, but I kept casting meaningful looks in the technician's direction during the process. I hope I rattled him, at least a little bit.

We had to wait a few hours for the results of our tests and the generation of the nanobots. We were faced with the question of how to spend the time. Most of the delegates chose to sit in a big library/cafeteria area and goof off. I left the two newbies and Meataxe to keep an eye on them with Lonely as supervisor; he had been around the block with us and knew when to call for help. Biggest risk seemed to be from paper cuts.

Right Honourable, Teddy Boy, Wallace, H'nuth and me decided to go for a wander. I knew if I stayed I would get into trouble, probably have a drink or two and then a few more. Time to fight that demon, I thought.

What was most surprising was the friendship of Wallace and H'nuth. We had picked up Wallace on Gamma 5, lovely planet, lots of tourism potential if you could avoid being kidnapped and slaughtered. He was looking for a change of career, a shift from being contract killer, a hit man. When we blundered through his town he must have seen something he liked because he was on the spaceship when we left his idyllic little abode. And H'nuth, our resident Tharl – what an addition to the NightWatch! H'nuth was a head taller than me, red skin, muscles and two little horns. Think of a devil without the tail - that's our boy.

These two hit it off and were now always hanging around together. Neither of them spoke much, Ted always felt right at home in their chatty silences.

We all stepped on to an external balcony to get a look at this world, the sun shone down, a few clouds were in a slightly yellow sky and a gentle breeze wafted against our rugged, manly cheeks. We could see across the city, a maze of spires, ramps, flying carts and what looked like people riding broomsticks. The view was quite beautiful. I may have sighed.

Wallace and H'nuth both found a sunny bench and opened their satchels. Now I kid you not - each of them took out a sketch pad and opened up a new sheet. Wallace seemed to be a charcoal man but H'nuth was into coloured pencils; they began to draw and chat. I gave Right Honourable the old raised eyebrows and nodded at our resident artists, he looked across and I was pleased to see his jaw drop a little. Not every day you see a hit man and a devil sitting drawing the butterflies. Surreal.

We left them to it, following Ted as he mooched around a corner. Before he disappeared he stopped dead still in shock at something he had seen, something around the bend out of my view. His face exploded in a smile and he took off at a run; Right Honourable and I increased our pace a little to see what all the excitement was about.

We found Ted sitting on one of the broomstick things, several were lined up on a low shelf with nothing between the edge of the shelf and a big, big, drop - I realised we were a long way above the ground. The broomstick was some form of transportation; it consisted of a long rail with one or two saddles over a huge engine, all shiny and metallic. Ted was on one of two saddles gripping a bar like the cross piece of a crossbow, the ends of the bar had padding for hands. Another alien was pointing things out to Ted who kept nodding enthusiastically; I think he was in Teddy Boy heaven.

As Right Honourable and I came up the engine on the broomstick roared into life. The alien hopped onto another saddle on Ted's broomstick, grabbed the steering bar from our boy, did something fiddly and they both accelerated off the balcony with a noise like thunder. Ted's tongue was out his mouth like a dog in bliss.

Another alien, this one in leather pants and top greeted us and asked if we wished a ride like our friend. Right Honourable said yes, was taken aboard a broomstick and followed Ted before I had a chance to draw breath. That left me like a shag on a rock, if I didn't go I would never hear the end of it so I agreed. Moments later I was hundreds of feet above the ground, going really, really fast, perched on a saddle behind some maniac who seemed intent on killing somebody – me, him, innocent bystanders, anyone would do. The noise was huge, like sitting in a thunderstorm, just a continuous roar.

We swung in tight curves around buildings, swooped over the pedestrians, scared the birds and chased each other across the sky. And all the time the wind beat across my face, the colours of the sky and terrain exploded in my vision, and the engine sent throbs of raw power through the saddle directly to my brain.

It was great.

When we returned from our rides we had the same expression, huge grins, windswept hair all askew, and eyes gleaming. Ted said, "We gotta get some of these."

Amen, brother, I thought.

****

In the afternoon we were injected with the nanobots. Yes, we willingly allowed these little horrors into our bodies and brains. Little beasties, crawling through our arms and legs. Occasionally, I gibbered.

We were told to stay quiet for a few days while they monitored our progress. If all went well we could return to the ship after three days. We would take a positive report and start injecting all and sundry with strange little vermin to swim through their bodies. I felt ill each time I thought about it.

Staying quiet was not a chore for the ship bred people, but us NightWatch got the fidgets after the first night. By about mid-morning on the next day we had played as many games of cards as we could stand – we weren't in a siege or trapped by bad weather; there was no reason to be confined to our small barracks. These rooms were palatial; each held four bunk beds, one on top of the other – I always claimed top bunk because I outranked everybody else. My roommates were right Honourable, Teddy Boy and Meataxe; our door opened on to a small corridor from which other doors led to similar rooms containing the rest of the delegation and the other guards. Lonely was doing a good job of strolling about, the newbies were happy to stay in the rec room with the delegates and watch videos, read or chat. Wallace and H'nuth sketched. But the rest of us were bored.

Bored, bored, bored.

Teddy Boy suggested another ride on the broomsticks and we all agreed, Meataxe was curious after hearing us talk so he came too. For the next few days we went back and forth to the broomstick site and learned as much as we could about these devices. Money wasn't a problem, we paid when we needed but most of the time other riders were happy to just sit and chat, showing off their machines, yarning about great rides they had been on. Sounded great. We were shown how to ride solo and by the time the third day came around we were good enough to ride comfortably alone. The four of us would hire out broomsticks and rattle around the city, hooning and yahooing like lunatics.

On the morning of our last day, we paid one last visit to the broomstick site and picked up some of their riding gear. Big jackets with gaudy colours, we walked around dressed alike and thought we were just it. We devised a dozen new names for our fearsome foursome, most unrepeatable. We stuck with 'Devils', it just seemed to fit us well and the shop where we bought the gear had a design printed on the back of our jackets – a red circle with little horns, flaming horns. The flames were my idea.

By the time we returned to the shuttle embarkation point we had terrorised several innocent citizens and well and truly worn out our welcome. Time to go. On the trip back to the mother ship we sat together trying to devise a plan to convince Magic we each needed a broomstick. A big one, with lots of shiny bits and a loud, loud engine. Oh, yeah....

Our conversation was so deep and colourful I forgot to be terrified by shuttle travel.

When we disembarked back on the big spaceship my boss was waiting for me. He was standing off to one side and beckoned me over. I didn't like the vibes I was picking up; he stood with feet slightly apart, a serious look on his face. I gave him my biggest smile and said, "G'day, Magic, what's up?"

He nodded towards an exit gate and moved off, I fell in step beside him. "Man in Black wants to see you, Val, we may have a bit of a problem. And when I saw 'we' I mean 'you.'" He fell quiet and I sure didn't feel like chatting. We entered the gate, pulled it shut behind us leaving us in a small, windowless room. Magic pushed one of a series of buttons on the wall and the floor shoved against our feet, bloody rooms can move on a spaceship. We rose several decks and finally stopped at the Big End of town, the level with offices for the senior crew. And the Man in Black was certainly senior, he was the Head of Security for the whole ship.

We found his set of offices and entered a small foyer area with a couple of gatekeeper's desks, plus two guards. They were Tharls, my favourite species. But my biggest surprise was to see my old pal Wilks sitting at one of the flunky's desks. Wilks, the man who loved a bit of paperwork, never met a regulation he didn't like. There was no middle ground to my relationship with Wilks – I either wanted to love him or kill him. Sometimes on the same day.

Magic greeted the main flunky, said the Man in Black wanted to see us. While he was being polite I nodded to Wilks and then spent the rest of the time giving the Tharls my best stone face. I could never tell with Tharls, some were keen on killing me and since I couldn't tell them apart I just assumed every one I met was a mongrel. Except for H'nuth. My life can become complex.

After a couple of beats the main door opened and we entered the inner office to have what was probably going to be an unpleasant interview. Unpleasant for me.

The Man in Black sat behind a big desk, bigger than the one in Magic's office This one was just as shiny but there were all sorts of bits and pieces scattered across its surface – papers, folders, little machines which probably did clever things. I hadn't been in this room before so I was interested in seeing how a fellow earthman made a nest at this level. The Man in Black was our original Captain for the NightWatch, the man who had stood up to defend the weak, the man who had told the rulers of the City they could not just torture, kill and maim the helpless. Not when he was around. He still dressed in black, still had the neat ruffles of white at wrist and throat, still had the coolest little beard and moustache – the man just reeked class. He was my hero.

"How are you, Charles?" he asked. "Good to see you again, Val. Sit down, we need a chat." Magic and I sat in two comfortable chairs in front of his desk, the boss continued, "Val, the crewman you assaulted in your bar fight on Deck 3 has been found murdered. You have been charged with the crime."

"Don't sugar coat it for me, sir, just tell me straight," I replied.

"Don't be a smartarse, Val," said Magic.

"When did I do this?" I asked.

"Last night," said the Man in Black.

"Like hell!" I said. "I've been on the planet for the last few days. Couldn't have done it."

"Of course you didn't do it, you big goose," said Magic. "But someone's out to get you."

"What's going on here?" I asked. "Have I got a big sign saying, 'Pick on me'. How come whenever there's a victim to be found it's yours truly?" I confess to feeling a little bit harassed. They ignored my sense of outrage, just carried on.

"What do you think, Franz?" asked Magic. "Could be we're closing in."

"I think so, Charles. While you blokes were having your stroll on Gamma 5 I may have turned over a few significant rocks, let the odd snake come out in the open." They both sat and thought, I just sat. I can recognise thinking when it's happening. "Might help if we do a bit of stumbling in the dark, blunder around a bit and tread on toes, what do you reckon?"

Magic smiled his nasty grin, "Good plan. Val's our boy, he can blunder with the best of them. What do you reckon we turn him loose?"

"I'm sitting right here, you know," I said, "I can hear you."

The Man in Black said to me, "The crewman who laid this murder charge against you is a maintenance tech on Deck 1, Crewman Jucthaz. One of us must convince him to cough up a name, someone's put him up to this, someone not too bright. You will not be interviewing him, Val. we will need someone with gentle interrogation techniques speaking to him. You are many things, sergeant, but gentle ain't one of them. Stay away from him." He looked directly at me, "Do you understand?"

I nodded. "Good," he went on. "Any fool can read a manifest and see you were planetside." He picked up something about the size of a prayer book and pushed some buttons on its surface – it must have had a light in it because I could see reflections in his eyes. He seemed very comfortable with all this gear.

"What have you got there, Franz?" asked Magic, "A new toy?"

"How long have you two actually been on board this ship?" The Man in Black had no problem answering a question with a question.

I kept my mouth shut, if these two guys wanted to have a gabfest than it was above my pay scale. I was just the hired help. Magic shrugged and said, "Well, let's see. We came on board, had about a week here, and then got stuck in that death trap of a Market. Returned after six months on the planet and we've been back about, I dunno, two weeks? What do reckon, Val, two weeks?" I nodded my agreement.

"I've been on board the entire time," said the Man in Black, "learning all their little ways. Learning about their cute technology and its inherent sense of infallibility. They rely on machinery, on gizmos and doodads. I've been learning about their tech, and this thing," he waved the tablet around, "is one of them. Do you two keep a notebook or journal?"

Magic pulled out a pencil and some bound sheets of paper – I was impressed. When I realised they were both looking at me I understood they expected me to have something to write with. "Uhh, no." Saints Above, I sounded weak.

Magic said, "I also keep a journal in my quarters. Valentine, get yourself organised and start acting like someone I can rely on." His voice was level and calm, no hint of emotion. He was merely laying out his expectations of me. "I know you can write and I know you've got a brain. Bloody well start using it."

My first reaction was a blossoming rage, quickly followed by heated embarrassment. These two guys weren't treating me like a schoolkid, they needed me to be on top of my game. I spoke through red flushed cheeks; self-control seemed to be the order of the day, not my normal hit first and think later response. My first thought was to apologise but I understood this was not the right reaction either, they didn't want someone on the team who just apologised and then screwed up again, they wanted someone who could pull their weight.

"I hear you, Magic. I'll sort it out."

I held my breath a little as they both looked at me for a few heartbeats. Had I just confirmed I shouldn't be in this room?

The silence stretched until the Man in Black spoke again, "Good enough. Let's move on." He waved the tablet shaped object, "This thing is an electronic notebook, you write on it with anything, finger, stick, quill, anything. Then it keeps what you've written as a neat copy. And get this, we can send messages to each other if we all have one of these notebooks. How good's that? I'll get you one each."

Magic beamed, I groaned inwardly, more stuff to learn; my brain hurt.

"Right, off you go then, gentlemen" The man in Black dismissed us, turning back to his desk to seek stray bits of work lurking in the corners. "Try to stay out of trouble, Valentine," he said, "Stay away from Jucthaz and stop picking fights you can't win." Good advice.

Wasted on me.

When we left his office I was going to have a little chat to Crewman Jucthaz on Deck 1. I decided to take Wallace and H'nuth with me, H'nuth because he knows the ins and out of shipboard life and Wallace because he is, like me, a mean bastard at heart.

And I was feeling like a right mean bastard.

Chapter 3

Wallace and H'nuth joined me for the little excursion down to the maintenance deck, we wore our standard coveralls with the Security shoulder patches; we didn't take any heavy duty weaponry, it was only a chat, after all. Since blasters were prohibited while on the ship – yes, I know about Teddy Boy but it's a braver man than me who would separate that particular guardsman from something which goes bang – most people confined their instruments of mayhem to clubs or knives. Sissy little things which only hurt people, if you want to do real damage then you needed something like my war knife. This was as long as my forearm and carried in a special sheath strapped to my left thigh; if we went anywhere serious I also carried my sword and maybe even a hammer. I do like a big hammer.

But today I wanted to play nice, so just the war knife; my companions probably carried their own choice of dangerous implements but I couldn't see any visible items. With anyone else I might have thought they were unarmed, but not these two characters, I think even their smiles were lethal.

We found the right maintenance bay and entered a large open area where various transport mechanisms sat upon special beds. One of the beds carried bits of machinery and was elevated to about head height with a technician strolling around the outside taking notes on a pad. Closest to us was a slightly raised shuttle with the legs of a human being protruding from underneath. As we approached the legs they twitched occasionally, accompanied by a grunt and a clang as the technician did improbable things to the underside of the damn thing. Hit it again, pardner, I thought.

I asked the legs, "Are you Crewman Jucthaz?" They stopped moving so I tried again. "Hey, you down there. Are you Jucthaz?" I kicked the sole of one foot with my boot.

The technician lay on a little wheeled trolley and used this to shoot out from under the shuttle, it caromed into my feet and made me hop to one side, rubbing a sore toe. By the time I had recovered my dignity the technician had stood up and was watching me do my little dance. I was starting to get cranky and wound up a good head of steam, ready to let it out over this dill who runs people down; I raised my head, opened my mouth and froze. The technician was a woman, her coverall was unbuttoned and I saw a sizable amount of cleavage, big cleavage, lots and lots of cleavage. My eyes were locked on her chest.

"Howa...hu...wababa..," I said.

"Nicely phrased, handsome," she said, "Something I can do for you?" She came to about my shoulder, hair tied back under a scarf, bare arms showing a few grease marks. One delicate hand held a large spanner.

I tried again, "Wea...whoohuba..bubbaaboo...." I still couldn't move my eyes of her chest, my brain had long since gone off in disgust and left the idiot at the controls.

"You're drooling, honey," she said. "Want to try to find my face?" She had a lovely golden voice, not harsh or accusing. Or sarcastic.

Birds may have sung.

H'nuth came to my rescue, "We're looking for Crewman Jucthaz? I understand he's on duty down here."

The girl answered without taking her eyes of me, probably amused by the large cretin reduced to incoherent jelly in front of her. "He's in the back storage area finishing a stocktake," she waved an arm in the direction of a large mesh gate. "Go on in, he's probably fallen asleep on the foam padding again."

Wallace took my arm and said to the girl, "Thanks, I'll take dopey here with us. Hope he hasn't offended you."

She smiled and said, "No, he's alright." As I turned to leave, she spoke to me "See you around, cutie." She slid back under the shuttle while my whole world hung on one word – 'cutie'.

"She called me 'cutie', Wallace," I mumbled. "Me – cutie. She said that, she did." My brain hadn't quite returned to full control.

"I heard" he answered. "Poor girl is obviously sick. After we've seen Jucthaz, why don't you come back and dribble on her some more. What colour's her hair, by the way?"

"She has hair?" I asked as we reached the mesh gate to the storeroom.

****

The gate was unlocked so we entered the storage area; large, heavy duty shelves jutted out from each wall leaving narrow gaps for access, boxes and spare parts lay stacked on pallets down the wide, central aisle We found Jucthaz at the rear of the storage area, squatting down beside some boxes and looking at one of those hand tablets the Man in Black showed me. As we came up he ran a hand scanner over some stripes on the box, checked his tablet for data and stood up. He found us three beefcakes standing very close, blocking any exit to the door. I hung back and kept in the shadow of a big shelf unit; he was alone and far from any help. Just the way I like 'em.

"Can I help you fellers?" he asked nervously. He was a big man, about the same size as me without the nicks and scars – they cost more. He looked like he could handle himself a bit, probably good in a brawl but I didn't get a sense of quiet menace from him. Not like with Wallace, he wears menace as everyday dress. Most people feel nervous around Wallace because he communicates with the frightened rabbit part of our brain, the bit which is keen on running and hiding.

Wallace scares me and I've seen a bit, I guess being a contract killer breeds a certain casualness to death. They see their victim and do the deed without fuss. None of the posturing and posing many brawlers develop at the start of a fight. Wallace would just walk in, kill someone and walk out again while most of the onlookers were still standing open-mouthed. A job's a job, he once told me, best to get it done quick. As a result, he had this way of looking at you which made you think he was working out the best place to put the knife. I was glad he had retired. I hoped he had retired.

So there was poor old Jucthaz, facing three mean looking characters, one of whom was standing in deep shadows. He shuffled a bit but seemed to cheer up a little when he saw our Security badges, probably thought he was safe. We kept quiet a few more beats, letting the tension build, no expression, no threats, no knuckle cracking. Just standing, looking at him.

He wilted a bit more, "Uhh...is there a problem?"

"We understand you witnessed a murder?" H'nuth finally asked. "Perhaps you could tell us what you saw." I stayed at the back, pretty sure he couldn't get a good look at me. H'nuth sort of dominates the eye.

"Ohh!" relief washed over him "Of, course. Yeah, dreadful thing. Last week I was in the bar on Deck 3 and saw this man trying to pick a fight with just about anyone. Guy was a drunk but mean with it. You know how it is, some of these weasels can't hold their liquor. Well, I was having a quiet ale with my buddy, Crewman Don'elk, when this drunk walks up and picks a fight with one of the other patrons – someone I didn't know. People tried to calm him down but he wasn't having any, the drunk, I mean. He took a swing, missed and fell on his face. When he stood up he pulled a knife. A few of us concerned citizens disarmed him and threw him out of the bar."

"Would you recognise this drunk if you saw him again?" asked H'nuth.

"Oh, yeah, no problems. Last night we were there again, in the bar, I mean. When the bar shut Don'elk and I headed home. Off to one side of the bar is this small storage space, a few bins and stuff, not much. When we passed it, we saw the same man - the mean drunk from the previous week - he came out with a knife in his hand, and it was dripping blood. He took off before we got to him but we heard moans from one of the bins. When we looked inside, we saw the body of the guy from the bar, the one the drunk originally picked a fight with last week. He coughed and died before we could get help. The big fellow had killed him, must've had some sort of grudge. When Security arrived, we reported it. I identified the drunk from some photos. His name's Valentine."

There was a bit of quiet after this series of revelations, some of it was true, the bar fight from last week probably happened as he said. Except for the bit about pulling a knife. I never take a weapon when I go drinking. I drink to relax; I carry a weapon to hurt or kill. Those two pastimes don't go together. My dad taught me if you pull a weapon then be prepared to use it, you don't wave it around to scare people, it's not a prop, it's not a game. Pull it out and stick it in someone or shoot them. But don't posture.

Not me. I learned a lot at Ostend. You see me with something pointy in my hand then someone's going to end up dead.

"So," said our beefy technician, "have you found him yet?"

"Yep," Wallace said, "We know the location of Valentine."

"Great!" said Jucthaz. "Is he under arrest? In the cells?"

"Nope," I replied, stepping forward. "He's standing in front of you."

Jucthaz wobbled a bit then tried a bit of bluster "You can't touch me! You can't hurt me!"

I wasn't following his logic, I grabbed a handful of his shirtfront and pulled him in close, nose to nose. "You may be wrong, friend." I said. My right fist was balled into a nicely compact lump, ready to be firmly placed on his nose. As I pulled it back to pick up a bit of swing, H'nuth placed his own meaty paw over my fist.

"No, Val, he's right, we can't touch him. If he lodges a complaint after this interview and has any marks on his body then you lose all credibility." My Tharl companion was making sense. Pity.

Off to one side I heard Wallace make a ripping sound, Jucthaz pulled himself out of my reach and started to gloat "You're going to get spaced, you moron. Who do you think you are, coming in here? Touch me and I'll scream loud and long to Security, you'll all get put out the airlock. Not a mark on me, boys, but I can sure mark you!" He started to throw a punch at my long suffering nose but was interrupted by a very loud and solid blow to his ribcage. Wallace had bundled up a wad of the packaging materials and used it to give Jucthaz a solid, meaty hit. I liked him all over again.

"Wallace!" shouted H'nuth. "Stop! We can't have any marks on him." Wallace hit the crewman again, eliciting a very satisfying moan from him as he sank to the floor.

"No problems, H'nuth," said Wallace, winding up for another blow. "Little trick I learned. Confine the blows to the torso and thighs, use a wide, soft bodied instrument and there will be no bruises." Jucthaz was on the floor, arms around his ribs. When he saw Wallace raise the padding again he covered his head. The blow fell heavily on his unprotected thighs. "Want to ask him any questions, Val? I can keep this up for some time, no problems."

The things you learn in this job, I thought. I squatted down beside a cowering Jucthaz and asked, "Who told you to set me up?" No answer, I stood up and said, "Hit him again, Wallace."

After a bit of a beating the crewman soon talked. His friend, Don'elk, was also his boss. They had been hired by another party to press charges against me, they had to fabricate the charge, plant evidence and do all the grunt work. But they were lazy and organisationally challenged so they fell back on the bar incident to find a victim. They killed the poor slob from the bar and just claimed I had done it. Very creative, this bunch. I explained how I had been on the planet for the last week, especially the previous night, and asked him how he was going to explain such a critical bit of detail.

He gurgled a bit, said, "Oh," and went quiet. "Can we make a deal?" he asked.

I love a good deal. After a bit of discussion, we came to an agreement. He agreed to claim mistaken identity and the charges against me would be dropped. We agreed to stop hitting him.

But he was still a murderer, I mentioned this snippet of information to him. "No, not me," he said. He told us Don'elk was the killer but Jucthaz was too afraid of his boss to testify against him. This set me up with a dilemma, Don'elk was a killer and also involved with setting me up - but I had no evidence.

In the days of the City, the NightWatch would have found a dark alley and just slit his throat. Another dead body in a dark alley wasn't going to cause a lot of fuss. But I had the impression people on a spaceship would take a dim view of some of our winning ways. People probably knew where other people were - if I killed Don'elk I would be charged with murder and be back at square one.

This would take some thinking; we may have to adjust some of our normal operating procedures like violence and death.

My head hurt.

"Psst!" This noise came from the front of the storage area. I turned and saw a figure outlined against the brightness of the maintenance hangar. Wallace stayed with Jucthaz while H'nuth and I moved off to confront, fight or talk to this new figure. Any option was possible, I breathed a small sigh – more complications.

It was my beautiful Shuttle technician; she had the loveliest smile. H'nuth nudged me and I decided to look past her out into the maintenance hangar; this way I wouldn't be distracted by her charms.

"You three bozos might want to know Don'elk is headed this way," she said.

"Why are you telling us this?" asked H'nuth.

"I'm not just a pretty face, pal," she replied. Slight dribble and gurgle from me as she continued, "I got the impression you weren't members of the Jucthaz fan club – fine with me. But his boss, Don'elk, has eyes everywhere so when you came in here one of them must have called him down. If you guys have done some damage to Jucthaz I won't shed a tear, but you could be in a bit of trouble. Don'elk's sent some Security goons to check up on you."

"No problem," I said, "we're goons too." She looked at me funny, I pointed to my shoulder patch. "Security. And we haven't left a mark on our boy." I cocked a thumb over my shoulder to the prone figure of Jucthaz as he lay groaning on the floor. Wallace had lost the padding and was leaning against a shelf being casual and unconcerned. "Thanks for the tip but we're fine."

She smiled at me and my stomach flipped while I tried to seem all manly and in control. "What's your name, cutie?" she asked.

"Valentine," I squeaked before dropping my voice and saying, "Sergeant Valentine of the NightWatch." Somehow my shirt was too big, my feet stuck out and I was itchy around the neck. My hands seemed to want to flap about and my brain kept stopping and starting. I was a mess.

She patted my cheek and said, "So you're Valentine," before turning and leaving the storage area. I stayed with my tongue around my ankles and H'nuth chortling softly until the guards arrived.

****

Chapter 4

"My name is Corporal Kam'thad" said one of the Tharls, "who are you gentlemen and what is your business here?"

I was impressed, polite requests from the civil authority was a rarity in my world. More learning for me, I thought. H'nuth introduced himself and identified us as members of the NightWatch. Kam'thad paused at this piece of information, his gaze travelling over each of our faces. I could almost see the wheels turning; no idea what they would come up with but at least we weren't dealing with a hit first and ask questions later type. Like me, I sighed.

Kam'thad asked H'nuth to stand to one side of the storage room, when Wallace introduced himself he also asked him to move over and stand beside H'nuth. My turn next.

"And your name, sir?" asked the Tharl.

"Valentine. Sergeant Valentine." No way around it, I thought.

Kam'thad spent a few more silent moments looking into my eyes, I did my best to squint up into his face – standing next to a Tharl is never good for the ego.

"Valentine?" he said.

"Yep," I confirmed. Bits of my anatomy were seeking to be elsewhere, my testicles had already pulled themselves up into my body cavity, my stomach was tensing for the blows. I was pleased I could keep the sappy grin on my face.

"Would you please step over there, sir?" he instructed. I ran the sentence through a few times seeking clarification – didn't get any, finally I decided he meant what he said and took up a position alongside Wallace. We stood together like schoolkids being addressed by the head boy, I was waiting for the fight to erupt; after all, I had killed a significant member of the Tharl hierarchy and caused the death or imprisonment of several others. Some of his pals on the ship were bound to be feeling antagonistic towards me.

"We have received a complaint concerning a crewman being assaulted. Would you gentlemen know anything about this situation?" he asked.

"Yes, they would!" came a loud cry from the back of the storage area. I had forgotten about our buddy Jucthaz, he chose this moment to step forward and point at us in great indignation, "They have been beating me, I was foully assaulted by the three of them. I demand they be arrested."

Kam'thad said, "Indeed, sir. Assaulted, you say."

"That's what I said; they hit me again and again. I can barely move for the pain." Jucthaz held a rib and leaned against one of the shelf units – bravely keeping erect, poor lamb.

"Would you please remove your shirt, sir?" asked the Tharl. He turned to the three of us while Jucthaz stripped and asked to examine the backs of our hands; we dutifully held them up, I knew what he was looking for – torn knuckles, split skin; the sort of thing you pick up when a fist smacks someone in the mouth. Naturally we were all pristine; I had some old nicks and bruises but it was obvious they had not been gained in the last few minutes.

Jucthaz stood before us, bare from the waist up and not a mark on him. Kam'thad poked his thumb into the crewman's side a few times trying to find some evidence of the frightful beating; I mentally applauded each time he winced. Finally he told the crewman to get dressed.

"You may lay charges if you wish, sir," he said to Jucthaz, "but I must advise you there is no evidence to suggest an assault took place. You may, of course, seek independent medical opinion but if called upon to testify I would have to state I was unable to validate the charge. What do you wish to do?"

Jucthaz steamed and blustered, abused the system but didn't go as far as calling these Tharls inept. He finally spat a few words to me, "You haven't heard the last of this, Valentine!" before storming out of the storage area. From where I stood, I watched him meet another man. Judging by the frantic arm waving I guessed he was telling his friend about how we had gotten away with the assault. I took a good long look at this friend; I can remember faces very well and I made a mental note to have a quiet chat with this character at some point.

My unpleasant thoughts were interrupted by Kam'thad, "You would do well to avoid this situation again." He looked at each of us in turn before coming to a rest on me, "Let's be quite open about this. I know you assaulted that man, I would guess you used something padded to avoid leaving a mark; it would be interesting to search this compartment and see if such an instrument is present." I thought of the wad of packaging Wallace had used, it would be obvious to an experienced copper we had used it. And I was beginning to suspect Kam'thad was just such a copper. Damn.

But he wasn't cross; neither was he giving us the old soldier's wink and a nod. He was just telling us how it was. "If I come across any of you using this method again then I will be unpleasant for some time. Unpleasant and tenacious in my follow up. Do you understand me?" he asked.

I nodded, not even bothering to deny or justify the situation. H'nuth and Wallace grunted assent.

"Good," continued the corporal, pacing back and forth in front of us. "Now I know Jucthaz and his partner, Don'elk, I know they are thugs and bullies, perhaps even murderers. The question is, what are you? You wear the uniform of Security, a uniform I take some pleasure in wearing. I will not share it with thugs and killers."

He stopped in front of me again. "Sergeant Valentine, you did the right thing when you exposed those in our ranks like Chayla who would use their position to bend the law. Some bear you malice for this act – I am not one of them. Understand me, Valentine, I am the law and I do not bend. I suggest you leave this area and avoid any future contact with Crewman Jucthaz. I understand he will shortly be summoned for an interview into the charges against you.

We crossed the main hangar deck, ready to return to Magic and fill him in on the latest developments and the fact his favourite sergeant was no longer a wanted felon. En route to the lifter – I'm learning new names for moving rooms – I decided to see my favourite female Maintenance Technician. Wallace whispered to me out of the corner of his stubbly, scarred mouth, "Try not to dribble too much, son."

We found her in the space between the shuttle she had been repairing and a large trolley of tools and parts. She was on her back, coughing; as we came up she rolled to one side and spat out blood and some teeth.

It was obvious she had been beaten, and beaten badly.

I hurried to her side, Wallace pushed me out of the way and examined her. He was doing the right thing, we had discussed what the ship people call first aid but I had zoned out during most of the lectures. Fortunately, Wallace knew a thing or two about life threatening injuries. I stayed near the girl's head and stroked her hair, making soft reassuring noises while Wallace felt a lot of soft female bits. Any other time and I might have made a smart-alec comment, but not now. H'nuth stood over us keeping guard.

She had lost some teeth and would have bad bruises but no broken bones. By the time Wallace had finished his examination she was leaning against me in a manner I definitely liked; she raised one hand over her head and softly caressed my cheek. While keeping up the hair stroking I asked, "What happened? Who did this?" I had a fair idea. "And who are you?" I felt I should know.

"Lydia," she said. "I fell over, all my fault." Wallace's eyes met mine over her hair, he kept a stone face but I knew he was thinking the same thing as me – she was lying.

"You're lying," I said. My mates and I have hit enough people to recognise a beating. It was Don'elk, wasn't it?" She pulled herself to a sitting position, pulled her hair back into a ponytail and began securing it with a knot. She shrugged and kept her eyes down.

I stood up, "Right," I said, "I'll ask him myself." She put one hand on my pocket and pulled herself to her feet, as she rose her arms came around my neck. I stayed very still as she nestled her head into my shoulder.

"Don't," she whispered. "Please don't." She went quiet before continuing, "If you want to help then take me to Sick Bay where I can be patched up." I had no idea what a Sick Bay was, but Wallace knew. He put a shoulder under Lydia's arm, I took the other and we carried her out of the Maintenance Bay. I would be back; H'nuth stayed as rearguard in case someone else wanted to have a go. I was certainly in the mood.

We left Lydia in a large room filled with beds and strange machines. Before saying my farewell, I promised to return and check on her the next day. She promised to be there, and to teach me what a Sick Bay did and how it worked. A win-win deal.

We left to report to Magic. Then I planned on having a Deep and Meaningful conversation with Don'elk.

****

Our captain, Charles Althorp, aka 'Magic', listened to our report of the questioning of Jucthaz and finished with my somewhat heated account of the beating up Lydia had endured. He asked for a few points of clarification before dismissing Wallace and H'nuth. He asked me to stay.

When the others had left he asked "Whose idea was it to go and see Jucthaz?"

I didn't like where this was going and decided to get it out in the open "It was my idea, Magic. The other two came along for moral support, probably thought I was acting under your orders." Here it comes, I thought, another roasting for my impetuosity; I could handle being yelled at. It made Magic feel better, let us both get on with our jobs – I considered each time I was bawled out to be a landmark in my career. A way to keep score.

"'Acting under my orders'," he murmured. "Why would they think that?"

"Well," I began, my mouth storming ahead without consulting the brain, "I'm your sergeant. Makes sense, doesn't it? Natural chain of command and so on." I felt he was being remarkably calm. He was silent for a while so I continued to shoot myself in the foot, "You're always giving me orders, little tasks to do. In their defence, they would have assumed I was doing something for you." Come on, mate, let me have it.

"Do you mean they trusted you?" he asked.

I let out a breath, "Exactly! They trusted me to...oh, hell." I got it, I abused their trust. Bugger, Bugger, Bugger.

He twisted the knife, "And I trusted you."

"Come on, Magic!" I exclaimed, "Don't play the wise elder with me! All right, maybe seeing Jucthaz wasn't the smartest thing I've ever done – but I got a result!" I'd worked myself up into a bit of a state by now, it's easier to seem angry if you really are angry. And I thought anger might get me out of this mess, deflect the conversation. Make it uncomfortable for all concerned and soon we could move on.

Magic went quiet for a while and I was hoping my little ploy had worked. His next comment seemed to justify my relief. "Things go alright down on the planet? No problems?" he asked.

I breathed a small sigh of relief, "No problems, all went well." Time to go, I thought and asked "Anything else? And look, I'm sorry about the Jucthaz thing. I'll be more thoughtful next time." Always good to do a bit of bowing and scraping.

"Next time," he mused, "yes... next time." He paused before continuing. "What did the civilians think of the whole process? Getting a bunch of – what do you call them? – nanobots inside their skulls. Anyone worried about it?"

How would I know, I thought; oh, right, I was the mission leader. "No," I responded, "we're all good. Bit of a shock at first but once we got used to the idea it all went without a hitch." My mind was wondering if Lydia had any emotional entanglements; my mind should have been paying attention.

"Without a hitch," he repeated, "...without a hitch...what about the woman who had hysterics when she received the injection?" he asked.

My mind chose this moment to go blank, "Uh..." I said.

"Did you know tensions were running high within the group? Not the Security people but amongst the delegates? Apparently there were some heated discussions over seating at meals and similar protocols. It seems whenever you were needed it was impossible to find you."

This was not going well, I thought I was free and clear after the Jucthaz thing and I'd used my only negotiating technique – anger.

Magic ploughed on, "Did you know some critical decisions were made regarding security by a newcomer to the Watch? Did you know ....well, let's just say you weren't around." He stopped and looked at me, he was calm, in control and listing all of my defects on the mission. There wasn't a damn thing I could do about it.

The excuses flooded into my brain, reasons why it wasn't my fault, why I wasn't to blame. In one of my rare demonstrations of good judgement I bit my tongue and kept quiet. My captain began to become heated and I began to really worry. When Magic gets angry, lesser men flee.

"What bloody good are you, Valentine?" he said, voice rising in indignation. "Saints above! You're my sergeant! A responsible position, a man I need to be able to rely on! And you're bloody useless!"

He stopped, I was ashamed of myself, hurt over the accusations and trying to stoke the embers of resentment deep in my breast. I wanted to mouth a few platitudes but still I kept quiet.

"This was your chance, Val!" he continued. "This was an independent command! And not once did you talk to any of the delegates to see how they were faring. Not once did you meet with your men and discuss the mission. Not. Bloody. Once. No, you were too busy off having a good time, thinking of yourself and your own selfish needs. You drink too much, you don't think of others and you're bloody unreliable."

He sat back, exhausted; I slumped in my chair, emotion draining all my energy. I tried to marshal some counterarguments, some means of justifying my appalling lack of leadership. And then I realised something, I was trying to think of ways to defend myself - I was only thinking of me. I wasn't angry over false accusations. They were all true. Subconsciously, I had accepted all Magic had said about me. When I dragged this realisation out into the cold light of reality, I was ashamed of myself.

Bugger.

Magic had been sitting with his eyes downcast, he now raised them to me and asked, "So, what do you want to happen here, Val?" I didn't think this was fair, I shouldn't have to set my own punishment – it was his job.

Fortunately, I had another attack of good sense and shut up; why was it his job? Who was in control of my life? Surely it was me? If I expected Magic to decide these issues then I was effectively giving him permission to run my life. How was this a fair thing for him or me? What did I want to have happen? Good question. I could stay on as sergeant or quit. But if I was going to stay then I had better sort myself out.

Perhaps it would be easier to step down and let someone else take the rank. I started to form the words for my resignation.

I sort of expected the door to burst open and someone to announce a disaster. A distraction would occur to interrupt this moment. I would be saved from talking or deciding any action. Or Magic would receive a radio message which would mean we all had to put aside our own, petty issues and solve the bigger problem.

Something should have happened to stop me from saying I resigned. A thunderclap, a noise – anything.

I got nothing, life went on.

He sat there looking at me, I opened my mouth to resign.

And stopped.

I liked being sergeant. It wasn't the rank, the power or the respect I was getting. I felt I was doing something worthwhile, I was a force for some of the good in the world - I liked being able to solve problems, I liked having people depend on me. I didn't want to quit.

And Magic had just told me how badly I had stuffed up.

"I'll fix it," I promised.

Not a good time then. Eternal moments went by as he sat and stared at me. I stared at him, I wasn't going to beg or plead. I offered my service – the choice was his.

"About bloody time," he grumbled. "Now piss off."

****

Chapter 5

That night I met with a few of the lads in a bar, not the one on Level 3. H'nuth was Wallace-less so we decided to inflict ourselves on L'on-li, otherwise known as Lonely for obvious reasons. The three of us sat and yarned for a few hours and I stayed sober. Baby steps. Lonely complained of a touch of nausea and headache so we called it a night.

We left at a reasonable hour and I was debating checking on Lydia before getting my head down when Lonely staggered against a wall. He hadn't been drinking much, I put his stagger down to a stumble because he was still young enough to trip over his own feet. He straightened up, leaned against the wall and moaned; H'nuth and I moved to him in time to see his eyes roll back into his head followed by a soft crumple onto the floor.

I knelt down and checked his pulse, rapid and irregular. The First Aid training I had finally started said this was not a good thing so H'nuth and I grabbed an arm each and we bundled him down the corridors to Sick Bay. We entered the now familiar room and dumped him on a bed, H'nuth went in search of a technician while I stayed with my young friend. I saw Lydia a few beds away and she gave me a sunburst smile. I gawped at her and did my best doofus impression, an imbecilic grin accompanied by foot shuffling.

The Sick Bay seemed remarkably full, certainly more populated than it was when we had brought in Lydia. A ripple of shock entered my brain as I recognised many of the occupants from our mission to acquire the nanobots. I cudgelled my brain trying to recall all the people on the expedition, part of my mind reminded me of my dereliction of duty. Again. I needed to know real information, who was on the mission and who was in Sick Bay. H'nuth had returned with a physician who started checking Lonely so I grabbed the

Tharl's arm and asked him if he noticed anything about the people in the other beds.

He scanned the room and said, "Many of them appear to be the humans who accompanied us down to the planet. I cannot be sure, most of you look alike." My hand was still around his arm and it was growing hot, his arm was becoming warmer.

"Are you all right, H'nuth?" I asked.

"A mild fever, nothing of concern," he replied with a slight wobble.

Yeah, right, I thought. Humans and H'nuth with the nanobots were getting sick – I was concerned. The physician had finished checking Lonely so I had him give H'nuth the once over, he was soon tucked up in his own bed and complaining like a baby. Honestly, some people.

I had the physician contact Magic, Lydia had come out of bed to ask if she could help. I told her to return to her bed and get well, she ignored me and sat on the end of Lonely's bed so I had her use some of the ship's communications to find the locations of Meataxe, Wallace, Right Honourable and Teddy Boy. Meataxe was in a bar with Right Honourable – no surprises there –Teddy Boy was in the armoury practising with things that go bang and Wallace was sketching an engine.

"Get them down here for a medical check up," I told her.

When the physician returned I had another task for him. "Get me a list of all the people on the Mission to the planet, have them report here immediately. Contact your boss or bosses and tell them we may have a situation." As he turned to go another thought occurred, "How many people have received the nanobot injections, the ones we brought back with us from the planet."

His reply made my stomach do a little flip of presentiment, "Nearly all personnel have received the injections. The Scouting Mission told us there were no side effects."

Until now, I thought, until now. Again, my mind flicked threads of guilt through my brain – I should have done a better job!

Lydia interjected, "I haven't had my shots yet. Between working on the shuttle and being beaten up it sort of fell through the cracks. From what I see around here I might just put it off a bit longer." Wise girl, my Lydia.

Magic arrived with more physicians, I told him my misgivings, "It looks like all of the humans who had the injection are in this room, all sick. H'nuth was the only Tharl and he's here too. I'm waiting for the others who were with us to be checked out. We could have a problem."

He spotted the flaw in my logic, "Why aren't you sick?"

Good question, I was unsuccessfully pondering an answer when Wallace, Meataxe, Right Honourable and Teddy Boy arrived. They all looked disgustingly healthy, Meataxe swayed and slurred his words but I assumed he was just drunk again. The physicians checked them out and then gave me the once over – we were all fine.

"Let's get out of here and find a place to talk," instructed Magic. He pulled rank on the physicians, "Get all the members of the Scouting Mission down here and check them out," he told them. "Contact me with results." He nodded to me and the lads and led us out of the Sick bay back to the area used by our Security contingent, someone had scrawled our name in very decorative text on the entry walls – "NightWatch."

We sat around his office, giving Meataxe a piece of floor where he fell asleep; whenever he became too noisy one of us would roll him around a bit. It's funny how some actions are almost unnoticeable – we've always looked after Meataxe and this was just another occasion for doing so, a bit cleaner than a tavern, not as comfortable as a stable. You roll the dice and take what comes.

"I repeat," said Magic, sitting back into his chair. "Why aren't any of you sick? Every other human on the expedition is down in Sick Bay with a fever, except you. What makes you different?"

Right Honourable had a go, "Perhaps the sickness keeps away from members of the NightWatch? Professional courtesy?"

Teddy made his disagreement snort, Magic said, "H'nuth and Lonely are in the Watch. Try again."

I admired Right Honourable, he never let a little thing like being wrong stop him from trying again. "But H'nuth and Lonely are a pair of late joiners, blow ins, Johnny-come-latelys. The evil plague must recognise their essential newness and so not accord them a full measure of respect."

Teddy Boy snorted again while I ran the last statement back and forth through my mind trying to work out what Right Honourable meant. Wallace destroyed the argument, "I joined with H'nuth and I'm not sick."

Right Honourable put up a valiant rearguard, "Not yet, dear boy, not yet." He gave each of us his best meaningful look before sinking back into a comfortable chair with fluid grace.

"Forget it, Right Honourable, that's not the answer," stated Magic. "You're all in the Watch and not sick; Lonely and H'nuth are in the Watch and are sick. Why?"

Sometimes my mouth skips telling my brain what is going on, this was one of those times. "We're all from planets," I said. "Lonely and H'nuth came from the ship – or have been on the ship a long time. Is that the common thread?" I listened to what I had to say along with the others – and I thought it made a bit of sense.

While bits of my brain congratulated other bits, Magic came to a decision, "Not a bad theory, Val. Ted," he instructed, "use my computer and find out if any of the other mission personnel are from a planet." We all know Ted has been burying himself in all ship related technologies, he was the most qualified of us to use a computer quickly. "Right Honourable, contact Sick Bay and find out what's going on."

Right Honourable and Teddy Boy moved to different machines on Magic's desk and began doing things I should know about – again I resolved to change my ways, but not today. Tomorrow, when things have settled down, I would change, I would begin to learn about this stuff. Tomorrow.

I made myself useful by finding some water and pouring it over Meataxe, his spluttering gave me a small amount of pleasure. Mean spirited and petty, that's me. Wallace helped.

Right Honourable had the face of one of the physicians on a screen, the report was not great. The non-humans from the mission had turned up and been examined by means peculiar to their makeup – they were all sick and becoming sicker.

Magic spoke at the screen, "How are the humans? They have been affected longest, any change in their condition?"

I saw it all, the physician opened his mouth to speak as a loud, continuous beep erupted from somewhere in the Sick Bay – his face disappeared from the screen. I recognised an alarm sound when I heard it. We all gathered around the desk looking at a now empty communications screen, in the background we could see some shelves and a wall, but we heard desperate sounds. I understood some of the phrases barked back and forth off-screen, the physicians were trying to save someone. The beep was shut off and was replaced by other sounds, clicks and jolts, commands from physician to physician. Finally, a palpable sound of resignation washed through the speakers.

The physician reappeared on screen, tugging a mask from his face. His eyes wore that angry look, an anger generated by a sense of inadequacy, the feeling of failure. I recognised it easily.

"The first human brought in with the illness has just died," he stated in a monotone. "If the others follow this pattern, we will lose all humans in the next six hours." He looked directly into the screen, his eyes boring into all of us but his message was for me and me alone, "What have you brought back to my ship?"

Magic turned the screen off, we all sank back as if from a race. "Lonely's down there" he said.

"What are we going to do?" asked Right Honourable.

Sick Bay was full of people who had depended on me, humans and non-humans. I saw their faces; I saw Lonely and H'nuth. They were all dead men.

"I'm going back to Sick Bay," I announced. I needed to be there when it happened, when the people I was responsible for paid the price for my leadership. I needed to sit beside Lonely and H'nuth and keep them company as they began their final journey. Magic looked at me for a couple of beats, I wouldn't be surprised if he knew what I was thinking – he nodded and I left. Alone.

****

The corridors were impossibly bright and clean, lights illuminated every crevice, no foul odours in the air. Along the walk I discussed things with myself, my body was on this spaceship but the rest of me was struggling. Time for some honesty with myself. I had been avoiding all things to do with the ship in an attempt to deny I was here – when my brain put forward this thought the rest of me chewed it over and found the premise reasonable.

I didn't want to be on a spaceship, I wanted to go home, back to my smelly city. I had been running away from reality, just like our poor, mad first sergeant.

Was I going mad? I wondered.

No. Or at least, I didn't think so. Having these sorts of quiet conversations helped me deal with my existence, I had been having them all my conscious life. I talk to myself but I'm not mad. Sure. You're just jealous because the voices in my head talk only to meeee!

Get a grip, Valentine, I told myself as I pushed through the doors into my own personal purgatory. A room full of the dead and the dying.

Lydia was sitting beside H'nuth's bed and bathing his head with a wet cloth. Physicians hovered over other comatose forms. All the humans and H'nuth were unconscious but the eyes of the other aliens who had accompanied me down to the surface gleamed with fear and apprehension. I nodded to Lydia and moved to the first of these conscious aliens.

That part of my brain keeping a running commentary on my life was trying to draw my attention to the physical appearance of this alien. He/she/it was thin as a rake with three eyes across the forehead and long skinny arms ending in three slender, supple fingers. My brain was insisting this was weird, and when was I going to start gibbering?

I ignored me.

"My name's Valentine," I stated, "Sergeant Valentine of the NightWatch." He looked at me with big eyes and slowly nodded. I continued, "Could you please tell me how long you have been on the ship?"

He didn't reply so I tried again, "Have you always been on this ship?" He shook his head in denial.

I was becoming exasperated, "Can you understand me? Are you wearing your Translator bead?" I asked.

The alien nodded his head and went back to gazing at me with his round eyes. Did he understand me? I think so, but because he wasn't talking it was hard to work out what he really meant. The Translator beads had their limitations. I stood there trying to work out a way through my dilemma, frustration growing.

Could I hit something? Usually helped.

A small hand crept on to my shoulder and Lydia said, "Maybe I can help, handsome?" To my credit I neither jumped nor drooled, I waved her forward and stood aside to let her try her conversational skills.

But it was to me she directed her first question, "What do you want to know?" she asked.

I told her I wanted to find out if any of the non-humans who had been on the mission were from a planet like me. Or had they been on board the ship for a long time?

"Why?" she asked.

I waved an arm and said, "Because I am not sick. Nor are Teddy Boy and Right Honourable. Wallace also seems to be doing fine. But humans who have been on the ship for some time seem to be coming down with a sickness." I looked around me and added, "And H'nuth, but he was the only Tharl with us on the planet."

"Ship dweller for six standard years," said my bed-ridden alien. I looked at him, curious and mildly annoyed he could give an answer now. Why not when I asked him? He was keeping up with me and said, "Not deaf. Not stupid. You ask bad questions." He shut up and so did I.

Lydia gave me a hug – she was very free with body contact and it was seriously derailing my brain – and suggested "Why don't I ask the other non-humans? Make myself useful. I don't want to just lie in my bed while all around me are sinking; very scary." I agreed and she moved off to start her questioning.

Lonely was still unconscious, I asked the physician how he was doing and got a non-committal grunt, "Soon be dead, like the other three."

"Three!" I exclaimed, "I thought we only had one death."

He nodded with his head to the back of the Sick Bay, "No time to move them out." I looked to where he was indicating and saw three sheet covered forms lying on beds separated from the rest of the patients by a discernible space. A space made up of more than just the absence of life.

The sheet on the furthest body quivered.
The body sat up.

****

Chapter 6

"Urgh...," I said. The physician continued on with his duties ignoring my attempts at speech. I grabbed his shoulders, straightened him up and turned him to face the sitting corpse. "What's going on?" I asked.

We stood side by side and watched the body slide its legs over the side of the bed, the sheet fell down revealing a skinny, naked torso. Its eyes moved around the room, head turning to gaze at the other occupants of the Sick Bay. I felt it was seeing the room for the first time, registering the presence of the opposition – the living.

Another physician ran to the seated body, he was yelling for assistance and a whole lot of other medical jargon which went right over my head. I didn't understand what was happening, my eyes refused to accept a corpse sitting up – therefore, it wasn't a corpse! I turned to my neighbouring physician, intending to question the accuracy of his diagnosis, and so missed the next instalment. A loud scream drew my attention back to the now standing ex-corpse, but it wasn't him doing the screaming, it was the physician who had moved up to examine this medical miracle. He was holding a hand to his head.

His ear had been bitten off, I watched the recently deceased chew on something and swallow. I can put two and two together and came up sick. My physician began yelling at others on his staff and together a whole bunch of them ran down towards the grisly scene. Not me, I can recognise an accident waiting to happen.

I looked around and found a large metal pan, it was empty for which I was grateful. Having seen similar pans filled with a variety of nauseating blobs, I didn't fancy going into a fight holding someone's liver. Our hungry friend had regained a grip on his first helper and had buried his jaw into a fleshy forearm. More screams, of course. Everyone seemed to be doing it.

I pushed through the crowd of physicians and helpers who were now moving away from the chewing dead man, if he was dead. I hoped he was, if not he was going to have to do some major apologising. Finally, I was able to grab the man who was being fed upon and pulled him behind me in between bites. His left forearm was down to the bone, an ear was missing, blood everywhere. I felt right at home.

My hungry friend swallowed what was in his mouth and stepped towards me, mouth open, bloody teeth and gums hankering for a bit of Valentine, medium rare.

"How're you doin'?" I asked, slamming the heavy metal pan hard up into his head, this was a killing blow. He wouldn't need to later apologise for chewing on a crewmate. The pan also spread his nose across his face, the nose ejecting copious amounts of thick, black gunk. The muck looked like old, pus-filled blood and he died. Again.

My blow pushed him back onto his bed and he lay there, spreadeagled, eyes pointed at the ceiling, motionless.

I stood over his fallen body, panting, still holding the now blood-streaked pan. What had happened here? Using the toe of my boot I nudged the feet of the again-corpse, looking for a reaction, a twitch. Nothing, he was dead, I would guarantee it. But then, so had the physician. I walked back to the rest of the personnel in Sick Bay as they huddled in two groups, one fussed over the man who had been chewed up - he was moaning – the rest clung together like shipwreck survivors – bit of moaning from them, too.

Lydia came and gave me a hug; perks of the job and one I was keen to prolong and relive. Her hair smelt soft and glowy, she certainly felt soft and wonderful. I closed my eyes and luxuriated in the warmth of human contact, one not trying to kill me. I've had girlfriends before, I'm not a complete novice, but my idiotic brain always gave a running commentary on my actions with women and frequently criticised my choice of partner. Now this part of my higher order faculties was mercifully silent, a bit of gruesome action tended to make it run and hide. Violence and alcohol kept it at bay.

I felt her arms stiffen around me and begin to softly shake my body. In my blissful reverie I hoped this meant she saw me as more saviour than thug, possibly someone she could take on romantic walks. My daydream of quiet dinners with soft music was derailed as her shaking became more and more frantic, I opened my eyes and leaned back to gaze into what I hoped would be an adoring face. Instead, what I saw was wide-eyed terror, not quite the reaction from my future girlfriend I was going for.

She shook me some more and eventually my brain kick started, sounds came online and I realised the quality of noise from my fellow citizens had taken on an unusual note. I suspect Lydia may have reached the end of her patience by now because she violently twisted my body around so I was facing away from her and back into the main body of the Sick Bay. At first, I put it down to yet another feminine rejection until I saw what had grabbed everyone's attention. It was worth grabbing.

The body of the man I had hit was rising from his bed.

I could see the depression where I had hit him between his two sunken eyes, the rest of the nose was still spread across his face. The blood and gore around his mouth combined with fluid dribbling from his eyes made quite the sight. Haven't seen anyone as pretty as him since retaking some old redoubts during the Siege of Ostend. My squad found some week old bodies after the rats had been at the buffet, I recall being eloquently sick before my corporal told me to grow a pair and get on with the job. Ahh, lost youth.

The body stood up and started walking towards us, not shambling or shuffling, a reasonably normal gait. He paused at each bed and seemed to examine the occupant before moving on, I hoped he wasn't still looking for a snack. The other three sheet-covered dead bodies were passed up before he came to H'nuth. The big Tharl obviously wasn't appetising and our dead man moved on to the next bed.

This one contained Lonely, my human squad mate. Before I could act he had passed by my companion and moved on to the beds containing the still conscious non-humans. He looked at each one for a few beats before turning away, rejecting them as a side dish. As he did this assessment, each non-human reacted the same. Wide eyes, sheet pulled up to nose for protection and utter stillness as the decision was made.

The hungry corpse passed each bed and then turned to the next available snack, Lydia and me.

I react well in an emergency, generally my body knows what to do and does it. Later my brain catches up. But this time I had been found wanting, I had stood still while this thing had walked to each bed and carried out his inspection, it was only when it started walking towards Lydia I moved. My only excuse is that I hadn't come across a lot of walking corpses before. Counting this character my total number of walking dead was ... one. I was a little inexperienced.

But there was no way I was going to allow Dead Guy to get at my girl. As he walked towards us I took a two-handed grip on my metal pan, stepped in and hit him again. This time I put all my beef into it and struck him nicely on the chest; I felt ribs crunch and down he went again, plopping onto his backside.

Weird thing was, he made no sound, no reaction. Generally, when I belt someone, they give me some audible feedback. Anything from a scream to a groan but nothing from this guy.

Lydia screamed in my ear, probably trying to compensate but it meant I was deaf on one side for a few beats. I gave her an accusing look and so was well placed to watch her beautiful big eyes get bigger. Very, very wide indeed. Unfortunately, she wasn't looking at me.

I turned back to Dead Guy and was not surprised to find him dragging himself to his feet. His face was caved in and his ribs were visibly flapping inside is chest. This guy should not be doing any light exercise, he should be dead. Dead and still. But up he got, he looked at me and the eyes were not dead but not alive either. Hard to describe, I'm sure something was looking at me but I wasn't sure *what* was looking at me.

He started walking towards me again, as he approached he raised his arms a little and opened his mouth. I could see were this was going but I'm not that kind of guy, I don't like to be eaten on the first date. I tossed my useless pan in his face; it had slowed him down but didn't seem able to stop him. In another small tray on a trolley beside me I saw a variety of medical instruments all shiny and clean, not dirty and stained like I would see on my own world. The physicians up here seemed to have a thing against dirt and rust in a wound.

I picked up one of the long, sharp and thin variety of instrument. As my hungry friend reached me I stabbed him in the heart with the sharp metal rod. For good measure I pounded the base of it with the palm of my hand and was satisfied to feel it thrust through his broken ribs and even poke a bit out of his back. I was sure his heart was somewhere in the vicinity of my weapon, maybe even skewered but at least damaged. My blow was strong enough to push him back a few steps, I waited for him to collapse. A punctured heart must mean this guy was dead.

No such luck, he stood still for a moment and then resumed his walk toward me, hands up and ready for the first course.

Now I can take a hit as well as the next guy, I can even think while in combat, I don't freeze or panic like most fighters. This has kept me alive; while the other guy is posturing and working himself into a frenzy I've already stepped forward and stuck a sword in his guts. Like I said, I react well around violence.

But not now, now I flipped out. This thing just kept coming, kept walking towards me and was ready to eat me alive. My brain packed and left, my bowels contracted and my testicles clawed up into my body cavity to around chest level. As Dead Guy's fingers touched my upraised arms – raised in some vague sense of protection from this horror – I screamed.

I kicked him in the stomach as hard as I could. He was pushed back and I stepped forward, spinning on the ball of my left foot. I pulled my right knee up to my stomach. I spun completely around until I faced back towards Lydia, but only for a beat because I had pushed myself into a complete spin and as I came back to face dead Guy. I extended my right leg and, adding the full force of my spin to the muscle of my right thigh, I hit him a tremendous blow with the base of my right foot.

I had learned this spin kick from a psychopathic killer while we were still on speaking terms. He's now dead, courtesy of my friend Teddy Boy and a blaster.

I swear my foot sank into Dead Guy's stomach all the way back to his spine.

He sank to the floor and I stepped on to my right foot to launch a kick at his head. At the same time as his backside was landing on the floor the toe of my left boot caught him on the chin snapping the skull back with an audible snap. He was flung backwards and lay still. I stepped up to examine the body in time to see a hand twitch and the legs begin to move again.

What did it take to stop this guy? I moved up beside his head and stamped down hard on his skull. I stamped again and again, bits of bone and brain stuck to the sole of my boot but I kept lifting my size nines and smashing them down into the squelchy mess. I think I was yelling, "Die! Die, damn you, DIE!"

After a while I stopped because my boots were covered in gore and they were only pounding a carpet of gristle, bone and blood. The skull was no more, one eye had skittered under a bed, everything above Dead Guy's neck was just paste. I leaned my weight on the end of one of the beds and stayed there, panting. A drop of sweat dribbled down my forehead and off the tip of my noise. Bit by bit my brain took control and turned on the hearing and thinking bits. I straightened up.

Everyone was looking at me, everyone was quiet. I took a step forward to Lydia but she shank back and joined the huddle of non-combatants. Even the fellow who had his arm used as an aperitif was silent as he sat on the end of a treatment table, one arm heavily bandaged and doped to the gills on painkillers.

But now they all looked at me with those eyes, those eyes that say you have scared the shit out of people.

****

Chapter 7

Couldn't blame them really, I'd scared myself. I hate being driven by visceral reaction, hate losing control. I don't mind being drunk, in fact I enjoy letting the control go – but I choose to let it go. Not like this, not the screaming heebie-jeebies reaching out of the darkness to take over.

Behind the huddled masses I noticed some new arrivals to our little party, a pair of Tharls wearing the Security patch. They also stood open mouthed and quiet.

"Uhhnh..," I said, articulate as always. "I...I think he's dead. Permanently." I took a few more squelchy steps and stopped. What's the correct etiquette for wiping brains from one's boots? "We need to get help," I managed to say before sitting on the edge of a vacant bed. Truth to tell, I was a bit done in; the emotional drain of my little scene was beginning to hit and I was feeling a heaviness descend on my limbs. My lovely Lydia came and sat beside me, she put an arm around my waist and just lay her head on my shoulder. Best medicine a man can have, I thought, a beautiful woman who cares for you; she held my hand and used her thumb to gently rub the back of my ugly paw.

"Thank you," I whispered. Her hand squeezed mine in response. I shut my eyes and thought about dozing off. Ahh, peace...

"Sergeant Valentine?" asked a voice.

I opened my eyes to see the flattened stomach of a Tharl standing before me, presumably the rest of him was nearby. I grunted a response. My eyes travelled up to the name tag and finally came to rest on his face.

"Corporal Kam'thad," I said, false cheerfulness beaming out of me. "Looking good, love the body work." My smile may have looked a bit forced, but here I was, trying to conduct a civilised conversation in a room where I'd just stomped one of the walking dead into a pulp. "Something I can do for you?" I asked. "I'm sure I've got a few moments before the next crisis." I lapsed into silence and just went with an inane smile, gave me more time to think about Lydia.

"Sergeant Valentine," said Kam'thad, "we have been sent to escort you to the cells." Behind him his companion shifted from foot to foot, a bit edgy with all the excitement.

Wonderful, I thought, the cells. "What have I done this time?" I asked, "And to who....er, whom?"

The big Tharl maintained a steady gaze, he wasn't nervous, he knew his abilities and his job. "The charge is murder," he stated. "Crewman Jucthaz was found beaten to death earlier this evening, a witness claims you were seen running from the area."

"A witness, eh?" I said. "Wouldn't be Don'elk by any chance?"

The big guy didn't change expression or stance, "I'm not at liberty to say," he said. "But I have already made a formal statement to the effect you were present during an earlier discussion with Jucthaz, an interview in which he maintained you had already beaten him."

I shrugged, "Always tell the truth, eh? You're a real altar boy, Kam'thad." He blinked and I guessed he missed the reference, "I haven't laid a hand on him, I'm a man of peace." As I said it, I realised it was a stupid statement, they'd probably seen enough of my recent bit of mayhem with Dead Guy to disprove any statement I might have about my gentle nature.

The silence built a little, they were probably wondering if I was going to object violently but I had used up all my emotional bank account. I was dead beat. When I stood up, I had the satisfaction of seeing Kam'thad take a backward step, his offsider even leaped a little. I take my pleasure wherever I can, being such a mean spirited mongrel.

"No worries, mate," I said, "I'll come quietly." I turned to Lydia and asked, "Please find Magic. Sorry, find Captain Althorp of the NightWatch and tell him I've been arrested. He'll know what to do."

All Security guards carry these funny little bits of material, two loops of a flexible substance which can be placed over a prisoner's wrists so he – or she – can be secured. Far better than hunting for a piece of rope, believe me, there's never a piece of rope handy when you want one. I took a few of them out of my pocket said to Kam'thad, "Give me a minute, would you?"

Without waiting for permission, I moved back up the aisle to the beds containing the other two dead guys. En route I stepped into the brainy sludge again, but didn't care – how weird is that? I used the loops to secure each of the dead man's wrists to the side of the bed; if these guys followed the example set by their recently deceased compatriot, we would be facing another two hungry corpses. If this did happen, I was going to be safe in a cell, lucky me. I didn't really care about anyone else on this stinking ship, my sense of being persecuted had lumped all on the ship together. They didn't like me and I didn't like them. This was my opinion of everyone except for two groups. the NightWatch, who could look after themselves, and Lydia. I did not want to have to worry about her facing off one of these monsters and having no one to help. I knew they took a bit of killing.

I squelched out of the room between the two Tharls, my boots making soft, squelching sounds as I left a trail of blood and bones on the shiny, clean floor. I hoped it was a bugger to clean.

****

I spent the rest of that day, and all the next day, in the cells. I wasn't mistreated or abused, just ignored. Magic came and visited, told me he was working on my freedom but it would take some time. I had a track record of violence and word on the street was I was a mean spirited, vengeful man who could easily beat a man to death. Graphic accounts of me stomping a man's head to a pulp gave a certain credibility to these stories.

I couldn't really complain, they were right. I was a mean spirited, vengeful man and I intended to demonstrate this to Don'elk at the first opportunity.

When would I learn?

Magic may have sensed I needed a bit of quiet, reflective time and I suspect he was going to leave me in the cells so I could think about life for a while. Bastard.

My evening meal was missed and I took this to be another manifestation of the universe working against me. No one came to visit, again confirming I had no friends.

Somewhere about this time God gave me a belt on the head and told me to stop feeling sorry for myself. His message was along the lines of, 'Get a grip, grow up and take a good hard look at yourself.' I've always had a robust relationship with my Maker, He pulls me into line when I need it. And right about now, I needed it.

I thought over Magic's comments, I reviewed my actions and came face to face with my own selfishness and arrogance. I had to start thinking how my actions affected those around me, I couldn't just live for my own pleasure and expect someone else to clean up my mess. Time to grow up. Bloody hell, I was turning into my father.

A scratching at my cell door interrupted my epiphany, moments later it opened.

"Val," whispered Meataxe, "we've got big problems." I could tell this was serious because he was sober and it was evening, usually he's slurring a lot more. And he was terrified. I don't know what worried me more, the fact he was sober or finding out what was bad enough to scare Meataxe.

Behind my surprising friend stood another mystery guest, Corporal Kam'thad. I stepped through the door and into my next nightmare.

"Dead guys are eating people, Val!" Meataxe said, disbelief wafting from every sweaty pore. "Eating them!"

Kam'thad leaned against one wall for support, "Your Captain needs you, Valentine." He slouched a bit more, this guy was not well, his normal red colouring looked washed out and orangey, I even had the impression his horns were wilting but it may have been my imagination; I'm not familiar with the look of a sick Tharl.

More surprises with his next statement, "We need you." He plumped one massive arm on my shoulder and leaned on me; I only sagged a little as I stared into his glazed eyes. "Get me in that cell, lock me in." I twisted a little and lurched my burden into my recent habitat; he sank against a wall and kept talking. "We had video of the Sick Bay, the camera recorded your fight with that...that thing. Your captain and I watched; it was so hard to kill."

Tell me about it, I thought, as he slid down to the floor.

"I'm getting sick, I don't want to turn into one of those things," he panted. "Find a cure, Valentine. Lock me in here where I cannot harm others. Already the humans have all fallen ill, the Tharls are next."

"How do you know Tharls are the next to go?" I asked.

He was slurring his words now as he sank to lie on the floor, "We put H'nuth next door in a cell after we arrested you. I watched you handcuff those other dead humans and saw the wisdom of restraining a dead one. H'nuth died this morning." My blood chilled for a moment, I knelt beside him, feeling very inadequate. He went on. "And then he came back. Came back as a monster." He took a breath, "Tharls are next." His eyes closed and his breathing became laboured.

I stood up and looked down at his large bulk, my mind not liking this picture. As I moved back into the corridor and locked the cell door behind me, I considered the implications. If everyone who received the nanobot injection became infected and died we would have a ship full of monsters. Flesh eating monsters.

How do I get myself into these situations, I asked myself. My inner voice didn't reply - bloody typical.

Meataxe gulped and said, "Magic wants us all to meet in our assembly room, the corporals are rounding up the rest of the Watch; I had to come and get you." He lowered his voice and looked around, no doubt worried we might be overheard in the empty corridor, "Val, I saw guys in a room drag another man down and eat him! They just bit chunks right off him!" He shivered, seeing Meataxe shiver is not an inspiring sight. I sighed.

"Come on," I said and we moved down the hall to the small ready room for guards looking after the cells. "What weapons have you got?" I asked.

He pulled out his sword and passed me a war hammer. Fair enough, I thought. I looked a question at him and gestured at the closed door. He nodded and I pushed through, he went right and I went left. We entered the room with weapons out, ready for anything; it was empty. I sank into a chair at a small desk bristling with technology, I was looking for a clue as to what to do next.

"Where are the guards?" I asked.

"Dunno, Val," he answered. "We started getting alarms at the start of the evening, crewmen falling sick, the Sick Bays filled up quickly, we started putting people into their cabins. Magic had us lock them in, all the people we found. The ones in Sick Bays we strapped to their beds like you did the two Undead." He stood peeking through the partially opened exit door, sword in hand, eyes bulging a little.

"Get a grip, Meataxe," I said, "What's this about people eating each other?" I had a fair idea about the last question but I needed an up-date. "Meataxe," I sighed, "the guy I, er, stomped on, he was eating any bit, not just brains." I pushed a few buttons on something which looked familiar, I think I saw one like it on Magic's desk. A list of little pictures appeared on the screen, beside each picture was an empty box. I'd been awake enough to know you pushed the screen on one of these empty boxes if you wanted to access that picture – thank you Teddy Boy. I recognised one of the pictures as the shoulder patch all Security guards wear, I assumed it meant this picture would connect me to the Security section. I pushed the corresponding box.

He twitched a bit more. "Are we going to head off soon," he said. "I'm feeling a bit nervous here. Feel safer with my mates."

The screen cleared and I saw another list of pictures, five of them. Each picture had another box beside it; great, what the hell does this mean? "You haven't got any mates, Meataxe," I replied, pushing the first button. A voice came out of the speaker, a slurry Tharl asking for help.

Okay, I thought, let's just keep pushing buttons until someone from the NightWatch answers. "Have so," said Meataxe, "I do have mates, Val. You're my mate, aren't you?" I looked up to see his scared face beseeching me from the doorway. Poor bloke, he'd been fighting his own battles, coming to grips with losing his home, his planet. We were all he had.

"Of course, I'm your mate, you dill," I said, all care and compassion. "Listen, do you know how to contact the NightWatch through this thing?" I wasn't hopeful, I'd seen Meataxe struggle with the concept of opening a window.

"Last icon on the Security menu," he said, surprising the heck out of me. 'Icon' and 'menu' were words I understood. An icon was in a church and a menu was in a tavern. What was this big goose talking about?

"Come again?" I asked.

"The little pictures are 'icons', push the one with the Security picture," he said. "That brings up another list, it's called a 'menu'. Push the last one and you'll go through to the Captain's desk"

I looked at him, "Who are you and what have you done with the real Meataxe?" I pushed the last button, icon, picture, thingy...

"Is that you, Val?" asked Magic's voice from a small speaker grill. Last he knew I was in a cell, but somehow he expected me to call him from the guard's desk.

I looked at Meataxe, "How does he do this stuff?"

****

Chapter 8

"Val," said Magic, "Got a little job for you." His face in the screen had a worried look, I wasn't surprised.

"Good to see you again, too, Charles," I commented.

"Yeah, whatever, now listen up," he shrugged off my inherent sarcasm. "The whole ship has started to go down, looks like only people from a planet are immune, any planet will do. That's us, the NightWatch and a handful of other folk. I've got most of the NightWatch back here with me but you're quite a distance away; the rest of the survivors are scattered throughout the ship amidst the dying and the reanimated. Can't be good for them."

I bet, I thought, hiding from someone who wants to eat you wouldn't be a nice feeling. "What do you want me to do, Magic?" I asked. Meataxe was still nervous, holding the door open a crack and peering down the corridor, shuffling his feet and making me feel twitchy.

"The Man in Black is trapped in the Chief Trader's quarters," he said. "You have to go and get him out." Our original Captain - The Man in Black. "We're cut off from those areas, too many Undead roaming the corridors. You're closest. Get him and keep him safe until we can find a way out of this mess."

"No worries, boss," I said. No idea how to do it, but now was not the time for nervous Nellies, Magic needed to know the job would be done. "How bad is it?"

"We're stuffed," he replied. "All the humans have gone the full route and are either Undead or alive and being chased by Undead. Tharls are in the process of dying – then they reanimate, as you well know. Everyone else is either sick or comatose, I've sent out a ship wide alert for everyone to seal themselves in their cabins. Val, this ship carries thousands of people, even if most are locked away it still leaves hundreds roaming the corridors. Mostly the humans, we caught on too late for them."

He looked off screen a moment, nodded and then continued to me, "We've got to secure Life Support and Engineering before some drongo stumbles into something and hits a switch. How do you feel about losing power or having all the airlock doors open simultaneously?"

"Not good," I agreed. "How do I find the Man in Black?"

"Follow the blue line on the ceiling," he replied. "Each major section of the ship has a line joining it to the command centre, green is Life Support, blue is Trade, black is Security, yellow is Engineering and so on."

I looked up at my blank, featureless ceiling. "I can't see any lines," I said. Meataxe shut the door hurriedly and activated the lock. He leaned his back against the door and looked around frantically. Part of my mind was trying to follow Magic's directions and another part wondered why Meataxe was acting strange. Stranger than normal, I mean.

"Of course not, you dill, they're only in the corridors. Leave the room you're in and get to a main corridor, then follow it until you reach Franz. We're going now to secure those vital areas and pick up any strays on the way. I'll leave Ted to man this communication system; we can link up through him." He left the screen and I saw Ted slide into the chair.

This gave me a moment to ask Meataxe, "What's up?"

He mouthed a word, difficult to make out through all his facial hair so I said, "Huh?" Concise as ever.

Ted spoke from the screen, "Better get a move on, Val, the corridor between you and us is full of human Undead, all looking for a feed."

I realised what Meataxe was saying, "Think they've found us, Ted. Meataxe just spotted some coming this way. We've locked the door, should be alright." The door started to shudder as a body slammed into it, I saw it buckle.

"Or not," I said, standing up. There were three doors from the room, the one behind me led to another set of cells; another - the one through which we had entered - was currently being pummelled by our local Undead and the final door led to parts unknown. Unknown to me. "We've got some options, do you know where these doors lead." The door was going to give way any moment, no time for advice from Ted. I grabbed Meataxe by the shoulder, drew my hammer and waited while he followed my lead and readied his sword. Which door? The cells were probably only one way in and out, that left the last door. It could be a corridor or room, could be empty or filled with teeth. Which way?

Worst case, the unknown door opened to a narrow corridor full of Undead, we would have no room to move. I dismissed the doorway to the cells; it was only one way in and out. Considering the door we entered from was already populated by the free lunch crowd, any other option was a bonus. I opened the door to parts unknown, dragging Meataxe with me.

As we left, the Undead broke into our room, growling after their disappearing food. I also heard Ted's voice come from the communicator, "Go back through the cells, they have another access to the corridors, your other door leads to the Tharls' muster room."

A day late and a dollar short, Ted, I thought.

I slammed the door shut and turned around; the muster room seemed empty. Empty except for the handful of Tharls lying on the floor, dead or comatose. So far, so good.

A dead Tharl began to stand up.

****

I locked the door behind me, which should gain us a few moments before bad things happened. I leaned my back against it and faced the slowly reanimating Tharls. Beside me Meataxe was very quiet, mouth open, forehead glistening with sweat; I hoped he was a terrified as he looked because I wanted some company.

Tharls are big, bigger than humans; their red skin, little horns and muscular appearance adds to the terror factor. In fact, I thought the first Tharl I ever saw may have been a real devil - before I killed him, of course. So now we were facing a bunch of them and my experience with the reanimated corpse in the Sick Bay led me to assume they were going to chow down on me and Meataxe.

I did not feel well, perhaps I should have chosen door number one. Meataxe moaned a little, a strange, nervous gurgle from deep in his throat. My bowels echoed the sound.

Behind me the door kicked as something heavy and no doubt hungry slammed into it.

Some days it doesn't pay to get out of bed.

****

I put my hand on Meataxe's arm, restraining him from attacking the Tharls. There was something different about this scene, we weren't being attacked. At least, not yet. There were three Tharls in the room with us, three Undead Tharls. A blaster can kill a Tharl, swords and hammers will also do the job but the chances are you will end up dead yourself. They are very hard to kill.

The room was too small for us to dodge around them, we were trapped. The only plan I had was to imitate a piece of wall. Meataxe and I stood very, very still. Shallow breathing, mouths open, eyes terrified. The terror came off us as a wave, both of us were almost catatonic. Being trapped in a room with the Undead can change your perspective on life.

The Tharls stood up from where they lay and looked round, none made any noise; no words, no growls, nothing. They sniffed and stared, they carried out each of these actions to each other and then turned to face us.

Oh God oh God Oh God.........

They sniffed us and stared. But nothing else.

As we stood and watched they began to move off, eventually leaving the muster room and entering the corridor. They didn't seem to be driven by any sense of direction or group decision process, they just wandered off.

Why weren't we attacked?

Behind us the door continued to be pummelled, Meataxe and I pushed back but I knew it was only a matter of time before it gave way.

I said, "Let's go." Together Meataxe and I ran from the door and into the corridor, I glanced over my head and saw a bunch of coloured lines across the ceiling – never noticed them before –but there was a problem. Which way? Left or right? The door behind us slammed open, human Undead tumbling in. I took a gamble and ran off to the right with Meataxe blundering behind me.

A dead Tharl stood in the corridor ahead of me, could I run around it before it decided it wanted a snack? In my clumsy terror, I nudged its shoulder as I ran past but received no reaction – what was going on here? I needed to think this out a bit but I was conscious of whatever was coming through the doorway behind us in the muster room, pretty sure it wanted to eat us. I pulled Meataxe around a couple of corners, hoping we had lost our immediate pursuers.

In retrospect I realised we were lucky not to have run into any other human Undead. But there was a scattering of Tharl Undead around us and none of them showed us any interest after the initial look and sniff. Time for an experiment.

A stupid, stupid experiment. An absolutely brainless idea. Why do I do these things to myself?

"Stay here," I told Meataxe and stepped in front of a Tharl Undead. With my buttocks tight enough to open bottles, I waited while it walked closer. As it reached me, I took a deep breath and leaned into the approaching creature. My hand was clenched around the handle of my war hammer hard enough to leave grooves from my fingers. It came closer, I broke wind, and it stopped, paused, and then stepped around me.

I just about fainted with relief, my body feeling all loose and boneless. On the upside, I hadn't soiled myself. I think. Out of the corner of my eye I could see Meataxe's face showing astonishment and disbelief at my continued survival.

Meataxe said, "Val!" He seemed stumped after this statement so he tried again "Val, you could have been... eaten."

Slumping against the wall I said, "Undead Tharls don't eat humans."

****

It made sense to me. Back in the Sick Bay the Undead had bitten a human; then it had looked and sniffed at the other dead humans, the conscious aliens and the unconscious bodies of Lonely – a human – and H'nuth – a Tharl. The creature had walked past each of these beds in order to attack Lydia and myself, more live humans.

And now I had shown Undead Tharls ignored live humans. I had a hunch, "Meataxe, listen to me. The Undead only attack living members of their own type. We have to be careful of human Undead, but we should be able to ignore everyone, or everything, else."

"Are you sure, Val?" he asked. "Maybe that one just didn't like you?"

"Thanks for the vote of confidence, mate," I said. "And no, I'm not sure. But that's they way I'm going to play it."

In a husky whisper, he said, "I don't wanna be eaten, Val."

"We play the hand we're dealt, Peter," I said.

"Val, you never call me by my real name. No-one does," he said. I looked at his face, his two worried eyes peering out from all his hair. Meataxe had a heavy black beard and wild, unruly hair.

"Just on special occasions, mate," I said.

He looked around and saw another Undead Tharl coming up behind us. Meataxe might have a lot of flaws – on second thought there was no 'might' about it, he had a lot of flaws – but he certainly didn't lack courage. Based on nothing more than my word, he stepped in front of the wandering Tharl Undead and waited. I was impressed and humbled, he believed in me. The Undead stopped, sniffed and then moved around my quivering friend.

"I think you're right, Val," he said – bit late if I was wrong – "but we still have a few loose cannons after us." He gestured towards the corridor we had just left, three human Undead hove into view. They seemed to be searching, doing a lot of sniffing and looking so it didn't take them long to spot us. They didn't break into a run but their walking took on a pronounced urgency, a sense of purpose and direction. Unfortunately, it was our direction.

I looked up to make sure we still had a blue line above us, tugged Meataxe's arm and we moved off, away from our fan club.

****

We ran on, participants in a very strange race down the long corridor, the human Undead always pursuing, always there. Occasionally we would have to step around an Undead Tharl and let me tell you it is one weird little dance step. The first few times we did it I bunched my shoulders waiting for the grab which never came; I would pull my elbows and arms in close to my body, tuck my chin into my chest and try to run. It is very difficult running in this hunched up twisted way, my brain tried to help but my gut wasn't fully convinced we were safe. Must have looked like a constipated dog.

We slowed going past any open door and then sped up, just in case any more hungry people came out to say hello. So many questions went through my mind, - how did the Undead track us? Why don't Tharl Undead eat us? Why weren't we all sick?

"Val," panted Meataxe, "why aren't we sick?"

Surreal. "Dunno," I replied. Why do people think I have the answers to everything?

"But you have to know," he said. "You know about stuff. You always know what to do."

I flicked a quick glance at him, he wasn't poking fun at me, he was serious. Hell's teeth! When did this happen? When did I get to be the answer man?

"Bugger off!" I replied, "I just make this stuff up as we go along. Now shut up, the corridor turns up ahead; we'll need to be a bit careful and have a look around the corner before we run into more strife. Remember, keep an eye out for a blue stripe on the ceiling."

"No worries, boss," he answered. I'm sure I detected a tinge of smugness in his reply, a little bit of satisfaction that I did, in fact, know what to do. He's a bloody idiot.

I stopped and slid against the wall as we reached the corridor, Meataxe right behind me. We were both used to this sort of sneaking and I knew I could rely on my partner not to do something stupid. He had gross personal habits, a casual acquaintance with personal hygiene and thought a fart joke was the pinnacle of humour; but put him up the pointy end when things were going bad and he became someone else – a man you could trust with your life.

"Watch for those guys behind us," I said, and snuck an eye around the corner. The corridor was empty up to a large bulkhead door, no other Undead of any sort, no other doors. "We're clear," I said and moved into the new corridor, the blue line still above us and going straight towards the closed door up ahead.

Meataxe ducked around after me, "They're still back there, Val, still after us. But they aren't running, just a fast walk. Why aren't they running?"

"Shut up, Meataxe, and let me look," I replied. Keeping my head low to the floor, I peeked back around the corner into the corridor we had just left. Some distance away I saw our pursuers moving in our direction. They couldn't see us and had slowed, eventually stopping. Each of the three stood and looked around, I think I saw nostrils twitching, couldn't be totally sure. I just got the impression they were sniffing. After a few beats they moved again, heading towards us, but still not running. Why weren't they running? How many questions would I ask myself before my brain exploded? Arghhh!!

"Come on," I said and we moved down to the closed door. "Do you know how to open this thing?" I asked my companion.

He pursued his lips, looked at the door, thought a bit, looked at me and said, "Nope." He gave me one of those looks that say you will have an answer to whatever the problem is and I trust you.

Great. "Look for one of those keypad thingies, like the ones on all the other doors" I instructed. Why was this door such a big deal? Then an answer came – finally! – maybe this was the main door into the Trader's quarters, maybe behind it we would find the Man in Black and he could do the rest of the thinking while I went back to plain old hitting. I'm good at hitting.

"Over here," Meataxe said, he had found a flip down plate which opened to reveal a set of buttons, each with its own little icon. 'Icon' - my new word for the day. We both looked at the buttons and then at each other; we both shrugged, neither of us knew which was the right one to push. We had a choice of six buttons, two rows of three.

Around the corner behind us came our three hungry corpses, I saw them pick up speed and move towards us with renewed sense of purpose. They still didn't run and made no sound; I don't count saliva dribbling out of open mouths as a sound. Time for a decision,

Meataxe just looked at me calmly, waiting for the miracle, waiting for bloody Mr Hero Valentine to do something. Fainting sounded about right.

I looked at the buttons, searching for meaning, what did those icons mean? I recognised the button to shut the door, it must be standard but the normal open door icon was not there. What sort of idiot designs these things?

A comment Lonely had once made came back to me, he had worked out the right button to push in another situation; he said he just chose the shiniest one, assuming it was the one most often used. I reached out and pushed the cleanest button, the door slid open and we stepped through. Once inside I pushed the close door button and the large, heavy door slid back into place, cutting us off from our fan club.

Meataxe was beaming at me, I wanted to hit him. "Don't say a word. Not a bloody word," I snarled.

****

Chapter 9

We definitely were not in the Chief Trader's quarters. Not unless he had a skewed viewpoint on interior decoration. Before us lay a large, open expanse containing a variety of machines and shuttle craft. I recognised our location; we were in the maintenance bay where I had first met Lydia.

Meataxe looked a question at me. I said, "We must have gone the wrong way when we left the Security section, the blue line went left and right; I guess we should have gone left." In retrospect it was an understandable mistake, the blue line connected lots of sections with the Chief Trader, I had just picked the wrong option. Sigh.

And the only way back was through the bulkhead door and our dinner guests.

From behind a shuttle craft came a bunch of human Undead, sniffing. They saw us and began moving in our direction. I was just considering reopening the bulkhead door and taking a chance on just three meat lovers when a door on the closest shuttle slid open.

"Hello, handsome," said Lydia, "care to join me?"

We ran, the Undead were about the same distance from the open door as us, but we were running and they stayed with a walk. Weird. They were still several paces behind as we both charged through the doorway of the shuttle, I'm leaner and meaner than Meataxe so I got there first but he was only one step behind me. Lydia hit the controls and the door slid into place, she flew into my arms at the same time as the pounding started. The Undead wanted to join us.

"Hello, lover," she said, and I really hoped she was talking to me. "Don't worry about those creeps outside, they can't get in through the door no matter how much they pound their fists." She gave me a pretty serious hug and then released her grip; this girl had my head spinning; I didn't know if she meant what she said or if she was just friendly. Really, really friendly. Right Honourable can talk to girls very easily, Horse has his own special brand of charisma but I always felt clunky. But this beautiful, gorgeous woman had called me some special names. Did that mean I could make some assumptions?

My brain reminded me we were trapped inside a shuttle craft by flesh eating Undead and would I give the lovey-dovey stuff a rest for a bit. Right, back to work, I thought.

"What's going on, Lydia?' I asked. "How'd you end up here?" the pounding continued outside with no sign of abating.

"Hello, Lydia," said Meataxe, eyes downcast and voice all serious. It was all he could do to stop drawing pictures with his toe and twirling his hat. If he had a hat.

She stepped up to the big goof and rubbed a hand down his cheek, "Hello, Peter," she cooed. My oafish companion gurgled with pleasure and wiggled; he just needed a tail to wag. It was just embarrassing. Then she moved up to the control section and sat in one of the pilot seats. Before Meataxe could recover from Lydia's charm, I grabbed the other seat and plopped myself down; Meataxe came out of his reverie and realised his missed opportunity. I smiled at him, an evil, mean-spirited smile. He leaned over the back of Lydia's chair and sighed with pleasure. Bastard.

"You called him 'Peter'?" I asked Lydia, I tried to put some mild accusation in the question.

She smiled at me, "I can't really call him Meataxe, can I?" She turned and beamed at him, "The darling man." The idiot slobbered over her chair and made gurgling noises; it was enough to make a man sick. She flipped some switches and a few screens came on, one showed the view outside the door. We saw a gaggle of Undead – not sure what the collective noun is – all of them trying to hit the door. All to no effect. First bit of good news all day.

"There they are, Val," she said, "and they're they'll stay. I speak from experience. When I found myself in a room full of hungry dead people I shut myself up in here. They all pummelled the door for a while and eventually gave up and wandered about." She gave me a friendly smirk, "Until now."

Then she hit me with the big one, "What do we do now, sweet cheeks?" she asked. Great, someone else looking to me for solutions.

"No idea," I answered - honesty above all else, that's my motto. "Got any suggestions?"

"Well," she said, "I wanted to get to the bulkhead door on the far wall." She pointed at a screen showing most of the Maintenance area, I saw another big door, similar to the one from which we had entered. "But," she went on, "the access panel was damaged when one of the technicians tried to escape. He was trapped against it and eaten. Bit yucky, really."

I bet; by looking closely I could see a smear against part of the wall and a mess of rags on the floor. From what Lydia had just told us it wasn't just rags, it also held the grisly remains of a human being. "I can fix it," she said, "but not in the time it takes those freaks to find and eat me. Didn't fancy that idea so I stayed here, waiting for a hero." She batted her eyes at me.

I had to admire her composure under pressure. Sitting trapped in this box while awful things roamed around outside couldn't have been a pleasant experience. And she had no way of knowing if any help would come. My girlfriend's a tough chick.

"The Undead chased us, but only at a walk," I said, more thinking out loud than starting a discussion. The others stayed silent, recognising the random nature of my mumbles. "I can move faster than they can walk. If I go outside and run, they'll come after me." My logical brain was doing a bang-up job of planning, but my emotional brain was listening on in horror. "Once they're all after me you can go fix the door. When it's open I'll dodge the bad guys and run after you. We shut the door and all's well."

It should work; the plan had a few holes but they were all mine. I needed to keep going while I had some enthusiasm for this totally ridiculous course of action. "Let's do it!" I cheered.

They both looked at me in astonishment. "You're out of your skull, Val," stated Meataxe. If they catch you, it's all over – Valentine buffet!" He shut up, looked at me and finally came out with, "No, I'll be the bait, they can chase me."

Lydia stayed silent, I said to Meataxe, "Forget it, I'm going. You cart around too much beef to be light and nimble whereas I, on the other hand, am just poetry in motion. A blur when I move."

"More like a smudge," he grumbled but he didn't keep the argument going.

"Meataxe, you need to be first through the door when Lydia opens it." I was thinking of the next step, more hazards ahead. "There may be more hordes of the Undead in there so you get to be appetiser; should give her more time to get back here. If you're in trouble I'll try to help but I may be a bit busy. You'll be on your own."

He shrugged agreement, "No worries, boss." He's a tough bastard. No bloody imagination, that's his problem.

"Right," I said, "let's do it!" I readied myself at the door, my adrenaline pumping while the bowels did their normal dance. How do I get into these situations - thumb in bum, brain in neutral. I love my job.

Lydia remained motionless, gazing steadily at both of us, "If you boys have quite finished beating your chests, we might resume our conversation. Honestly, some people." She turned back to the screens and pointed at the view of our shuttle door, "Notice anything interesting?" she asked.

I looked and saw her point; we still had a bunch of Undead beating the door. Not as many as at first but still more than one. And even one Undead is a tough customer.

"Right," I muttered. I lowered my hammer, feeling somewhat cheated. "Right....let's just...wait..." I sat down, Lydia smiled and patted my knee, congratulating her backward child.

****

After about half an hour the last Undead sauntered off and we regathered for a quick departure. While we were waiting, we had discussed other options but kept coming back to our original plan. Lydia would open the door and I would sprint out waving and hollering. The Undead would chase me - this was not my favourite part of the plan. When the way was clear, she and Meataxe would run for the door where she would fix the controls. They would open the door and, if clear, would enter the new corridor. I would cunningly slip past my pursuers and join them, shut the door and ta-da! All of us would be safe.

It had a vague chance of succeeding.

The door opened, I ran outside and tripped.

I slid along the shiny floor for a few feet and came to rest in a nice clear space. Looking up I saw my arrival had generated some interest, the original bunch of Undead were a little spread out but they soon sniffed me out and turned in my direction.

"Hi, guys," I said. "Can I play too?" Up I leapt and off I ran, yahooing and capering about, taking them away from the desired door controls. I hoped. Soon I had a little entourage of fans after me, none still at more than a fast walk. I quickly moved into an empty space between a pair of shuttles and ran into the back of another Undead. Talk about surprised.

I bounced off its broad back and realised I had run into an Undead Tharl. That was the good news, it meant he wasn't going to eat me. Yay. The bad news was he had a few buddies with him and most were human. This bunch had just been standing around, doing whatever out-of-work Undead do, when muggins had interrupted their little tete-a-tete. I stopped only long enough to bounce off my new acquaintance while behind me the original crew had moved a few paces closer. It was time for some creative dodging and weaving with a minimum of tripping.

I found a few more Undead, scattered in ones and twos throughout the Maintenance deck. Pretty soon I had run out of new places to find them and since they were following me none were watching as Lydia and Meataxe ducked out of the shuttle. They quickly moved to the door panel. No Undead saw them because they were all watching me, and in order to keep their attention I was whooping and hollering, leaping about, waving my arms and gradually moving away from our target door.

Oh, please, Lydia, I prayed, don't be too long about this.

I had run out of places to dodge, the Undead had formed a loose semi-circle around me, not through any deliberate plan, they just came from all parts of the huge room to see what the excitement was about. At a rough guess there were about thirty of them, too many for me, even on a good day. When my brain came up with this statement I giggled, pity I was the only one to appreciate my humour.

They walked forward and I stepped backwards, occasionally glancing back to check for obstacles. The only thing behind me was the corner of the Maintenance Hanger, each of the walls were bare; no ladders, hanging cables, odd bits of rope, no doors either. The net around me now consisted of all my new friends, mouths open, walking shoulder to shoulder. No gaps.

I told my brain this would be a good time to come up with a plan. Time to consider options - when faced with an obstacle there are only three ways to get to the other side: go over, go under, or go through. Go through – not a chance, I could charge at them but a misstep or trip would let one of them grab me, and it would only take one, one hand, one moment of inattention and I would be lunch. Too big a gamble.

Go under – steel deck, no pipes or trapdoors. That route was just not physically possible.

What's left? Go over? Right, time to fly; another giggle snuck out.

I managed to climb the wall by placing my back into the corner and placing my right boot heel onto a convenient bolt. Up I stepped, my hands found grips and I looked down to find a space for my left boot heel. By this means I got to about four feet off the ground, both boots on a bolt and my hands gripping some old shelving brackets jutting out of each corner. But this was not going to be far enough, the Undead were about six feet away and bunching up nicely, good table manners, no pushing and shoving, just a dense mass of teeth and appetites.

I had to go higher. Without any handholds I decided to just use my feet. By placing each boot heel a little higher I could go up a bit further. Balance was the key; I didn't dare look down because I would have fallen. My fingers walked up each wall of the corner, head back and eyes straight ahead. My entire concentration was focussed on each boot; I would stand with my weight on whatever stuck out of the wall for a few inches and use my other foot to search for another, higher support.

And all the time the Undead got closer, if they could reach any part of me they would drag me down and that would be the end of yet another glittering career. They didn't make any noise so I had no idea how close they were. I did not dare risk a peek down as I moved in case I tipped forward and fell. Each moment I expected to feel the clammy grasp of fingers around my legs. Up I climbed, eyes straight ahead - discipline, discipline discipline, I told myself. Sweat ran into my eyes, leg muscles trembled; I felt I was swaying like a tree in the wind.

Fear and apprehension roamed freely throughout my body and mind, spreading chaos, uncertainty, doubt and my old friend, blood-curdling terror. I've lost count of the number of times I have been truly and utterly terrified; not just scared, not frightened, I mean fear so great your intestines go to water, muscles liquefy and the blackness descends into your brain. Shit-scared is such an appropriate term.

I ran out of places for boots, no matter how hard I raised a foot I could not find any more ledges. My feet recognised the shape of the shelving brackets my hands had found and I knew there was no higher ground, I leaned back into the corner as far as I could, about a millionth of an inch, and lowered my eyes. Head still, chin tucked into chest, eyes down; I saw my adoring fans.

Deep breathes, Valentine, I told myself as I gazed into a sea of open mouths and outstretched hands. None touched me, I couldn't see those closest to the corner - and so closest to me - but it seemed a good bet I was safe so long as I stayed where I was. Whoopee.

Off in the distance I saw Lydia and Meataxe standing in the open door, my beautiful girl had got it to work. They were both looking at me, standing very still and watching my impromptu artistic grouping. A little tableau - 'Fool trapped by Undead.'

They waited. I waited. The Undead drooled a bit more.

Right, I said to myself, can't stay here all day. Got places to go, things to do, people to see. My brain had packed it in, so while I was considering the options my body decided to do something. Without thinking it through, I launched myself off the brackets, boots kicking as hard as I could, hands pushing from the wall. I had already dropped the hammer hoping it hit something in the head, maybe an eye.

I dove over the heads of the Undead, a beautifully executed forward dive, body at full stretch with hands gracefully extended. It was a bit of a hoot, really, the way their heads all turned to watch me in flight. I hit the floor behind the last Undead, my hands and arms outstretched to take the shock. I tucked my chin into my chest, pulled my head in and did a smooth forward roll. As my legs spun over my head, I pulled my right leg into a bend behind my left leg which I kept only slightly bent, foot ready for the impact. I rolled onto my right leg and used it to raise my buttocks off the ground, my momentum pushed me forward and I completed the roll by standing on my left foot. I kept the movement going by breaking into a run, flat out for the door, still Undeadless.

Sometimes I even amaze myself.

****

Chapter 10

As soon as I was clear Lydia hit the close button and the big bulkhead door swung down to seal off my recent buddies. Lydia flung herself into my chest and gave me another massive hug. A man could get used to this, I thought. Over her shoulder I gave Meataxe a wink. He just kept repeating, "Bloody hell, Val...bloody hell...," and looking at me like I won the annual beer drinking competition.

Reluctantly, I broke the clinch and looked over Lydia's head, no blue line. She saw my gaze and asked, "What's up, Val?"

"We need to find the Chief Trader's quarters," I explained. "We were following the blue line but I went the wrong way and ended up in the Maintenance Hangar. And where are we?"

We were in a room, a very strange room. Behind me was the door back to the Maintenance Hanger, the only other exit from the room was another door on the left wall. This worried me a great deal because I knew what lay behind the left wall – nothing, just the emptiness of space. I generally survive by ignoring bad things and so far I had been able to ignore the very bad thing of thinking about space.

But now I was confronted with a doorway to the outside and my skin crawled a bit. Violence gives you a boost, a person can handle weird stuff during a fight because the blood is running hot - there's probably a medico who could explain why but I didn't need to know the details. Suffice to say, I could deal with strange and scary in a fight, no problem. But this wasn't a fight, this was me standing calmly looking at a door to emptiness, a door in a very thin wall, the only thing keeping the nightmares at bay. My stomach descended, my mouth was dry and I felt the beginnings of panic. Just think about it, how can you deal with the idea of floating in nothing ... arghhh!!!

"This is a Ready Room for external maintenance," said Lydia in answer to my question. "That's my gear there." She pointed to a hanging suit, complete with helmet; it reminded me of full plate armour except it was not made of metal but rather something soft. "Well, not really mine, just the one I use most of the time."

I was a bit slow on the uptake and asked, "Why do you want to wear one of those things?"

She looked at me, "Like I said, Val, for external maintenance." I looked blank. She patted my arm again and said, "Sorry, love, I forget you're a bit new to all this." She walked over and held up a sleeve from one of the suits, "I put this on, pick up one of those tools," she gestured at a long rod with an end like a trident, "then I go through the big scary door and walk around the hull of the ship checking things."

My brain gurgled for a while, drool formed in the frontal lobes, stomach flipped back and forth.

I looked at this wondrous woman, standing there with a smile on her face, all normal and nice. My brain tried to imagine her putting on the suit and going outside to the great nothing, it didn't like it, "Er..." I began, "You mean you actually go and..."

Meataxe interrupted my free fall panic, "Val," he asked "what are we going to do? That's the only door out except for the bulkhead back into the Undead."

The only door out - the Undead didn't look so bad now, I thought. No way was I going into space wearing nothing but a shiny helmet and funny clothes.

"We could go through the inspection hatch," said Lydia, totally oblivious to my state of mind. I was hoping she thought I was in deep planning mode and didn't suspect my gibbering fear. She looked at me expectantly, waiting for the great leader to be wise.

"Inspection hatch?" I managed to say. She pointed to the ceiling, in one corner was a grate; looked marvellous. I felt a bit better, "Where does it go?" I asked.

She looked at it for a moment and said, "I think it leads to the interior maintenance walkway which runs around the ship. It links the various technical hangers, storerooms and the like. The next room," she pointed at the wall opposite our entry bulkhead, the wall without a door, "should be the Artificer's Workshop."

"Right," I said, "let's try it. Meataxe, you go first, I'll boost you up, then Lydia, then me." He grunted agreement, didn't even ask why he was going first. He's a good man in a tight spot, but he was also a big man and not light on his feet; I just couldn't see him doing the necessary unaided leap from the floor to the lip of the grate if he was last man. As it was, he would be able to reach down and grab my hands, he's a strong bugger.

I cupped my hands, he stepped into them and I lifted; the climb took many, many grunts from both of us. He put one foot on my shoulder and another on the top of my head, after first attempting to stick it into my open and gasping mouth. The taste of Meataxe's shoe will stay with me for a long, long time. He used the walls for support as he reached for the latch and unhooked the grate. Pushing it up, he was able to reveal our access manhole. The lid crashed back out of sight, I heaved his feet further and he managed to get his arms up over the lip of the opening. With a bit more thrusting, panting and cursing we were able to get him through the hole. I watched his feet disappear and stood back to wait, hoping for the best. I spat a few times.

Neither of us had mentioned the presence of Undead up there but I knew he was thinking it. Before he went through the hole, he had put his knife between his teeth, ready for action. He looked like a fat, sloppy pirate. I knew a knife would be useless against the Undead, putting a piece of steel through one's heart hadn't slowed it down at all, but I wasn't going to remind my friend of this piece of information. He needed to feel some security.

Moments later a bearded head peered back through the hole, "All clear," said Meataxe, knife no longer visible. He lowered his arms ready for Lydia, she stepped onto my hands and very slowly stood up, leaning against my face for the entire upward journey. I felt bits of female which were very definitely tasty and delectable, the thigh was particularly pleasant. I'm a lost cause.

She reached Meataxe's outstretched paws and he easily pulled her up. As I watched her lissom form rise above me, all thoughts of Undead went out of my head. Other thoughts rushed to fill their place, unmentionable thoughts. Really great thoughts.

She disappeared through the hole. I stood watching, eyes fixed on her point of exit, mind wandering down lascivious pathways until Meataxe dribbled on me. "Psst!" he slurped. "Come on, Val, I think I can hear something up here."

I had no weapon, no knife, axe, sword or blaster; my trusty hammer was back amongst the Undead. The only thing I saw was the long tool near the suits; this was a rod about six feet long and tipped with two broad pieces of metal. It looked remarkably like a pitchfork with only two tines, pity these tips weren't sharp. I took it, at least I could swing it and hit something hard, the tool did have a nice weighty feel, and threw it up to Meataxe. He shuffled it back out of sight and then reached down for me.

Suddenly he seemed to be a long way up.

I backed off and took a running jump, leaping as high as I could towards my dangling companion. He grabbed both my hands in his and we both grinned at each other, the effect was partially spoiled by a piece of moisture coming from him onto my forehead. Such is life.

I managed to haul myself up and through the hole; Lydia was waiting with my pitchfork and soon we stood erect on a metal walkway. Faint lights seemed to be embedded at intervals around floor level, these gave enough illumination for me to see the walkway extending ahead and also disappearing behind us. The rest of the space was quite open, one vast, dark cavern containing chutes, large pieces of machinery hanging in space, pipes and cables dripped from all areas. There was no proper floor, just our narrow path, about two feet wide without any guard rails, below the walkway was the ceiling of the room below us. Lydia whispered, "We go that way to the next grate." She pointed ahead and off we went, this time I was up front.

She didn't need to explain why she was whispering, I could hear the shuffles, the sound of footsteps. We were not alone up here.

The metal track we walked on rattled softly as our boots found their way through our very own Hell straight from Dante Alighieri's 'Inferno'- Right Honourable had read us bits from his copy but I couldn't see any Virgil up here. But we had other company, we heard other feet; not as far behind us in the dark as I hoped. I led the way with Lydia inserted between Meataxe and myself. Sounds off to the right made me start, I wasn't worried about them until I saw another track join ours up ahead a little, joining from the right; make that lots of tracks. All these walkways seemed to be linked. Oh, joy.

Lydia was taking peeks over my shoulder as we edged along, me waving my trident in feeble little circles while Meataxe occasionally stumbled and pushed us both forward. Like cats, we were. "There's the access hatch down to the next room" she said. I saw it, too, lights from the room below shone up through the holes in the grate; it didn't run the full width of the walkway, just a narrow hole. I assumed this was to allow crewman to still walk back and forth without falling down an open hatch.

"Val...," Meataxe began nervously. I looked behind and saw my comrade staring at an Undead moving towards us on one of the cross walks. It was followed by a conga line of hungry friends. Time for us to pick up the pace.

I reached the metal trapdoor and bent down to open it. There I was, stupid weapon in one hand, another hand feeling for a latch, my head down and bum up. Mr Hero. This is not the pose one hopes to strike when hearing approaching footsteps from ahead. Looking up from my gawky position, I saw legs walking towards me from the other end of the walkway. I was staring up into the hungry mouth of an Undead, reaching for my head.

From my bent position, I jabbed forward with my pitchfork. They wouldn't stop him but maybe I could force it back. The two prongs hit the Undead in the chest and caused it to take one backward step. I was happy with the situation; it gave me time to get to my feet and braced for a proper blow. This time, as the thing stepped forward, I thrust hard. Again, the prongs didn't penetrate but I forced Mr Hungry to stagger backwards quite a bit. If he had been alive, he would have some broken ribs.

This gave me time to check behind me to see how Meataxe was coping. He was facing a line of the Undead, some of them had travelled from the cross tracks to our track and were heading towards him. He was waving his sword but I knew it would be no protection, we had to get out of here. I bent down and pulled the trapdoor open, then straightened up to give my own dinner guest another jab. It staggered back but no real damage was done. The hole to the Artificer's room now stood exposed, I was on one side of the opening, Meataxe on the other and Lydia between us, squashed on the remaining piece of walkway surrounding the opening. A real cosy grouping.

"What do I do, Val?" asked a nervous Meataxe. Lydia was squashed between the pair of us, but she was a real soldier, she didn't say a word, scream or grab on to us and demand to be saved. We either got out of this or not, no room for maybes.

"Meataxe," I commanded, "drop into the room! Jump down and be ready for Lydia, you also have to keep any Undead in the room away from here. Move!" This was an easy command to give but a dreadful order to receive. If one of us was going to be lunch I didn't want it to be Lydia. Meataxe pushed past my girl and stepped into the hole without another word. What a guy. I heard his grunt when he landed while giving my own Undead partner another push. I could keep this up all day, the stupid thing didn't seem to realize it could just push past my pitchfork, or duck under it, or jump over it. It just kept walking forward, again and again. Have to admit, though, his level of tenacity could wear a man down.

After another push I turned to Lydia and told her to jump through, she dropped down as a line of Undead reached for her shirt. Her eyes came up to mine, I saw her lovely form plummet down and I pushed the trapdoor shut. I didn't want our grisly friends dropping on top of her.

I wasn't in a good place. There was one Undead on my side of the trapdoor, this was the guy I kept pushing back. Another bunch of them came on from the other side after following Meataxe. Both sets of Undead were almost upon me, I could push one lot back but not the other, sure I could keep up a bit of a dance but muscles tire. These characters didn't seem to know when to stop.

Again, I jabbed the prongs at my single Undead, aiming for another chest blow. I missed, instead hitting hit his neck. The tines of my pitchfork went on either side of the thing's neck, therefore my forward jab wasn't powerful. I started to pull the pitchfork back and hoped to get in a proper hit, very worried he would just reach up and grab the haft of my almost useless weapon.

He didn't even try, he just kept walking forward, pushing against the pitchfork as I pulled it back. The weapon was still around his neck and doing no real damage so I changed direction to walk forward into him. With me keeping the pitchfork pressed against his neck, he stopped. He tried to continue but he only had the muscle power of the crewman's body, an off-balance crewman. I was expecting a surge of super strength – by now these characters seemed to be tougher than normal people but the big pushback never came. He just stood there for a couple of beats trying to push against my solid muscle mass. He did growl a lot. And gnash his teeth. Not a good look. We had a stalemate.

Before I could get too happy with this standoff, I felt a finger brush my neck. Company's coming.

The walkway was narrow, Undead behind me, a single Undead ahead of me and surprisingly no terror from my internal organs, I guess they thought I could handle it. Smart alecs.

I pushed forward a few steps against my lone opponent, it had trouble walking backwards and, after about two paces, tripped over its own feet and sat down, I kept the pitchfork where it was and pushed his head back so his whole body was flat on the walkway, face up with my pitchfork forming a line between his neck and my arms. Before those behind me caught up I took a step and a leap and, using the pitchfork as a lever, I sailed over the flat body of my sedentary muncher. I landed near his head, changed my grip on my weapon and faced back the way I had come, I now faced a line of Undead trying to step over their prostrate companion. I was hoping for a bit of comedy, maybe they would all fall and trip over their prone friend and I could have a good laugh but no such luck. The first walking Undead stopped at the feet of its prone companion; they all stopped and waited for the fallen one to regain its feet at the start of their line. It then turned to face me, I now had a line of Undead looking to join me for lunch.

Oh, boy, never a dull moment.

****

Chapter 11

I backed up several steps, throwing anxious looks behind me. The line of Undead to my front continued to advance, step by step. I was separated from my companions, cut-off from the hatchway by the line of Undead. Behind me the walkway continued to other parts of the ship. Other parts no doubt full of more Undead. Right, I thought, time for a bit of action.

I'd had enough, enough of spaceships, of aliens, of stupid, stupid things in my life over which I had no control. As the Undead stepped their way towards me I felt a rage rise within me, a rage I had been able to drown in alcohol and stupidity. A rage which started when circumstances took me out of a familiar world and made me have to deal with too much, too much strange.

The first Undead was almost on me, behind him were another four or five, off in the darkness I heard other noises, footsteps, shuffles, no voices, no pleading.

You want me, boys, I thought, you have to come and get me. And you better bring a big stick.

I yelled, not a scream but a full-throated yell. I yelled and ran forward, eyes glaring and lips pulled back from my bared teeth. The yell drew together all my frustrations, all my fears and my anger into a palpable force. When my pitchfork hit the first Undead it was backed by months of emotion, I wasn't really there anymore; the part of my brain involved in higher order thinking was subsumed by the animal, by the manic forces of my inner primal beast.

The first Undead caught the full force, the pitchfork pushed into its chest, the blunt tines doing terrible damage to the body. I pushed hard, pushed and ran forward. I learned a thing about Undead here, I learned they might be walking teeth and hard to kill, but their strength came from ordinary muscles. Nothing superhuman here. So, when I hit the group like a frenzied bull, my rage fuelled momentum pushed the entire group back. They fell down, arms and legs all askew, tangled in each other. I left the pitchfork sticking up out of a ruined chest, stamped on another's face and found myself facing the trapdoor, the trapdoor into the Artificer's room. It was the work of a moment to throw it open and leap into the gap.

A hand grabbed at me as I stepped into the hole and plummeted down, the fingers catching in my coverall. As I plunged past the metal lip, I heard several cracks and felt a slight tug. Then I was falling towards a floor containing my astonished friends.

Meataxe broke my fall. I didn't completely land on him but he threw his arms up to catch me and managed to slow me enough to prevent any broken ankles. Always knew he was good for something.

I lay in an untidy bundle on the floor; Meataxe was getting to his feet after my sudden descent. Off to one side I heard Lydia gasp, "Val..." I sucked in some deep breathes, rolled onto my side and slowly brought mind and body under control. I heard Lydia speak in a low tone, "Are you...are you all right, Val?"

The noise of blood thundering in my ears subsided enough for me to gather some coherent thoughts. "Yeah," I said, soft and slow, "I'm good."

"Val," she said, "you were trapped by them, by those things. You were cut off from us, how did you.... you came back to us," She buried herself in my chest and sobbed. I was beginning to think the price for a Lydia hug was a bit steep.

"Uhh, Val," said Meataxe from one side and behind me. I turned my head to see him; he was looking at my back. He stepped forward and swept my back with his sword in a brushing motion, I felt a loosening on my overalls followed by a sloppy thud as something hit the floor. When I looked down at my left boot, I saw a few fingers and part of a hand on the floor; someone up there must have had a good grip once. But not anymore. Trying to keep a hold of my clothing as I plummeted through the trapdoor had put quite a strain on the muscles and joints. Gotta hand to those Undead, they don't like to let go.

My two companions were giving me funny looks again. "Come on," I said, "let's get out of here before any more bits rain down." We moved off into the body of the Artificer's Room. The open trapdoor was a risk but any plummeting Undead would probably break something. I was hoping for legs. We would be alerted to their entrance by the wet, splatting sound.

This room was a workshop; long benches ran down each wall, plus a few more in the centre. Machines of strange design stood around behind tiny protective fences, machines which sent a seductive come hither to some blokey part of my brain. I had an urge to chop and saw, plane and drill.

Meataxe and Lydia kept their distance from me after the initial hug, maybe I smelled bad or something. Fighting a few hordes of Undead may well leave a certain odour; panic, fear and terror – maybe they had their own scent.

Racks held interesting arrays of tools, I saw a heavy hammer in its brackets, all shiny steel and glowy metal. It was mine, nearby was a workman's belt which I strapped on and thrust the handle of my new best friend through a convenient loop. I liked this room. I was considering which pointy thing to take when Lydia suggested we might want to hurry. Another rack held more of the pitchfork tools, I took one and gave another to Meataxe before indicating to my beautiful companion I was ready to go.

Any more Undead? Bring 'em on, I thought as we left the room and entered another corridor.

****

No one in sight, one piece of good news. The corridor was straight before finishing at a normal internal door at the end of the corridor. Another little door stood alone on the internal wall, not lockable, not secure, just a door, probably a storeroom. Above our heads the ceiling was still bare, where were the coloured lines?

"Lydia," I asked "where does that little door lead? And where are the lines, the coloured lines?"

Still keeping her distance from me, she indicated the door at the end of the corridor. "Through there, Val, it leads to the main corridor. The other one, the little one is a storeroom." She bit her lip and dropped her eyes, I felt there was more to come and sure enough she spoke again, "Val," she stopped and moved a step away.

"What is it, Lydia?" I asked. My shoulders hurt, I could feel the tension knotting my muscles, my hands seemed to be sticky with blood. They weren't, of course, it just seemed to me I had a talent for causing blood and gore to come out of people. Or Undead, or things, probably cats and dogs too. I stood before her conscious of the weight of the hammer and the potential of my pitchfork to do damage.

"It's just...," she began before stopping. Then she did a brave thing, she stepped into me, looked up into my face without making body contact. I was thrown a little, prior to this session every time she had come within range, she had hugged me or touched my arm; done something to link us together. Now she stood with her arms by her sides, I could feel a big statement coming on and didn't like it much. Here is where she would say she didn't like me.

She took a deep breath and said, "You're a scary man, Valentine." Another moment while I studied her eyes, all liquid and moist, all shiny and fathomless. Then she smiled, hugged me again and my muscles relaxed, my shoulders sagged and my headache lightened, "I'm glad you're here. With me," she said.

I didn't exactly turn cartwheels but I warmed to the idea of her liking having me around. Just a nice feeling. So I did my best to clumsy it up and said, "Good to know. Look, when we get to the blue lines, will you know which way to go? I don't want us to head in the wrong direction again and end up like last time." My brain was sending recall messages to my mouth by this stage but it was too late, I was focussed on getting the job done. "Don't want to end up in the Maintenance hangar again. Wrong way."

"Not quite the wrong way - I was there," she said and I realised my gaffe. I stumbled over my tongue for a bit and she watched the show before putting me out of my misery. "I understand, sweetie. And I know how to get to the Chief Trader's quarters. Follow me." She strode off leaving Meataxe and me standing, we glanced at each other and ran after her. This was some girl.

I caught her arm and said, "Now slow down a bit." She stopped and the three of us stood together, "Meataxe and I have been doing a fair bit of creeping through this ship, it's not a pretty sight, Undead everywhere. No bodies yet but we'll see some more, let's just do a bit of planning before we run off half-cocked." I couldn't believe what I was hearing, I was talking about planning first before taking any action. Was this me talking? I am so grown up.

Most surprisingly of all was their reaction, they both lowered their heads and mumbled, "Yes, Val," and, "Sorry, Val." Then they looked at me, expectantly.

I shook my head, is this what Magic has had had to put up with all these years?

"Meataxe," I ordered, his eyes met mine, all aquiver to follow my commands, "Go and check the last door, see if it's locked." He trundled away, happy in the service. I turned to Lydia and she snapped to attention, giving me a brisk salute, "Now cut that out!' I said.

"Sorry," she replied, "just getting in the mood." She lowered her voice and spoke very suggestively, "What can I do for you, big boy?"

I stepped back from her, aghast. "Will you stop!" I said, "It's hard enough for me to think with you around, you're just so...so bloody gorgeous!" I panted a little. "Look, this thinking and planning is not what I'm good at, it's all a bit new. I can't do it if you keep distracting me, can you just, sort of, rein it in a bit."

Meataxe waved from the first door and moved off, without further instruction, to check the storeroom door. Now he was showing some initiative – when would it end? Lydia placed a small hand on my arm and said, "I'm sorry, Val, it's just my way. I work with men all the time and the way I've learned to get by is to play these little games – I'm sorry, I won't do them to you anymore." I didn't like where this was going, was she going to stop being nice to me? I felt my face burn red and my mouth opened and closed a few times. She stepped up and kissed me on the cheek, "I like you, Val, let's see where this takes us when we're a bit safer."

I nodded, gulped and let my brain run in circles a few times yelling, "SHE LIKES ME! SHE LIKES ME!" I finally got a grip and asked her, "How do we get to the Chief Trader's quarters? And why isn't there a blue line in this corridor? I was told all corridors had those guidelines."

"Not all," she replied, Meataxe was at the little door now. "This is an internal corridor for the Artificers' Section," she continued, "it runs from their workshop into the main corridor. Just behind the last door," she nodded to where Meataxe was checking, "we'll connect back on to a major corridor and we'll see the blue line, plus others, of course." I guided Lydia's arm and we trotted up to join Meataxe standing outside the storeroom door.

He pushed the door and it swung open, wide open. He looked at me and said, "This one's not locked, Val." I knew it wasn't locked because I was looking at a human being standing on the other side of the now open door. It was my old pal, Don'elk, the thug who beat up on Lydia. I smiled my happy smile.

I knew he wasn't an Undead because Undead don't faint when they see me.

****

We entered the room and quickly shut the door behind us. It had lots of shelves and cupboards with a large table in the centre. On the floor were scattered some opened boxes, various bits and pieces of equipment and the unconscious form of Don'elk. I squatted over him and slapped his face a few times until his eyes flickered. As he regained coherency, I sat back on my haunches and waited for his face to show signs of life. "Hiya," I said, when he opened his eyes.

Then I hit him, a good solid punch to the jaw.

Chapter 12

He went limp and still again. I stood up and dusted my hands off against the seat of my pants. Meataxe started poking in the cupboards and shelves, Lydia sat on the table and swung her legs back and forth, she gave me a smile. We all waited for Don'elk to come around again. I may have whistled a bit.

A groan announced his return. I bent down and helped him to his feet by grabbing a lot of shirt plus chest hair and pulling straight up. His eyes watered a little when I finally let him go. He put one hand on the table to steady himself and that's when he caught sight of Lydia. She smiled at him, he choked and stammered but didn't fall down again.

"What are you doing here?" he asked.

"Shut up, Don'elk," I said, "We'll ask the questions." Meataxe found several cupboards locked, he looked a question at me, I nodded and he began to break open the doors. Always keep the kids occupied.

The little weasel in front of me was responsible for hitting Lydia so straight away I didn't like him. He was dressed all in black, definitely not the standard crewman's coveralls. "What's with the fancy dress, weasel?" I asked.

"I don't know what a 'weasel' is," he replied. I slapped him again, just an open palm but I've got a big hand and I put a little zing in it. His eyes watered and I could see a very nice imprint of my hand begin to glow on his cheek.

"Stop hitting me!" he yelled, "Just cut it out!" He stepped back a little and pulled himself erect, "You're in a lot of trouble buddy!"

Lydia had stopped her leg swing and watched the pair of us expectantly, I could tell she was reacting to Don'elk's manner and tone – unfortunately her reactions were based on a fear relationship she had with this thug. It was the little things I picked up on, her slightly widened eyes, the held breath and tense posture. It all began to say she was subservient to this man in front of me. Don'elk was picking it up as well, his chest puffed up a little and a touch of arrogance crept into his stance.

"You would have to be that clown, Valentine, the one who's going to get spaced for murder." He straightened his shirt and smoothed the hair back out of his eyes, "I don't know how you got out of your cell, buddy, but you're done for. Unless..." and the little weasel leaned forward conspiratorially towards me, "...unless you start getting smart. I can fix things for you, but you'll need to change your attitude. I might even have a small job for you, I could use a bit of mindless muscle in our current circumstances."

Meataxe had stopped breaking into lockers and was watching our little tableau, probably wondering why I hadn't broken this guy's neck yet. To be honest, I was mildly wondering the same thing myself. I was showing admirable self-restraint in this situation. My normal verbal interchange would be a few, "Oh, yeah!" statements followed by the odd insult about the guy's mother and then we would start to whale on each other. Sometimes I came off second best and sometimes I was the last man standing. Don'elk wasn't a big guy, a reasonable person would conclude I was the bully. Quite right, too. I've never been bothered about hitting people smaller than me, just means I have to lean down a little.

A part of me was wondering why this guy was still vertical and hanging on to all his teeth. The same part that marvelled as I spoke to the weasel in tones of conciliation and supplication. I was all ears, eager to hear what I had to say.

"What kind of job?" I asked. "And what circumstances are we talking about?" Brilliant, Mr Policeman, incisive questioning coming out of the old brain. See, I'm even sarcastic to myself.

Don'elk gave me the look I have seen many times, the one where someone thinks they are smart and I am just a dumb clown. "Surely even you have noticed the mayhem on board?"

I nodded a little, my face showing all the intelligence of a log. I let my mouth hang open a little, it's always a nice touch and lets the civilians think you would have trouble walking and talking at the same time. Meataxe was leaning against a locker; he's seen this show a few times and enjoys the last act. Poor little Lydia didn't know anything about it, of course. She must have thought I was being cowed by the ferocious charisma of Don'elk. Her eyes were much wider now and her mouth was well and truly open in apprehension.

The weasel gave a theatrical sigh, "Space! Preserve me from muscle bound fools." He stepped away from the wall and gave another look to the poor dumb animal. That'd be me. I tried to dribble but couldn't quite manage it. "Come with me" he sighed, "You three can earn your keep by running interference for me with the infected crew - I need to meet some friends coming aboard soon." He turned to the open doorway and poked his head out. After looking both ways he signalled us with a proprietary wave, "Come on, I need to get to the Control Room so I can signal my pals." He turned to check the corridor once more.

Lydia was looking frantically at me, worry etched into her every feature; poor lamb, just not used to my little ways. I placed my large paw on Don'elk's right shoulder and got a good grip, "What do you think..." he began to say but lost his train of thought as I grabbed his other shoulder and lifted him into the air. I bounced him of the ceiling a couple of times and then threw him against the wall on the other side of the corridor. He hit face first and left a small blood smear as he slid to the floor.

Meataxe followed me out of the room with a very confused Lydia behind him. By the time I reached him, Don'elk had managed to get up on to all fours and was watching the blood drip from his nose into a slowly growing puddle on the floor. To take his mind of it I planted my big foot - complete with lovely, nasty boot – into his right buttock and pushed hard. His face hit the wall again, this time with more of a crunchy sound rather than the normal thud.

"You may have a touch of concussion there, old son," I said. "I've been learning First Aid – aren't you the lucky one?" He rolled over onto his back and lay there at my feet, his nose looked broken – I'd confirm that later – and his face was covered with blood and snot. It's amazing what comes out of your eyes and nose when you cop a few good belts in the face, it's very embarrassing.

He looked at me, swivelled his eyes to an amazed Lydia, took in a smiling Meataxe – never a pretty sight. "What?" he slurred, "I thought you...?"

"Yeah, well," I said, "there's your problem, Don'elk, old buddy." I stood over him and placed a foot on his chest, by leaning I could squeeze his ribs down towards his backbone. Or by leaning down a lot I could snap a few off; the things you learn, eh? "You might be putting too much faith in this thinking business. I don't go in for it much myself, more of a slugger than savant."

I shifted my weight some more to get comfortable, this caused me to squash my companion and he gasped with pain. I gave him my most winning smile, "So, here we are, eh? What's new with you then, Donny, seen any good plays lately? Up to anything much?"

He gazed up at me and I saw the hate enter his eyes, chalk up another enemy for Valentine. "You're a dead man," he said.

"Sorry?" I queried, leaning down harder, "Couldn't quite catch what you said." He gasped as my weight came onto his ribs; I bent over so he could see my eyes. "Want to run that by me again?"

He flicked a glance to either side, no help anywhere, "Look," he gasped, "What do you want? We can make a deal here." I took the weight off his ribs and stood up.

"What's going on, Don'elk? What's all this about an infection? And who are you planning on meeting?" We stayed that way for a few heartbeats as I watched the rat cunning come back into his eyes, I wasn't going to get anything out of him as long as he thought he had something to bargain with. He opened his mouth to speak but couldn't keep the smile from his face.

I spoke before he could get a word out, "Nah, don't bother, I couldn't care less about what you know. Meataxe," I turned to my fellow watchman, a man who had the brain power of a small slug but a man who had been around the block with me a few times. "Meataxe, bring over the pitchfork thing, I reckon it'll make a great little cattle prod for our friend here."

We both ignored Don'elk, his questions and entreaties, his threats and cajoling. I pulled the poor slob to his feet and spun him around and then stuck the tines of the fork around his neck. Meataxe picked up on what I was about and found some tape and cord in the storeroom, within a very short space of time our new best friend was securely trussed on the end of the pitchfork. By holding the pole, we could push and pull him around as we pleased. He stopped complaining as he realised we weren't talking to him but he had one final stab at communicating with us great unwashed. "Okay, okay, I get it," he said, "I'm your prisoner, yeah, sure, fine. So now we go somewhere and we start all over again. You know, at some point you'll have to negotiate with me, I'm the only one who can help you. Even if order is restored on the ship, you'll need me on side to avoid more charges. So you can't kill me."

"Meataxe?" I queried.

"Yeah, Val?"

"Reckon I could kill this guy?"

"No problem. Want me to do it?"

"Nah, I've got it covered," I gave him the pole and moved to stand in front of Don'elk. "Donny, old boy, you seem to be labouring under the misapprehension I give a shit. I do intend to kill you, put your mind at ease on the topic."

"But you can't!" he wailed.

"Course I can, easy as pie"

"But I'm helpless"

"And your point is...?"

"I'm your prisoner! You can't kill a prisoner, that's.... that's not fair!"

"Ah! I see the problem," I said, "You're thinking Meataxe and I are civilised people, that we are bound by the conventions of ship board life." I slapped the palm of my hand against my forehead as if I just had a brainstorm. "Yes, of course, perfectly natural assumption, especially considering we're wearing these nice clothes and shiny boots and all. Tsk, tsk, tsk." I looked at him pitifully, "Thing is, Donny, we're the NightWatch and we really couldn't give a shit about being fair, being nice or being reasonable. We're mean bastards. Kill a prisoner? Every day of the week. Spot of torture? No problem. Saints Above, you little worm, I could quite happily squash your nuts and watch you bleed out in front of your mum while eating lunch and I wouldn't be bothered. In fact, I've done it before, haven't I, Meataxe?"

"The bloke in Ostend, Val? The one with the printing press? Boy, did he squeal for mercy as you cut bits off him, he must have taken a whole day to bleed out in front of his wife. And kids."

I mentally grimaced, he was embellishing it a little; the guy didn't have any kids. Still, the big oaf's heart was in the right place.

"Here's what we're going to do, Don'elk" I continued. "We're going to wander onwards and see how far we can get. And you're going to be our front man, yes indeed. I reckon if we all stay behind you and poke you ahead of us with this pitchfork thing then any of these Undead that want to munch down on us might see you first.

It'll give the three of us a chance to hoof it away from the scene of the feast. What do you reckon, worth a try?"

"But you can't do that!" the little snot moaned. "You can't just force me ahead of you!"

I pondered a moment, "No, shouldn't be a problem. If Meataxe and I take turns I reckon we should be able to manage; we're both young and strong. Well, I'm young; how old do you reckon you are, Meataxe?"

I watched Don'elk spasm while Meataxe and I softly debated his age. Our prisoner was being ignored by us, completely sidelined and of no interest to us at all. At least that's what I was hoping he was thinking.

"Wait!" he said as Meataxe poked the poor slob forward a few steps. Don'elk tried to push back with his heels but he didn't have the strength or the grip. "Wait! I can tell you things! I can help you!"

"Sorry, mate, not interested. Besides, this looks like it's going to be fun. Let's go and see what's behind door number one, eh? Come one, Donny, try to get into the spirit of things." I nodded to Meataxe and smiled happily at Don'elk as my partner pushed him along the corridor towards the far door. I turned to Lydia and extended an arm, "Care to go for a stroll, sweetcheeks?"

She was giving me a funny look but took my arm anyway. We moseyed after the pair ahead and I patted Lydia's hand in my best reassuring way. She flicked a glance at me and said, "You are a ruthless man, Valentine."

"So I'm told," I replied. "Don't see it myself."

By the time we came to the door, Don'elk had exhausted himself. He tried to flop to the floor and make it impossible for us to move him but Meataxe just angled the pitchfork up a little until the cords and tape cut into Don'elk's throat. He quickly realised sitting down meant he ran out of air and so clambered back to his feet and kept walking. I left Lydia standing next to Meataxe and out of Don'elk's line of vision when we reached the door. But I moved up to stand beside our prisoner, shoulder to shoulder we faced the door, mere inches from our noses.

"How good's this, eh, Don'elk? Could be anything behind the door. How about a small bet? I bet when I open it we'll find...let me see...two, no, three Undead. Right there in front of us, what do you reckon? Want to take that bet?"

His eyes bulged with terror. Combined with his snot and blood covered face he looked like the poster boy for mindless terror.

"Not a gambling man, Donny?" I asked as I stepped to one side and flipped open the cover on the door controls. Giving our captive weasel my best beaming smile, I pushed the button which I hoped would open the door.

It did. And facing Don'elk was one human Undead, about twenty feet away. Deadguy reacted to the opening of the door and turned to greet our little troupe. With a shuffling gait he stepped towards Don'elk who promptly let go of his bladder.

I had a quick peek into the compartment and said, "You should've taken the bet, Donny, there's only one of our Undead brethren...but he looks a bit peckish. We might just leave you two to get acquainted. See you, mate."

Chapter 13

Don'elk stood transfixed. I couldn't really blame the poor slob; when I saw my first deadguy up close back in Sick Bay I gawped a bit. Still, I did think old Donny was stretching things out a bit, I mean to say, he hadn't moved all – just kept his gaze fixed on the shambling diner and let bodily fluids run out of his various orifices.

Meataxe leaned into the rod, probably anticipating Donny making a break for it. Yeah, like that was going to happen.

I smiled back at Lydia, just gave her a happy grin and a wave but her mind seemed elsewhere, she seemed a little pale and distracted as she gazed at the little drama unfolding with Don'elk. He had begun to make interesting gurgling sounds as Deadguy lurched into grasping range. You just can't pay for this sort of entertainment.

Don'elk soiled his pants again, this was getting old. I felt I had made my point so I pulled out my hammer and thumped Deadguy on the forehead – there was a distinct cracking sound and the front of his skull moved to the back of his head. Stuff came out his ears and he fell down.

The rest of the compartment was empty of personnel, living or not, so we trundled in. I noticed Lydia giving the new corpse a wide berth. It continued to lay very still on the floor, my blow to its head seemed to have finally terminated its life. I had been thinking about this for some time, the one in Sick Bay - the one whose head I pulped - stayed dead after I got through squashing its brain. I hoped a solid blow to the head or a decapitation would do the trick. So far, so good.

We let Don'elk sit down and positioned the handle of his pitchfork so he could have a chance at breathing, he certainly wasn't going to run off anytime soon. Meataxe and I examined this new space, both of us were trying to act all casual and unconcerned because of what we saw. We had both noticed what took up prominent positions in the centre of the room. Big shiny engines looking for a good time.

Two broomsticks sat there, all gleaming with spiky bits sticking out; they made me drool just looking at them. I sauntered over, making out I was examining the walls and so forth; Meataxe did the same, silly sod even put his hands in his pockets and whistled a little tune. But we both ended up standing in front of the broomsticks and exchanging big drooly grins.

"Val," he said. "What do you reckon about these? A bit of alright, eh?" We moved around and gloated over the various bits on each broomstick; both machines were held upright in some sort of brace mechanism and stood facing the outer wall of the spaceship. I couldn't help looking at this wall because part of it was taken up with an exit door, it was larger than a normal door and covered with the strange symbols the crew used to communicate danger and such stuff. The big wheel in the middle did it for me, by turning it I could imagine opening the door and standing on its lip to face an eternity of nothing.

I froze up and stood there facing the door while my brain gibbered and I relived a very unpleasant period in my life. I had been strapped on a stasis couch next to a door during a shuttle's descent when the door blew out. We had been sabotaged. I spent a bottom clenching period of time as we fell howling towards the planet's surface – the shuttle did the falling and I did the howling.

Not a big fan of doors in a spaceship. Not a fan of spaceships actually. Or space.

My little reverie was mercifully interrupted by Meataxe, he had been tugging my sleeve for a few moments trying to get my attention. "Val...Val...what are we gonna do now? Val!"

"Get off me, you big lout, give a man a bit of space!" I pulled my arm out of his grip and clamped down on my nightmares. Lydia was sitting in a corner of the room, knees pulled up to her chest and arms tugging them closer; she didn't look like she was coping too well. I tended to have that effect on new acquaintances, after being dazzled by my wit and casual banter they were generally put off by some of my more personal habits. Like hitting people with hammers or stomping a man's head to pulp. I mentally crossed another female off my list.

"Go and look after Lydia, Meataxe, she needs a bit of gentle handling; must be a shock to someone like her to hang around us for a bit."

He looked at me funny and asked, "Come again? You want me to talk to her? Be compassionate? Me?" I stared at him for a moment and he must have seen something in my face because he turned away and said, "Yeah, righto. I'm going to be better than you at the moment."

He moved off and I did a self-check on how my life was going. Let's see now, remembered the sensation of falling to a planet while strapped into a malfunctioning machine? – check. Killed a guy by smashing his brains out with a hammer? – check. Treated a prisoner with sadism and derision? – check. Lost my new girlfriend? – check.

Everything seemed to be in order, I decided it was time for me to have another little chat with Don'elk. I sauntered over and nudged him with my toe before squatting down beside him on the floor. To sit comfortably I had to take the hammer out of my belt so I laid it on the floor beside us. Pieces of skin and bone seemed to have been imprinted on its face, I wiped it as best I could on Don'elk's coveralls.

"Don't piss me about, sport," I said, still not looking at him as I wiped the hammer clean. "I'm going to ask you a few questions now and I reckon you should answer them." I stopped talking and raised my face to him, giving him the opportunity to have a good look at my eyes and see who he was dealing with. "What do you reckon?" I asked.

He did his best to flinch back into the wall and I think he gave the bulkhead a real run for its money. "What do you want to know?"

I waved an arm to take in the room and, by association the spaceship, "What's going on here, Don'elk?"

He squirmed and said "They'll kill me, you don't know what…" He was interrupted by me raising the hammer and forcefully striking the deck next to his kneecap, the noise was sudden and intense. He jumped a little.

Over in the corner Meataxe was sitting next to Lydia, I could see them out of the corner of my eye. They seemed to be talking which I took to be a good sign; her head was slumped down a little but I think she was doing the talking. Meataxe was watching me, he had his worried face on but I put it down to the strain he was going through trying to be compassionate to a girl without putting his hand down her blouse. He didn't budge when I hit the deck with the hammer, he knew my little ways.

"Tell you what, Don'elk, let's assume you don't know me very well. Let's assume there are other people in this world you are more scared of than me. Let's assume that, shall we?" I looked at him pleasantly and he gave a little nod.

"Excellent!" I resumed. "Now I'm going to demonstrate your conclusion is, in fact, quite wrong." I took his hand and laid it flat on the deck and he let me do it. If you act all low key and reasonable people think you are, indeed, acting reasonably. I splayed out the fingers of his hand and then held his wrist so he wouldn't wriggle it around.

I lifted my hammer and noticed I had his complete attention; his eyes followed my raised arm very carefully. Especially when I brought it down on his pinkie finger, squashing that sucker flat.

Have you ever had that moment when you know you have been injured but your brain hasn't been fully informed? Like you're cutting up something and the knife slips, your eyes see the blade cut your hand and you know you are a heartbeat away from feeling the pain. That little pause is what Don'elk and I inhabited. I kept my eyes fixed on his and saw realisation dawn, the realisation that he had just had his finger crushed and the pain was about to come a-callin'. I smiled at him.

He screamed.

"Now, now, Donny," I murmured, "It's just a finger." I shifted my grip on the hammer and raised it again. "And it's not as if you get a lot of use out of it, come on now, who uses their pinkie for anything?"

I used my other hand to keep his wrist flat on the deck and pushed aside the remains of his squashed finger, this gave me a clear shot at the next one. "You might think I'm just all talk. Do you know, I understand that. I really do. So, I need to convince you I am a bad man. A very bad man. Quite awful, really." He wanted to scream but couldn't take his eyes off what was happening, I had raised the hammer and lined up his next finger for another blow.

I gave him my best smile and threw in a little wink as I brought the hammer down onto his next finger. This time there wasn't any pause and he went straight to scream. I let his wrist go and he grabbed the wounded hand and cradled it to his chest, I wiped my hammer off on his clothes again and leaned back against the wall. Off on the other side I saw the two faces of Meataxe and Lydia, hers was all white and shocked – I knew she was in shock because she was holding Meataxe's hand. He wasn't too concerned about my actions. Been there, done that.

"Have I got your attention now, Don'elk?" He stopped the screaming and just moaned but he was certainly looking at me with real intensity. "I'm not going to pussyfoot around, you little worm. You start talking now. If I think you're not being completely honest I'll just keep going with the rest of the hand – and I'll do all the fingers, one at a time, followed by smashing my hammer onto the knuckles. Quite happy to do it." I reached out and took a good grip on his injured paw and dragged it out again, "In fact, I may as well do it now."

"NO!" he yelled but I dragged his injured hand back onto the deck and spread the remaining fingers. "I didn't want to do it! They made me!" He began to sob a little, "Please, please don't...don't..."

I hefted the hammer and paused, it was a toss-up if he was telling the truth or not, I must have had my thinking face on because he launched into a rambling account of his nefarious activities. At one point I considered smashing another finger – must have pursed my lips in thought – because he became convinced I was serious about being a ruthless bastard. Heck, anyone who knows me could tell him that.

He was part of one of the black-market gangs aboard the ship, he seemed to fit in towards the top of the food chain and was responsible for organising the human part of the gang. There were other members of the criminal executive who looked after the different species who made up our happy crew. He really won my heart when he said the big boss was a Tharl. That was the point I considered breaking another finger. I generally don't like Tharls.

But Don'elk had visions above his station and had formed a relationship with the criminal element on the planet we currently orbited. The long and the short of it was he had arranged for this ground-based element to come up and take over the whole spaceship. I had to admire the brazenness of the plan; he had moved from petty larceny to Grand Theft Spaceship in fairly short order. Gotta admire a man with real get up and go.

I left him to bandage his injured hand as best he could with strips I tore from Deadguy's corpse. Don'elk didn't look too keen to use the bits I gave him but we were all out of clean white bandages. If we were back in the City I would have hacked the fingers off completely and then cauterised the stumps with a hot poker but it seems my ideas of First Aid were not totally in line with Life on the Modern Spaceship.

Lydia and Meataxe watched me wander about for a bit, I do my best thinking walking around – my brain seems attached to my legs. Eventually I plopped on the saddle of one of the broomsticks and beckoned them both over; Don'elk wasn't going to give us any more trouble in the short term so I left him to moan on.

"Pirates?" asked Meataxe, after I passed on the information about bad guys coming up to board us. "We got Space Pirates? How does that work?"

"I've heard of it," said Lydia. "From time to time a vessel disappears and it's usually written off as an accident. But then some of the cargo finds its way on to the market." Lydia stood a little away from me and kept flicking glances over towards Don'elk and then back to me. "But to take over a ship this size would be difficult, we have weapons, guards and, well, they would certainly take some casualties and even then the ship might be too badly damaged. The cargo could well be lost."

"Unless they found a way to incapacitate the crew", I said. "Don'elk tells me the nanobots we were injected with had a neat little side effect. They were supposed to knock everyone out for about 12 hours, long enough for them to come up from the planet and board the ship. He was on his way to open the main hatches when the side effect had a side effect."

"What'll we do, Val?" asked my fellow guardsman.

There it was again, the big question – as if I had a clue.

Chapter 14

"Lydia," I asked, being as gentle as I could, "why would it have been important for the pirates to have someone on the inside to open the doors? Someone like Don'elk?"

"Because of this very situation, spaceship captains like to be the ones who say who comes and goes on their vessels. Little tyrants, every one of them but they have to be. There are communication ports near each exterior hatch to accept an external link, anyone can contact the Control Deck and ask for permission to come aboard."

"Val," Meataxe was getting fidgety, "What'll we do?"

"What about, you know, rescue missions and the like. How would they get in if everyone on board was sick or dead?" Like now, I thought.

"They'd cut their way in, usually through a hatch but it would take some time. Especially if the people doing the cutting wanted to keep the ship in the best possible shape. Resale value." Lydia was talking to me a bit more now but there was definitely a wall between us. I can tell these things, what with my wide experience of women and all.

"Vaaal......," said Meataxe. He was hopping from foot to foot.

The big guy was suffering a bad case of the nerves. Here we were trapped on a floating hulk about to be boarded by pirates and we both knew about pirates. Cold blooded, cruel killers – at least the ones from our experience and I saw no reason why these would be any different. I was willing to bet some habits would be the same no matter what day and age we were in. Habits like killing the entire crew or selling them into slavery; it stopped the survivors from running to the navy or other authorities. "Go and check those lockers, Meataxe," I told him, perhaps a little activity would take his mind off our present trapped-with-no-hope situation.

"Lydia, you still say if we follow those blue lines on the ceiling, we'll make it to the Chief trader's quarters?"

She nodded, "But time will be against us, how long until the pirates arrive? And how are they getting here from the planet?"

I yelled the questions over to Don'elk.

"I don't know," he called back, all surly and resentful. Some people, eh? "They're coming up on Cargo Sleds."

I looked a question at Lydia and she said, "Cargo Sleds are just bigger versions of these Personal Sleds, like the one you're sitting on."

Meataxe had trundled back carrying a shiny coverall and helmet. "There's some of this funny looking gear in those cupboards but that's all."

"Those are emergency space suits, the life support packages would be nearby," said Lydia. I told Meataxe to dump the suit and get Don'elk.

"What are we gonna do, Val," he asked.

I sighed and ploughed ahead, "We have to find our way to the Chief Trader's quarters, that's where the Man in Black is. Once we find him, he can tell us what to do, especially since he probably doesn't know about this little pirate scheme. Now go and get Don'elk." The big guy lumbered off and I turned to the lovely Lydia.

"I need you with me, Lydia, here and now. I know you might not like the way I treated Don'elk, I understand you must think I'm some sort of thug and you'd be right. I am a thug." And a damned good one, I added mentally.

She looked at me and said, "You've always treated me right, Val. And Peter thinks so highly of you." My brain stuttered a little until I realised she was talking about Meataxe. "We've got pirates about to board the ship, it's infested with undead cannibals and we don't have anyone at the controls to keep us from crashing into the planet. We could lose Life Support at any moment." She was not cheering me up.

"Maybe we need a thug. A really, really good one." She hit me with another smile, put a hand on my shoulder and said, "What can I do to help?"

I gurgled until Meataxe rolled up with a very white faced Don'elk. Right on cue my buddy asked, "What are we gonna do, Val?"

"Can these Personal Sleds work inside the ship?" I asked.

"Don't be stupid, man" snarled Don'elk. "You can't ride one of these things down the corridors! They're unsafe in confined spaces, you'd end up killing yourself and anyone else you hit."

But it was Lydia's verdict I was looking for. She gazed at me for a few wonderful heartbeats before giving me a little nod. A nervous one, but I'll take what I can get.

"We just disable the stabilisers so the engine doesn't shut down," said Lydia "It's a safety feature to prevent people riding them in confined spaces." She smiled at me.

"Like the corridors of a spaceship?" I asked.

"Like the corridors of a spaceship," she agreed. "As luck would have it, I know how to disable this particular function. Part of my job is to maintain these particular Sleds; they belong to the Chief Trader."

A man of rare discernment, I judged. I strapped Don'elk's arms to his body and then tied him to the rear seat of one of the Sleds – I guess I couldn't call them broomsticks anymore. Meataxe would ride that one and Lydia would sit behind me, her arms encircling my manly torso. Lydia did strange things with bits of each engine and then unclamped the machines from their storage position. We started the engines which sounded absolutely fantastic in the confines of a room and lined them up facing the door. Meataxe and I looked at each other and exchanged big toothy grins, we revved the engines few times and then turned back to face the door.

A few moments passed before I realised we hadn't worked out how we were going to open the door. I felt like a bit of a goose until Lydia tapped me on the shoulder and leaped of the seat; she ran over to the door controls and flipped open the cover. With a quick look at me for confirmation, she opened the door and ran quickly back to resume her position behind me. She gave me a little extra squeeze. I think.

The next room was empty, just a long corridor and we really tore it up, blasting happily under the broad blue line.

Eventually we came up against the door at the end of main corridor except this door was open and beyond it was room with a whole lot of occupants, all of them Undead. I saw a mixture of humans, Tharls and a few representatives of the other various bric-a-brac who make up the crew of our happy spaceship family. They all turned to see us, our machines were certainly making enough noise to wake the dead, and the human members began to walk towards us with real purpose – I guess we were meals on wheels. The other Undead also started walking towards us but not with the same intensity as the humans; maybe they just wanted to check out the noise.

There were a lot of them, an awful lot. I considered just trying to barrel our way through but the chances of one of us being snagged and pulled down were just a bit too high. Lydia had a death grip around my waist which distracted me somewhat until I was brought back into the here and now by the sound of Meataxe's sled crashing to the floor. I looked behind and saw him pinned beneath the Sled while Don'elk jittered about – he had somehow managed to free himself from the Sled, a surge of strength probably coming from seeing all the revenants. But in doing so he must have knocked over the Sled and so doomed us all.

"Get away!" yelled Don'elk. "Get away from me!" He was yelling at the Undead as they trudged remorselessly towards us. They, of course, were homing in on him and my trapped buddy.

"Lydia!" I turned my head to speak to my companion, "Get off! Go and help Meataxe!" She looked at me for a moment and then jumped off the seat. Good girl, I thought.

The Undead were beginning to enter our corridor, Lydia couldn't get the Sled up by herself and Meataxe was at the wrong angle. Don'elk just hopped from foot to foot and gibbered. We were about to be engulfed.

I accelerated the Sled towards the doorway and the oncoming horde and then hit the control which braked the front of the machine – I think some sort of jet thrusters were involved but didn't really know or care. At the same time, I accelerated the main engine and the rear of the Sled swung around, there was a brief moment when I was sitting erect on a machine which was moving sideways into a herd of Undead. Some fun, eh?

leaping off a falling horse involves kicking your feet out of the stirrups and jumping, plus a bit of prayer. This was almost the same, especially the prayer. As I fell, I landed on my shoulder and bounced along the floor; the Sled landed on its side and also began to slide but its greater mass and nice, smooth surfaces meant it moved a lot faster than a cranky, swearing guardsman. The big machine slammed into the growing cluster of Undead and cleaned them all up, at least for a short time. I rolled to my feet and ran to Meataxe, screaming instructions to Lydia.

"Get Don'elk!" She scampered over to where the little weasel was wetting himself in horror again. The guy was going to be seriously dehydrated.

I picked up the downed Sled and jerked Meataxe to his feet, "Get this thing started! Lydia rides behind you." We had a chance if we could just get a bit of a head start, I hadn't seen any of these Undead types running so I was hoping we could move faster than them back down the corridor.

My sled had cleaned up the nearest group of people munchers but there were more coming. Even the non-human types seemed to have had their interest piqued. Meataxe started his machine and rode it over to Lydia and Don'elk, I was a heartbeat behind him.

Don'elk tried to jump on the back of the Sled but Meataxe busted him in the mouth, a nice meaty thwack – full of blood and teeth. I liked it.

"Back to the room which held the Sleds," I instructed him as Lydia climbed aboard; while I talked I cut the tape binding Don'elk's arms.

"What about you?" asked my sweetie.

"We'll be right behind you. Go!" Meataxe took off with a full roar leaving me and Don'elk to face the shambling hordes. With his nose dripping a variety of fluids he didn't cut a very heroic figure; in fact he looked a lot like the Undead bearing down on us.

"Ready for a bit of a run, Donny?" I asked.

He glared at me, "Do you expect us to outrun them? Is that your grand plan?"

"Almost," I smiled at him. "But I haven't got to outrun them, I just have to outrun you. Wanna live, Donny-boy? Let's go!" I took off without a backward glance.

It seems I've spent a fair amount of my life in running away from someone bigger or meaner than me. I'm not complaining, mind you, I'm still alive. You can't argue with that sort of result. This being so, I had no trouble falling into a steady but fast stride, I even risked a quick glance behind me. Not recommended for beginners because it can mean you slow a little and lose some rhythm. Not me, though, I'm a past master at looking over my shoulder as I run away from someone who wants to do me harm. I'm usually screaming at the same time.

Donny was struggling along manfully and I could see we were outdistancing the pursuit fairly easily, my hunch about their running abilities seemed to be confirmed. He was like my little canary they use in some mines, if someone caught and ate him then I'd know the Undead could move quickly. I gave him a little smile to keep his spirits up but I don't think he noticed. Badly out of shape, was our Donny.

By the time I reached the room where the Sleds were kept we had left the hungry gang some way back but they were coming. Still, I was feeling pretty pleased with myself for getting us all alive and in one piece out of the jaws of death. Lots of jaws. As soon as Don'elk made it into the room I hit the door close control with my hammer, I guess I was a little more frazzled than I was letting on because as the hammer hit the controls I thought to myself a gentle touch would have been enough. There was a spark and the doors started to shut but stopped before closing fully – a narrow gap remained. Whoops! Still, I thought, we're safe for a bit.

Meataxe spoiled my moment by asking, "What are we gonna do now, Val? They'll be here in a minute."

Lydia ran to the lockers and pulled out some of the emergency spacesuits; she thrust a set at each of us and started to climb into her own set. Meataxe and Don'elk followed her lead but I was made of sterner stuff and stood about helplessly.

The first few members of the cannibal crew had reached the door and tried to get through. I stood and watched several of them clogging the gap, perhaps their very numbers would work in our favour as they pushed each other out of the way. A great big fat crew member would be very welcome right about now, someone to get wedged good and proper. My three fellow gang members were now dressed in very stylish and shiny outfits. Meataxe was especially grotesque; he resumed his seat on the sled looking like a whale in a balloon. Lydia looked at me expectantly.

"Err....ummm?" I queried, waving the spacesuit at her.

"We have to get those doors shut," she said, waving at the gap through which we could all see grasping hands stretching for us. Sometimes popularity can be a real bitch. "The only way I know which will work in the next few seconds is to open the exterior hatch. The drop in pressure will initiate a failsafe protocol and the internal doors in this part of the ship will automatically shut." She looked hard at me, "Get dressed and hang on to the Sled."

I climbed into the suit as one of the Undead appeared on our side of the half-shut door, little sucker must have been able to squeeze himself through – you have to admire their commitment. We didn't have much time for checks but Lydia did give Meataxe and me a quick onceover to make sure we hadn't put our arms in the leg folds. She ran over to the external hatch controls and hit a big red button.

The door popped open and all the air rushed out into space. On the upside, the internal doors sealed shut.

On the downside, none of us had the Life Support package on our spacesuits.

Chapter 15

A few arms were sliced off when the doors shut but the biggest excitement happened to our Deadguy. The one who had, by leadership, grit and perseverance, managed to push past his weaker brethren and get into our room. A real go getter, the guy was a hero.

When the main hatch doors opened all the air and loose stuff got ejected into space; Deadguy included. He didn't look surprised, just a little bit more pissed off than normal as he floated out into the great unknown.

Of course, I was a tad busy at the time as he floated past me, I had my hands full of ABSOLUTELY NOTHING!

Lydia had grabbed a rail next to the door controls and was hanging on grimly, I guess the rail was put there for just such an occasion. Her feet were swept up and she looked a little bit comical but as I said, my mind was elsewhere and unable to fully appreciate her position.

Meataxe, the lucky bastard, just hung on to the control bars of the Sled and clenched his thighs onto its body. Probably clenching other parts of his anatomy as well.

Don'elk had grabbed a bar on the side of the sled, he probably knew what was going to happen when all the air rushed out. The more I know about this guy the less I like him.

But I had nothing but good intentions to keep me held down and so I joined the rest of the trash and gently floated out of the room. Across the metal floor I wafted, gentle as a breeze and totally unable to do anything about it.

Except gibber in terror, of course, and I was doing a bang-up job of that task. I thought the newly amputated arms floating out with me was an especially nice touch. They wafted along at my eye level.

The room sort of glided by, Meataxe turned his head to look at me and we exchanged sickly grins. At least he gave me a sickly grin, I just had my eyes bugging out and my mouth wide open – Mr. Hero.

And then there was the vast open space of the doorway, I moved in a leisurely fashion towards its gaping maw, I threshed and waved my arms and legs. I twisted and turned, I wriggled and performed some pretty spectacular contortions, anything to get me to stop, slow down or change direction. I think I pulled several muscles quite badly and may even have popped a shoulder.

Nothing helped, inexorably I drifted across the last few paces of floor and then I was at the threshold, the line which marked where the ship finished and space began.

Oh, Lordy, space. It is so big. So very big, and it goes on for like … ever.

I am a man of faith, I am a believer – hard to comprehend, I know, given my lifestyle and chosen profession but there you go, some things stick. I remember a sermon given by one of the priests of my youth who said God created the vastness of space, of all eternity. Let me tell you, I know a thing or two about the vastness of space because I floated out of the doorway and I was in it. Talk about big, space is HUGE! It goes on and on, I saw stars and lots and lots of black. Lots of black. All round me, up and down, to the side, I was in the middle of a whole lot of nothing, the vastness of space. Boy, do I know vast.

Terror just keeps on building; it doesn't seem to have a threshold or upper limit. I was sure I was at my absolute limit of fear before I left the ship but when I gently wafted out into the centre of the universe my emotions kicked in the turbo charger. My imagination populated the dark reaches of the universe with giant creatures, great big eyes, lots of teeth and tentacles. I expected at any moment one of these nightmares to notice me and lunge towards my frail, puny body. The monsters are going to get me! My stupid, stupid imagination ran amok inside my head, seeing boojums everywhere.

And of course, I listened to every word so I was in a total funk. Man, I have never been so scared because I knew I would just keep on floating out into the darkness and there I would die. Probably have a heart attack due to fear and stress. Or my air could run out, lots of options for me, not just monsters.

I didn't really feel the moment when Lydia clipped a cable onto some random hook on my belt. I didn't realise anything was different until two strong arms hauled me onto the outside deck of the spaceship. I thought the two strong arms were monsters finally getting me. I now know I have an immensely strong heart and it can take a few hits because the rest of the body was all for shutting down but that little sucker just kept on beating.

Lydia had seen my plight, launched herself to Meataxe's sled and retrieved a safety cable. She clipped one end to the sled and then dived out the main door to me where she clipped the end onto my belt. Meataxe hauled us in. I am not worthy to shine her shoes.

I came out of my funk when I realised Meataxe was holding both my shoulders and shaking me, his face looked all pale inside his helmet. He was standing directly in front of me with a concerned look on his face and seemed to be saying something but I couldn't hear a word. Space, you know, no sound.

I gave him a little imbecilic smile. Gradually I realised my exertions and, well, everything else, has caused my body to give off lots of interesting odours. I noticed the interior of my suit smelled really, really bad. I was sharing my helmet with what seemed to be the aromas of several graves and a well-used outhouse.

Someone spun me around and I was face to face with the beautiful Lydia, she pushed her helmet against mine and heard her delightful voice, "Val, Val, are you okay?"

She is rather angelic, a vision of a better world. I gave her another of my sappy grins and possibly drooled a little. She shook me a few times and gradually the old mind came back online, had a look around and decided to take over management again.

"Lydia?" I bleated.

"Oh, Val," my sweetie pie said. "You're alright! We've got you. Just keep your boots on the deck and you're quite safe."

I looked down and noticed I was standing on the outside of the spaceship. On the outside, right next door to nothing. Yet this was an improvement. I was a sick, sick, man.

Don'elk was still standing next to the sled, he had a death grip on it so he wasn't going anywhere. Pity.

A few deep breaths seemed called for so I put one of my hands on Lydia's shoulder and we just stood there for a few moments, she seemed to understand my need for a bit of quiet because she let me alone for all of ten seconds before touching helmets again.

"Val," she said, "we have to move. These suits only have a few minutes of air in them, we have to get back into the ship but we can't go through all those Undead. What'll we do?"

How the hell should I know, I thought, what do I know about spaceships? Why do people seem to think I know what to do? The latest technology I was aware of up until recent events was the printing press and the musket. A musket, for goodness' sake! And now I'm standing on the hull of a spaceship discussing the amount of air in a vacuum suit. Don't tell me God doesn't have a sense of humour.

"Are there any other hatches?" I asked. She just stared at me, I could see the expectant look on her face, all shiny with sweat behind the clear faceplate. Sorry, she wasn't sweating, she was glowing. My mum used to say woman glow, men perspire and horses sweat. I can believe Lydia was glowing but I was definitely sweating. And was it getting hard to breath? Maybe I had sucked in a bit more of the good stuff than a normal user would consume over the last few minutes. Panic does things to a man.

Oh, goody, I thought, so let me see now. The problem isn't being eaten by the Undead or swept into the great emptiness of space it's - hang on a minute, I'll get it – oh, yes. We're going to die of suffocation when our air runs out in these weird suits. Well, that's much better.

Lydia didn't answer me and I was wondering what this meant. Maybe there weren't any more hatches; maybe she didn't know. She grabbed my helmet again and we banged heads. "Val, we have to have our helmets in contact to communicate. The radios were part of the survival packs, we have to hear by sound waves transmitted through the suits.

Poor love, she probably thought I would know what she was talking about. How can sound wave? Does it also smile and go dancing? Still, I understood her message – if I want to talk to anyone then I bang helmets. No problem.

"How else can we get into the ship?" I asked again. Another thought struck me, "Can we find an entrance near the Chief Trader's Quarters and avoid having to go back through the crowds of all the uglies down there?" What the hell, worth a try, I thought.

"Come on," she replied. She took my hand – which made me feel all twirly – and led me back inside the ship to the Sled. It was only a step or two but I would have floated away if it wasn't for her guiding touch; I could cope with where I was – well, actually I couldn't but I didn't have the luxury of having a little melt down – but I could manage as long as I kept my eyes downward towards the deck and didn't look up. Or around. Or over my shoulder. Or think.

Life's a bitch.

Lydia climbed onto the saddle of the Sled and gestured for Meataxe to sit behind her. She indicated Don'elk and I would have to hold onto the rails at the sides of the Sled's saddle. I took a death grip on mine, pretty sure I bent it a little. Looking over at Don'elk I saw him doing the same, I don't think he had let his rail go the whole time since Lydia hit the door switch. Smart man, I thought. Lydia gave us all a nod, looked ahead, and pointed with her right arm off towards the right. She put her hands on the controls and the Sled slowly lifted off the deck by a hand's breadth and gently began moving forward, into the vastness of space. Perhaps it would be better the second time.

My bowels turned over.

Lydia guided the machine out of the doors and did clever things to get the machine - and its passengers - gliding across the external hull. The Sled eased along at a soft pace which to me seemed to be a flat out sprint. I found my magic boots being sucked off the deck by the pull of the Sled and I floundered for a bit before placing my other foot back down again; then it was pulled away in turn and we kept moving forward. I moved in strange bounds, floating in space for a few seconds before my next foot found the deck and clamped on again.

Those moments of weightlessness were not in any way enjoyable.

The deck wasn't smooth like the hull of a proper, God-fearing ship; one made to float in honest water. There were lots and lots of things sticking out of the surface, some single poles and then just knobby bits and even a few large box-like constructions which could have housed a complete wagon and its team. But Lydia seemed to know what was going on because she softly moved us around all of the obstacles until we came to a stop in front of another large box. This one was like a large guard's hut, big enough to shelter out of the elements but not big enough to lie down in for a proper sleep. I've tried, it can be done but it's not easy. Yeah, I know, sleeping on guard duty is a dreadful sin but you try living through a siege where you are on watch every night for six months. After a while the body can sleep anywhere; I know I can. I've got all the skills.

Lydia lowered the Sled to the deck and did something clever to the controls because I felt the machine settle firmly and almost stick to the surface. It wasn't going anywhere.

My breath was getting shallow, Meataxe swayed a little but stayed on the saddle. I had run out of air once before and knew what it felt like. Not good. I had to sneak into a smuggler's camp after Magic convinced me I could breathe underwater if I had a basket over my head. An upturned basket which he had sealed with oilskin and wax, he guaranteed it would hold enough air for me to slip under the smuggler's nose, come up behind him and then do my little trick with a pointy blade.

It never occurred to me to ask why he didn't do it himself if it was so safe. But he was management and I was labour and not too bright labour at that. I agreed like a puppy trying to impress his master. I probably even hopped back and forth and waved my tail. I was such a dork. The creek I had to slip into was murky and full of silt which meant I promptly lost my way once I was fully immersed. It was a new experience, standing underwater with a basket over my head, I stood taking it all in while I sucked down my air. I know, not too bright. At this point I realised I had no idea where I had to go, the water was cloudy and so I started walking in a random direction. All seemed well. Then the air ran out.

I was blind, lost, soaked and uncomfortable while walking into a dangerous confrontation. Is this the life, or what?

Because of this valuable life lesson, I know what happens when you run out of air. There isn't a gradual lessening of the air, it just stops. The last few breaths become a bit harder and that's all the warning you get before it becomes impossible to suck in anything else. And believe me, when you are underwater with a bloody basket on your head there is a strong reason to suck really, really hard. I certainly sucked, but nothing happened, the lungs just don't have anything to drag in. My brain did the usual and shut itself down, turning over control to any other part of my anatomy which thought it could do a better job. My liver probably took over, or some other ridiculous organ because I threw the basket off and surged upwards. My head broke the surface and I hauled in a few deep ones.

Talk about lucky. I came up under a small jetty and I could hear the smuggler's feet moving around above me. The rest of the night went pretty much as planned, a bit of mayhem, a few bodies and then home for a drink.

But I never forgot the sensation of running out of air, the last few hard breaths and then nothing. Makes a man panic.

I figured Meataxe was close to those last few deep breaths, he was shuddering on the saddle. Lydia came and touched helmets with me. "This door leads to an airlock which opens directly into the Chief Trader's Quarters."

"Can you open it?" I asked.

"There's a keypad over there," she pointed at a little box on the wall. "But I don't know the code, it's totally restricted access, only the Chief Trader knows the code." Pause. "We can't get in without the code."

The night was definitely dark - dark outside and dark inside. Sure, there were stars out there but the radiance they shed was dwarfed by the enormous sense of catastrophic failure I felt. This is it, I told myself, we walked all the way over this stupid hull under a pitiless void only to hear my girlfriend say she didn't have a clue. It was her idea, for heaven's sake!!

Meataxe started shuddering, his whole frame was twitching; any moment he would slide off the saddle and die. Closely followed by us. I've heard stories of heroes in their moments of crisis, how their mind works swiftly, how they leap into action and perform stirring actions. How they come up with THE PLAN. The one that gets them all to safety.

My mind was a complete blank. Not a thing, empty space; not even a clever phrase or pithy recrimination. Nope, when the big moment comes I found I am not the stuff of heroes,

I'm just a spear carrier.

Chapter 16

As I mulled over this interesting and possible final moment of self-revelation I felt Don'elk push past me and step up to the key pad. With a few deft motions he punched in a code and the door opened. Safety beckoned.

I farted in relief.

Fortunately, Lydia is the stuff of heroes because she punched Don'elk to one side as he tried to enter the airlock. I stood and watched dumbly as she dragged the great mass of Meataxe in with her and then waved at me to join them. Don'elk squeezed in with me and the door to the great nothing slid shut – my air was going; no amount of sucking was getting anything into my lungs. We stood together as little red emergency lights came on and vapour entered the room, the light stopped being red and became white at which point I closed my eyes and blacked out. All that air, I was thinking, it's all outside of my suit. But there's no air in here with me.

Ah, well, so be it. My brain closed up shop and got ready to turn out the lights.

My body tends to ignore my brain, probably very wise. My fingers reached up and unclipped my helmet as I was sliding down the wall, gusts of wonderful tasting stale air vented into my nostrils and I pulled the helmet off the rest of the way.

Lydia had already pulled her own helmet off and was busily removing the same thing from Meataxe. Don'elk was standing with a glazed expression on his face, helmet hanging limply from one hand as he sucked in the big ones.

"Donny-boy," I croaked as I waved at the keypad, "you've got a bit more explaining to do."

He lurched upwards and tried to push past us to reach the inner door, no doubt some glimmer of self-preservation gave him strength but the gallant effort was undone as he tripped over the large inert form of Meataxe. The big guy growled querulously as Donny fell across his ample gut.

"Gerroff," my mate slurred. I was relieved he seemed normal, or as normal as Meataxe could ever be. The big guy rolled over and braced himself on all fours before shaking his body like a dog with wet hair. Same sort of smell, too.

I stood up and peeled off the coveralls, Lydia was doing the same but she made it look way more interesting. I saw the other two gawping at her as she shimmed and wobbled lots of interesting bits of anatomy before standing cool and calm before us.

"Hi there, fellas, enjoy the show?" she asked.

Meataxe grinned, Don'elk dropped his gaze in embarrassment and I just looked neutral. My face may have had a touch of leer in it. Possibly some drool.

About this time my brain came back online and I looked around the interior of the airlock.

It was a small room, two doors only. One of which I knew went Outside to bad, bad places. The other, if Lydia was correct, led to the highly secure Chief Trader's Quarters. Which prompted me to cast my eyes back on to my old pal, Don'elk.

"I've still got the hammer, Donny. Now if you don't want to lose any more fingers you better tell us how you knew the code to this airlock."

He glared at us, which was about as threatening as being hit with a damp rag, before slumping a little and saying, "I was meant to open it after everyone was, you know, incapacitated from the injections." He searched our faces for a bit of compassion – not a shred did he find.

"Why not open the big doors into the cargo bays or hangers?" asked Lydia. "This entry is too small to take out anything large. Surely the codes to the main doors would have been easier to find?"

"You'd think so, wouldn't you?" said our boy. "But the Codes to those doors are changed at random intervals to prevent, well, someone on the inside giving them to an attacker."

"Someone like you?" I asked.

"Sure, I don't mind making a deal with the highest bidder. Hey, isn't that what this ship is all about. I was trading, that's all, just trading."

Spin that tale, Donny, I thought. Self-delusion has got me through a few tough ethical spots.

"Explain how you got the code to this room. Surely that'd be even more secure?"

"I didn't get it," he admitted. "I was approached by a guy and he set the whole deal up. He gave me the code and told me what and when things would happen. All I had to do was ensure the injections got given to everyone and then open the airlock when they arrive outside."

"And then what?" I asked,

"Well, then they would pay me off."

"Did you meet anyone else?"

"No, just this...guy...."

"So, you are not a member of the gang, not in with the big crowd?"

"Not yet, but I will be. This is a big deal, they promised me a big stake in their operation."

I looked at this little twerp and wondered how he had survived so long. "Let me get this straight," I said. "You met a guy in a bar and he talks you into this deal. The end point is when you open the exterior door to a bunch of pirates and they walk past you saying thank you in polite tones?"

"It wasn't a bar" he said.

"What?"

"It wasn't a bar. He arranged for the meet to be in a park. Last planetfall, we met a couple of times. I was supposed to get a couple of Survival suits – for humans - cross the hull and enter the airlock to the Chief Trader's quarters."

"What happens then?"

"I don't know, that's all I was told."

"You bring a couple of suits to the Chief Trader's quarters? That's it?"

Don'elk nodded.

"Are you always this stupid?" I asked.

"I am not stupid! He came with references. He was introduced! The deal was good."

"Whaddya reckon, Meataxe?"

"I reckon Donny here is probably dumber than me," replied the big guy.

I agreed. "If I was a nasty, violent sort of a guy," Donny gave me a surprised look, "five seconds after coming through the airlock door I would stick a knife in you. Probably accompanied by an evil laugh."

There was a pause for reflection as we each considered the deed.

"Still," I continued, "could just be me. Maybe these pirates are the honourable ones who pay their debts and keep their word."

Meataxe guffawed and a little bit of spray came out of his mouth. "Sorry, bit excited," he apologised. He looked at Don'elk, "You mullet."

"Anyway," I said, "It doesn't matter now because you are a changed man, Don'elk, you have seen the error of your ways. You are 'helping us with our enquiries' and keen to make good. Your mum would be so proud."

"Piss off," he muttered.

I punched him in the stomach. Pretty hard, too, judging by the way he collapsed and lay there writhing. "Now, now, Donny, ladies present and all. Now get to your feet and we'll see what's behind door number two – remember this game?"

"Hey," he choked as Meataxe dragged him up, "I saved your lives, remember, I got you inside when all was lost. You owe me!"

"Give him a big kiss, Meataxe, and let's get the door open," I said.

We set ourselves again with Don'elk at the pointy end facing the door as I pushed the button.

The door slid aside and I thought Donny was going to wet himself again. I nearly did when I saw the interior of the new room. Standing on the other side, directly facing the door was one of the Undead, not a human undead. The thing gurgled and twitched, rolled its eyes and leaned in to poor old Donny. Dead guy then sniffed my little buddy's chest and chin before turning away and shuffling off back into the room. Meataxe had a good grip on Donny and was able to hold the little fellow up when he fainted during the olfactory inspection. A moment's reflection confirmed Donny had, in fact, soiled himself. Ahh, the odour of fear, I know it well.

Dead guy was very well dressed which made me think he may have been one of the big shots up here on the Executive Level. The other distinctive point of interest was the fact he wasn't a human, or a Tharl. He was a Glitchen, that's my name for them anyway. A Glitchen is almost a human but has some distinct differences, the main ones being the vestigial insect carapace on their backs, multi-faceted eyes and really bad breath. I'm sure there are other, deeper points of dissimilarity between us but I never had the urge to investigate further.

And I guess the reason he didn't latch on to Donny for a quick feed was due to Donny not being a Glitchen. Donny's more of a worm than insect.

Being the fine upstanding sort of chaps we are, Meataxe and I pushed our buddy further into the room just in case the Glitchen had other friends with a more human dietary interest. Poor little

Donny must have been at his emotional end by now because he didn't give us any objections, even after he came too and realised what was happening.

The room we entered was indeed occupied by a few more individuals, all of them noteworthy.

Over near another closed door stood Wallace and a Tharl, neither were undead. They were still alive and kicking but obviously feeling the strain of current events. Wallace looked his usual unconcerned self except for a certain tightness in the lips while the Tharl had a distinct twitch about the old visage. A lesser judge of character may have suspected he was nervous but I dismissed the theory. A nervous Tharl does not fit in my worldview.

Both had blaster weapons pointed at us.

Dead guy stumbled about a bit which drew my eye to a Main Control Panel and the Big Chair. I guess this was where the Chief Trader would sit when he was, well, Chief Trading. Leaning against the panel was another human who looked like he was about to lose his lunch, he was dressed in Steward's Livery and was immensely forgettable. No sense of presence or style, no Charisma, no effortless force of personality.

Not like the dude sitting in the Chief Trader's chair. It was the Man in Black, our boss.

"Valentine!" he said, "you are an amazing man. How do you do it? You just keep on surviving; you just don't stop. Saints above, you came in through the Chief Trader's airlock!" The Man in Black chuckled, lowered his own blaster and gestured with it at Deadguy.

"May I have the pleasure of introducing you to the owner of the airlock, the most recent Chief Trader?"

I smiled weakly and became aware of a steady thumping, a gentle but insistent pounding which came from the door near Wallace and the Tharl.

"Everything alright here, boss?" I asked.

"Couldn't be better, Sergeant – or is it Corporal – I tend to lose track of your rank, you go up and down so much. So far, we remain uneaten. For some reason the Chief Trader doesn't want to give us a nibble; although he did get stuck into one of his stewards before we arrived, isn't that right, Jenks?"

Jenks was the colourless type looking ill, he took a breath and answered, "Yessir, that's right, sir. Fair chewed up my mate he did. Poor bugger got his arm chomped straight off. 'Course, then my mate turned and became 'one of them.'" He poked his chin towards Wallace's doorway and I pictured the unlucky steward on the other side thumping the door with his bloody stump; keen to get inside at the goodies. Sometimes I believe I have far too colourful an imagination.

The Man in Black caught my glance at the door and said, "Don't worry, Val, it's not the steward making the noise. Much worse, I'm afraid; the Chief Trader had a full squad of bodyguards, huge and horrible brutes, made for mayhem. It's them you can hear; they all became undead. All except Sergeant Thorl over there, he's got quite the turn of speed when properly motivated. The noise has been going on for some time and it does wear a man down. How are you bearing up, Thorl?"

The question surprised me, asking a Tharl if he felt alright was like asking a mountain if it minded a spot of rain. Then I remembered about the Chief Trader's Bodyguards, they would be Tharls.

Just like Thorl. The thumping was for him.

"Peter! What a pleasure!" said the Man in Black when he laid eyes on Meataxe. "Now I know we will be just fine. You and Valentine have a knack of sorting things out."

Meataxe gurgled and stood a little straighter; believe me he had a lot more straitening to go before he could walk erect all the time.

Still, our boss called him 'Peter' which still jarred in my ears. Doesn't anyone have a sense of propriety and whimsy anymore.

"Afternoon, Captain Franz," mumbled Meataxe, giving the boss his old title. "Good to see you again, sir."

"And who is this delightful young lady?" asked my Captain.

I gnashed my teeth. Bloody aristocrats, charming every bit of skirt they meet. Bloody pampered, prissy, over-indulged girlfriend stealers. Damn, damn, damn....

Lydia responded by standing beside me and taking my arm in the nicest possible fashion, "Technician Lydia, sir, Valentine saved my life."

I smirked. I was going for insouciance but missed the mark and ended up with smirk.

The Man in Black raised an eyebrow; there may have been a tiny smile. I felt my face heat up. Bloody suave, smooth, sophisticated member of the gentry; they always know how to act. I bet he wouldn't stand around shuffling his feet if he was standing next to a pretty girl.

"Stand still, Valentine. Saints above, you look like a damned recruit. Now smarten up and give a me a proper report." My boss, a man of the people.

I launched into the whole saga, from being locked up to us arriving at the airlock and Don'elk hitting the keycode.

The Man in Black looked across at Donny who was trying unsuccessfully to sidle away from Meataxe's hairy paw on his shoulder. "Tie that bastard up, Peter. We don't want him running around causing more mischief." Meataxe looked around the room, searching for inspiration. The bed looked heavy enough to secure him plus there were plenty of bits of metal sticking out of walls, all of which would do the job; but this is Meataxe we are talking about. We watched in admiration as he used some torn strips of bed sheet to lash poor old Donny to the Undead form of the Chief Trader.

You had to be there, honestly. Our little thug was up close and personal with his very own Deadguy – the Chief Trader kept looking at him and leaning in for sniffs. A fair bit of snuffling was involved and lots of drool and rolling eyes. Donny was rigid with terror; you had to laugh.

The Man in Black sat and watched the whole event, he gave Meataxe a lingering look before saying, "You two are certainly effective - not pretty or elegant - but certainly effective." He turned back to me. "Now, time to plan our next step. Magic and most of the NightWatch are in the engine rooms trying to keep the infected crew from doing serious damage as they stumble about. They've had to fight off a few large crowds of them, I understand it hasn't been pretty, all hand-to-hand stuff. Except for Teddy Boy, of course."

Naturally, I thought, goes without saying - Ted would have found a shooty thing.

He went on, "They've secured most of the 'at risk' areas but they can't afford to leave. Plus, they don't know what has already been damaged or what is needed to keep things going. Flying a spaceship is a bit out of our skill set." He paused as we considered the comment. Six months ago we were working with horses and wagons as the limit of our technology. We were far more comfortable with breaking things up – buildings, furniture, the odd member of the citizenry.

"I could help," said a small voice. We turned to face Lydia, "I'm a Technician," she said. "If I could get to the right areas, I can monitor what is happening."

"Thank you, Lydia," said the boss, "but you have hit on the key problem – getting there. We have been trapped in here unable to leave because the only exits go through lots of the unpleasant folk who may want to ask us for a meal. We are saved by that door," he nodded to the interior hatch behind which lurked lots of Undead. "It is heavily reinforced because these are the Chief trader's Quarters."

"What about the airlock?" I asked. "We got in that way, couldn't you put on some of those suits and leave."

"The suits are the problem, or rather, the lack of suits," said the Man in Black. "This is the Chief Trader's quarters with just the one suit, and it fits him." He nodded to the drooling figure nuzzling up to a terrified Don'elk. "He is most definitely not a human; his suit is no good for us."

"We've got human suits now" Lydia said, "The four we wore to get here."

A new voice spoke up, "But only one Survival Pack from the Chief Trader's suit."

We looked around, the speaker was Jenks, the Steward. Jenks was human and relatively nondescript, normally he would just be part of the scenery, invisible in the background. But not this time, this time he drew the eye and gathered up our attention. At least, the two blasters he was holding gave us pause.

I cleared my throat to say, in my best copper's voice, "'Allo, 'Allo, what's all this, then?"

Chapter 17

"Get over there," he barked, waving us all to one side of the room, well away from the door.

"I just bet you are the guy Donny met in the bar," I said.

"It wasn't a bar," muttered the Don'elk part of the dynamic duo.

"Shut up!" ordered Jenks. "You, girl," he waved a weaponed paw at Lydia, "untie Don'elk."

Lydia gave him a look, I guessed she doesn't take kindly to being called 'girl' by random criminal masterminds. She moved over and separated Don'elk from our previous employer. Donny staggered over to stand beside Jenks.

"Now then, put your hands on your heads and kneel on the floor. Don'elk, get their weapons."

The Man in Black, H'nuth and Wallace slowly sank to the deck, fingers intertwined on the top of their heads. Meataxe looked at me, "What'll we do, Val?" he asked.

I hope there will be a time in the future when we can relive that moment, that delicious little pause in our drama. Jenk's face was a delight to watch; I have to admit I was a little surprised myself. There we were at gunpoint, big guns, too. The two toughest blokes in the room (that'd be Wallace and Thorl, I'm just an interested amateur compared to them) had complied with the instruction without hesitation. Even the Man in Black was on his knees without a quibble and he had stood up to the Inquisition without blinking.

But there was good old Meataxe, too dumb to be afraid of the creep with the weapons, asking me for instructions. Even Lydia gave me an inquiring look.

A natural born leader, that's what I am.

Jenks shot the Chief Trader with his blaster and I dropped to my knees before his body hit the floor. Stupid I ain't.

"Do as the nasty man says," I said. Meataxe and Lydia took up the required positions and we stayed that way while Don'elk stepped around us and took the blasters away from the good guys. When he came to me, he took my hammer, I thought I might cop a belt in the head but before Donny could summon up his courage Jenks called him to heel.

"Keep the blasters on them while I get into this suit." Donny took up a threatening stance and I felt well and truly threatened. If they wanted to shoot someone else to make an example, I was sure Donny could come up with a name – mine. We watched Jenks climb into one of the suits and attach the survival pack to it; I wondered when the penny would drop for Donny.

"Give me the weapons and then you get into another suit," ordered our evil villain. Donny dutifully gave up his blasters and began to slip himself into something more uncomfortable. With one leg in and folds of suit intertwined around his arms and legs he finally got it and asked the question.

"But we only have one survival pack, how will I breathe?" he queried. Such a little voice, too – no self confidence in our boy, very low self-esteem. Pretty rubbish as a thug, I thought.

Jenks opened the airlock door and gave Don'elk back one of the blasters. Stepping into the small room he gave a final instruction, "Good thought. I will go and get you a pack, keep them covered until I send someone for you." As he shut the door he gave one final suggestion, "Shoot another one when I leave, set an example."

Hoo-boy, I thought, here it comes.

We all watched the airlock shut and gazes were drawn to the little set of lights above the door; these lights indicated the status of operations – some sort of safety precaution I was told later. At the time I didn't know what the lights were for so I wasn't distracted; at least, not as distracted as Donny. He was probably running through his boss's instructions and by then wondering if he was to be trusted. Hmm, let me think about that one.

I launched myself at Donny while his worried little eyes were held by these flashing lights, his blaster has wandered off course as his brain ran the odds of survival so he didn't get a good clean shot at me before I hit him about waist level.

Still, he did get a shot off. It zipped past my left ear leaving a little burning sensation in its wake but I was focussed on getting to my target so I didn't feel anything at the time. I'm sure there is a small part of my mind which keeps score over these little wounds, the nicks and bumps of life, and then gives you the bill when you relax. But that's why we have alcohol.

He sort of folded when my shoulder hit him, a little gasp expelled the air in his lungs and I was able to push the blaster to one side so any more shots would be well away from all of the highly sensitive folks. After I banged his head on the deck a few times he lost interest in the blaster, Meataxe gathered it and I stood up. We all looked down at Donny as he lay in a pathetic heap, the survival suit twisted around his torso, his nose had started to bleed again and he looked really, really miserable.

Fair enough, I thought, couldn't happen to a nicer guy.

Then the little bleeder started to cry.

What a wus.

The Man in Black gathered us together around the big desk after we tied Donny into the chair. We just looked at each other.

"We might have a bit of a problem here," our boss said, the master of the brief summation. "Right", he went on, "let's see what we need to do and work out a plan. We have a gang of pirates about to land on the hull, one of the ring leaders has been in this very room with us waiting for, I presume, the airlock to be opened by Don'elk. Hmm, now why would that be, I wonder?"

We all looked thoughtful. Well, I pretended to be thoughtful, Meataxe picked his nose, Wallace leaned against the table with a blank expression and Thorl seemed distracted. Probably the thumping from the other side of the main entry door. His dinner guests.

Lydia gave us the clue. "This main console holds the codes to all the exterior doors. They can be opened from here remotely or the codes can be downloaded and then input at each door. Did Jenks use the console at all?" she asked.

I continued to have no idea what was going on – what's a console, anyway? – so I did my manly silence bit and hoped someone else had a few clues.

"Yes," replied the Man in Black. "He said he could connect us to the bridge from here but when he tried, he was unsuccessful."

"Did he use a data stick?"

I turned to look at the Man in Black, intensely interested in the answer. At least, that's the look I was going for but I don't think anyone bought it.

The Man in Black thought for a moment, looked over at Wallace and Thorl for their input and then grunted, "Yes, I think so. At the time I thought it was all part of the log on routine."

I spotted my hammer and picked it up. I know where my strengths are.

"That's what he's done, then," said Lydia. "He's downloaded all the door codes and now he's gone off to let the rest of them in."

"Can we get after him, maybe grab him before he meets up with the others?" I asked.

"No Survival Pack," said Wallace.

Silence descended as we considered our options. My brain was stuck in a loop – find bad guy, hit bad guy, find another bad guy, repeat until finished – so I was not much use.

"Any ideas, Val?" the Man in Black asked me.

"How about I go out and find one of the pirates and take his Survival Pack?" I was very interested in what my mouth was suggesting; obviously it had decided some other organ had better come up with something. Seemed like a workable plan, too; of course, my bowels were dead against it – they reminded me of the Great Vastness outside the ship.

"No air, Val," reminded The Man in Black.

"The suits hold a few minutes' worth," I said, my mouth seemed to have it all worked out. The rest of me watched in astonishment. "Should be enough for me to find someone."

"And if you don't?"

"Fabulous motivation for me to succeed, sir. Dead keen, I am." Bloody hell, what have I done to myself?

There were a few moments of quiet while we all considered the plan. Lydia had a worried look on her face – score one for the home team, I thought.

"I'll come too," said Wallace. "I need a bit of exercise."

Thorl was very firm in his decision to come with us, "Me, too. I'd rather not wait around in here until I get eaten."

Meataxe shuffled his feet and murmured he'd prefer not to go through the whole running out of air thing again. He said he would stay inside with the boss and Lydia. When did he get to be so smart?

The Man in Black summed it up, "Let's do it, Val. You, Thorl and Wallace try to get a couple of Survival Packs, bring them back here and we'll make our way across the hull down to the rest of the NightWatch. Lydia, can you get those codes from the console in case we need to open a few doors?" My girl nodded, clever thing that she is.

"What about Don'elk?" I asked. "Do you think Jenks will really send someone back for him?"

They all gave me the look reserved for the idiot cousin.

"Oh, right," I said. I turned to our captive, "Looks like you've been left holding the bag, Donny. Now what are we going to do with him?"

"Kill him," stated Wallace. I really like Wallace.

"Probably," decided the Man in Black. "I'll give it some thought while you three are out on your stroll. Don'elk's eyes grew large and pleading. Like that was going to work with us.

"You can't just kill him!" declared Lydia. "Val, you can't!"

Why do people ask me this question?

"I can. No trouble at all – I know where to put the hammer – I reckon one good hit on the temple should just about do it. Are you sure you don't want me to get it over with before we go, Chief?" I asked.

"No, leave him. We may have a chat while you're gone. Pass the time, so to speak."

Except for Lydia we all were discussing the imminent demise of Donny in calm, casual and unconcerned voices. No stress or strain.

Don'elk was understandably agitated; after all, he was intimately connected to the topic. But Lydia seemed to be having a lot of trouble with it.

"Val! Val! No matter what he's done, you can't just casually hit him with a hammer. Not in cold blood. Val, you can't!"

Well, I could. And would do so if ordered, or even if I just felt like it. Three years in the Siege of Ostend is a wonderful apprenticeship for killing. Easy, casual slaughter.

On this note we three suited up and left to cause a bit of mayhem outside.

Or die.

Time to roll the dice again.

Chapter 18

For weapons, we had a blaster and my hammer. Wallace and Thorl searched the room for pointy things. We decided not to take the blaster outside, the Man in Black might need some heavy firepower if the interior door ever opened – besides, our aim was to creep around. I wanted to kill bad guys, my preference was to hunt as a pack and come at them from behind and to do this successfully meant we had to be quiet and inconspicuous. The quiet was easy, this was space, after all, and no sound carried. A stab in the back suited me just fine, I certainly didn't want to spread the alarm and draw curious pirates down upon us. Not keen on that. Not keen at all.

Wallace always carried a long thin poniard which I am sure he kept in hidden places about his person; places I never want to see. He also picked up a stylus - a writing tool which he took from the main console. I had begun to use these myself as part of duty as the sometimes sergeant of the watch – Magic like reports on all sorts of little things. So far, he had been happy to accept the works of fiction I had been presenting him but I always felt he knew I was just making them up. Who reads this stuff anyhow?

Thorl had found a knife and fork from an old meal; we were going to attack space pirates with cutlery. Seemed reasonable.

Wallace grunted as I poked him in the ribs with a misplaced elbow. It was misplaced because we were trying to all fit into the airlock; a Tharl takes up a lot of room. When we all had our suits on and the inner door had cycled shut, I put my helmet against Wallace's and said, "We can talk to each other if we do this?"

"Do what?"

"Press our helmets together."

"What about Thorl, can he hear us?" Wallace sounded quite tiny; the suits bring a man down to size.

144

"No," I said. I took a deep breath and prayed for some more patience as I dealt with a slower mind than mine. "The helmets..." I tried speaking a bit slower for the benefit of the great Unwashed "...have to be touching. Like ours are now!" I may have raised my voice a bit.

"Then why is he pulling my arm?"

How the hell should I know, I thought. Before I could ponder more on the vagaries of a Tharl's mind the big guy grabbed my head and physically turned it towards the outer door. Great, I needed a reminder of where we were going. And what are all those lights for? The flashing ones?

I sensed a problem, got the senses of a cat, I have. A sick cat.

A part of my brain dredged up information about flashing lights in an airlock – someone had started the cycle to open the outer hatch and I didn't think it was one of us. The door swung open to reveal three suited figures. Since these guys had just operated the opening mechanism, I guess they were a little surprised to see the three of us standing there taking up all the useful real estate. I know I was surprised.

My body reactions kicked in and I tried to raise my hammer but Thorl was standing on it. It's remarkably hard to swing a hammer when some great lump of an alien is standing on the hurty bit. I grunted and but it wasn't coming free from under his boots. This cost me a few precious seconds in reaction time. Normally I would have dropped the weapon and reached for another implement of destruction, but the circumstances were different to a nice quiet dark alley where most of my fights have taken place.

Crammed as we were into the airlock, we couldn't move very much at all. Our only advantage was the bozos in front of us seemed more surprised than we were. I guess they had planned on doing a bit of random pillaging before buckling down to the serious task of taking over the entire spaceship. I was, of course, presuming they were part of the pirate gang.

All of these thoughts sort of meandered across my tiny brain and filled in the gap between my ears. Wallace, lovely man of violence that he is, had already stabbed the pirate in front of him with the big stylus. I bet the Chief Trader never knew it had so many uses.

Thorl just stood there, no reaction at all. Very uninspiring. The pirate in front of me started to react, his hand dropped down to a rather nasty looking holster at his side. I did the only natural thing in the circumstances and head-butted him. There was a nasty jolt as the helmet of my emergency suit met his; I had perfected this technique after a Saxon had shown it to me in a bar. He insisted on giving me a practical demonstration during a heated discussion we were having over a wager. I had a jug in my hand and took the opportunity of investigating the relative strengths of a thick clay jug against a smelly Saxon's skull. The jug won but not before he had vigorously demonstrated his head butt against my poor old nose. I had practised the manoeuvre many times since then, all with great effect.

My blow against the pirate would have been even harder except I tripped as I lined up the backswing. He only got a bit of the pure Valentine effort and my helmet softened the blow. Even so, I drove the pirate back a few steps where he stood in what I hoped was a slightly dazed state. Yet another example of these people's lack of any in-your-face fighting style.

I struggled forward and grappled my opponent, hugging his arms to his sides in an attempt to keep him from getting a glove on to his weapon. At this point I was out of options; in fact I was very nearly out of everything because my head butt had opened up a small crack in my helmet where the face plate joined the rest of the outfit. I could see air puffing out as a pretty little cloud. It would seem emergency suits are not meant for hand to hand combat. In an attempt to stave off the inevitable I took as deep a breath as I could and hung on to my violently shaking companion.

Just once I would like a turn at being the guy who has the weapon.

I gritted my teeth and pressed my lips together as we lurched about the hull – must have looked hilarious. As well as holding my breath and keeping the pirate in a death grip I had to spare some concentration devoted to keeping at least one of my magnetised boots on the hull of the ship.

I promised myself if I survived this little waltz I would get well and truly terrified of the emptiness of space. But right now, I had my hands full, so to speak.

We swivelled around a few times in quite ludicrous circles and it seemed in no time at all I was beginning to see the blackness descend as I ran out of air. Suck as I might the pantry was empty. The good times just roll on.

We both started to go limp at about the same time. At first, I thought he was mocking me - watching the valiant hero in his death throes – until I felt a firm smack on the front of my helmet. I slid away from the pirate and started to turn gently. Even as I died, it seemed the universe wanted me to see how really, really big it was. I closed my eyes and consigned myself to a better place.

"Wake up, you useless lump," I heard a rough and unkind voice rasp in my head. Perhaps I had gone to the other place, no surprise really.

"Val!" repeated the voice. "Valentine! Get a grip, you've got air and Thorl's patched your helmet. Now help me get these three back into the airlock."

I opened my eyes to an unchanged view, unchanged but now greatly restricted by the patch which covered most of my helmet, especially the piece in front of my eyes. I could still see if I tilted my head back and peered down my nose, not the most elegant or heroic pose for a burly adventurer. But what really got my attention was the simple fact of breathing. No longer did I see the little hiss of escaping air.

In fact, I was feeling pretty buoyant- surprised but grateful.

Squinting out of my faceplate I saw Wallace and Thorl stuffing two of the three pirates into the airlock. The third was at my feet with Wallace's poniard sticking out of his chest. Love that man.

I floundered about and grappled the body over to the others, it's surprisingly difficult to walk on the metal deck of a ship with magnetic boots while pulling a body along by the arm. The finishing touch was the necessity of keeping my head tilted back so I could see. Judging by the way Wallace's shoulders were moving I sensed he was having a right old laugh.

After placing my burden in the airlock Wallace stuck his helmet on mine and said, "You take this lot in, the airlock won't hold us all. Thorl and I will check out their sled."

"How am I still breathing?" I asked.

"Thorl put some sort of patch on your helmet, it seems we all have them in those pockets on the legs." Pockets? What pockets, I thought.

"And he pulled the survival pack off the dead pirate and gave it to you. Lucky it held air, eh? Could have been any old gas in there." He clapped me on the back and stood up, gently pushing me to stand on top of the bodies in the airlock.

Sometimes Wallace is a bit hard to take.

I cycled through the airlock – the things you learn to do in the NightWatch – and stood waiting for the inner door to open. When it did, I was punched in the stomach, thrown to the floor and had a blaster thrust into my face.

Okay, I thought, this time I give up.

The helmet was pulled off me and I heard the Man in Black say, "Stop playing around, Valentine. For God's sake, man, this is no time for dawdling."

The sting of his remarks was softened by Lydia placing her soft arms and ample bosom around me. I do like an ample bosom.

"What happened, Val?" she breathed – and believe me, Lydia taking deep breathes can be quite a sight. "Are you alright?"

I struggled to my feet while keeping her close and clingy as I gave my report, "Found them outside, sir. Must have been about to come in as we were going out."

"How'd you kill them?"

Good question. "I, er, don't know."

"How can you not know?" asked the Man in Black. "And what happened to your helmet?"

"Uh, I broke it when I head butted one of the pirates."

Lydia's hand went to her mouth, "Val, those suits are just for an emergency, they won't take any strain." She pointed at the gear our dead adversaries were wearing. "And they've got proper exosuits on, it's a wonder you didn't smash your face plate."

I decided not to mention the fact I tripped as I hit him.

The Man in Black was examining the bodies, "One's got a hole over where I suspect his heart would be; another has a poniard still in him and this one's still got a stylus sticking out of his chest." He stood up, "Wallace, I presume?"

I gave him my best smile and decided to shut up.

"And where are Wallace and Thorl? Are they hurt?" he asked me. "I can't imagine they have much air left.

"I dunno," I replied. This report was not one of my winners.

"And where did you get this Survival Pack from?"

"Thorl gave it to me, took it off one of the bodies, sir"

"Good thing it had air, eh? And not some noxious gas." Meataxe chuckled; I was glad I could bring some light entertainment to the troops.

The Man in Black paused to gave me a look, a small stare, "I don't know how you've lived so long, Valentine." I decided to keep quiet since I had often thought the same thing.

"I assume," he went on, "they are doing a small recce out there. Let's see if we can get these suits of these characters and see what we have. Can we reuse these suits, Lydia? Even with the holes?"

"We should be able to; I can put some of the emergency patches on them. We're roughly the same size and these suits are made to be generic. There are a set of tighteners on them so they can be adapted for an individual. I don't suggest we use Val's suit again; it's been too badly compromised."

We started to strip the pirates and fix up the suits when we heard the airlock cycle again and the Man in Black prepared to stick a blaster into the face of whoever came through the door.

It was Wallace and Thorl, looking quietly pleased with themselves.

"Found a sled," said Wallace. "Big one. Thorl showed me a storage hatch where we found these." They held up some more suits and Survival packs. "We might be able to use them."

"Well done, Wallace," said the boss, "I understand you are a dangerous man around stationery."

Wallace looked blank, Thorl grinned and said, "An amazing fight, sir, I have never seen a body move so fast. When the outer door opened, we were all surprised, us and the pirates. I froze – just for a moment, as did the pirates. But Wallace reacted instantly, he plunged his knife into the first pirate's chest even before the door had stopped moving."

"How did you know it was a pirate, Wallace, and not one of the Watch who had made an escape?" The Man in Black asks good questions, but this was not one of them. I knew these guys weren't NightWatch; wrong gear, the way they stood, plus the fact no-one in the Watch would be able to cross the deck and come to the airlock door without help.

"Lucky guess, sir," replied Wallace. Excellent answer, full of detail and colour.

Thorl had more to say, I wasn't looking forward to the assembled throng hearing of my stumbles and trips but who can stop a Tharl when they get chatty.

"The pirate in front of me had begun to move, I was just about to engage him when Wallace plunged the pen into his chest! There could not have been two heartbeats between the door opening and him dispatching the two vermin."

"Commendable reaction time, Wallace," said the Man in Black. "What was Valentine up to during all this time?"

The Tharl blinked at the "all this time" quip but then opened his mouth to tell all and sundry of Mr Klutz.

"Bravest thing I ever saw, sir," said Thorl. "Valentine couldn't get to his weapon," and I know why, I thought - because some great slob of a bodyguard had his giant boot on it.

"Remember, Val was only wearing one of the emergency suits and the pirate was in full equipment. But that didn't stop him from acting! Again, as soon as the door opened Valentine was trying to raise his hammer but after an instant realised it was not possible. Instead, he hit the pirate with his helmet! With a fragile, lightweight emergency helmet! The blow pushed the pirate back but did him no real damage and so Valentine grappled with him before the wretch could draw his blaster." He gave me some sort of admiring look. I was fairly amazed at his spin on the story.

"And all the while his air was escaping from a crack in his helmet! Damage such as this usually results in a catastrophic malfunction of the entire suit as the internal pressure blows the entire face plate off." This was news to me, the words 'catastrophic malfunction' made me go all wobbly.

"I slapped a patch on his helmet as Wallace plucked the knife from the first pirate and then dealt with Valentine's opponent." He looked at me and said, "You are a very brave man, Sergeant."

Wallace rolled his eyes and Meataxe snorted, "Bloody stupid. Bet you didn't know those suits we were wearing can't take a hit, eh, Val?"

"I think I'll just sit down for a moment," I said, sliding to the floor.

Chapter 19

Now we had some more suits, three extra blasters plus a bunch of Survival packs. We could all leave and go.... somewhere.

"What do we do now, boss?" I asked.

"We have some options," The Man in Black was back in planning mode. "These undamaged suits mean we have some freedom of movement. However, we must bear in mind the damaged suits cannot take any real combat because they are already compromised. How good are those patches, Lydia?"

"Even with the patches they will be stronger than the Emergency suits. Still, I don't recommend any more of Val's physical style of combat." I returned her mildly angry glare with my best blank face and silently agreed with her. She was working at the Main console, fingers dancing over little knobs and levers as she spoke.

"More problems, though," she said. "Jenks did a few more things than just download codes. He's turned off the Main Console's ability to control a lot of stuff on the ship."

"Such as?" asked the boss.

"Normally this console can control internal emergency doors, the main engines and life support. It can function as a back up to the main controls on the Pilot Deck if needed. It gives the Chief Trader the ability to keep an eye on things - see those screens over there?" She indicated a wall of blank monitors, "Normally the Chief Trader would be able to use those to scan thorough various areas in the ship. Were they working when you arrived in here?"

"When the rest of the bodyguard were killed..." Thorl stopped speaking and looked at the door to the hallway. The thumping was very faint now but still there if you knew what to listen for. His face blanched a little.

"Had you received the new injections?" I asked.

"No, we were due to have them at the end of our shift."

The Man in Black finished the story, "We were attacked by groups of Tharls we encountered in the corridors while we escorted the Chief Trader back here. We were picked off one by one until only Thorl and I were left; when we burst into the room Jenks was at the Console and I didn't think anything of it. The screens were already blank and then the Chief Trader dropped dead. You saw him after he came back...to life."

"That's it then. He must have only had time to disable the controls and was trying to get the external door codes when you came in," said Lydia. "The console must be rebooted from the Main Engine Room, fortunately you have people down there, they could do it. What technicians do you have in your squad?"

I looked at the Man in Black, deeply interested in his answer, "We don't have any technicians" he said.

"You must have. All Security Squads have one certified technician." My girl liked to press a point.

"Not the NightWatch."

"Well, maybe your technician was infected." Wonderful the way she could ignore his statements and assume he was wrong; we were going to get on like a house on fire. "What about someone who is a bit smart around computers? Do you have any hackers in the group?"

"Lots of them," I put in. "Best hackers in the business. Got some great slashers, too. And for bashing, I'm your man." I smiled at my girl.

The Man in Black gave me the shut-up eye before rejoining the conversation, "Let's just assume there is no-one down there with the necessary technical skills." He leaned on the door to the airlock and casually rested a foot on a body of one of the pirates. "You said before you need to be down there to ensure the engines and so forth are not damaged. Why not do the reboot as well?"

Lydia nodded, "Someone will have to stay here then. When the Main Console is back online this room will be a potential risk. If the pirates get in here, they could fly the ship wherever they choose."

The boss tapped a thoughtful foot up and down a few times, I don't think the dead guy minded too much.

"Val, you escort Lydia down to the Engine room; Wallace and Thorl go with him. Don't fart about and get sidetracked. Lydia, get to the controls, turn this Console back on so I can see the screens – from here I will see what sort of state we are in. Can you override the exterior door codes from the engine room?"

"No, the codes are the overrides – they are meant to bypass everything else, not the other way around."

"Very well then. Once we have the engine room in hand and the monitors are back online, I can direct you to finding the pirates. Val, once we get it together I want you to send out some of the lads in small groups to do a bit of hunting."

"What if they open all the airlock doors, let all the air go out into space?" asked Wallace.

Good point, a bit ruthless but if you didn't mind wholesale slaughter then it made sense.

"That's awful!" Lydia was struggling with the idea of mass murder. "They wouldn't do such a gross act!"

"I would," said the Man in Black. Wallace and I both nodded agreement.

"The Emergency Doors!" said Lydia. "Remember! When we ran away from the...dead crew... we opened an exterior door to use the sled. The Emergency Doors shut automatically, the ship can't lose all its air. Unless...." Lydia turned back to the Console, I could see her shoulders sag from where I sat on the floor. "Jenks has disabled the command to shut all internal doors if there is a drop in air pressure. If he wants to vent the ship he can." She looked over to me, "We must have made our exit before he disabled the protocol."

Jenks would have fitted right in as a squad member of the Watch. I was going to have to kill him.

"We'll stick with the plans," decided the boss. Peter and I will stay here, Don'elk can keep us company; leave us a couple of suits and your damaged one, Val. Guess who gets to wear it if needed?"

I like the Man in Black, he has a real sense of style. It took Donny a few beats to catch on – a little incentive for him to help the good guys.

Lydia got back into her survival suit and attached one of the Survival packs. We had decided it was best if she did not look threatening, just in case we ran into nasty people. Wallace and Thorl picked up two of the new, undamaged pirate suits and began climbing into them.

I was a little slower, all the talk of patches and broken suits had caused me to think of the dangers inherent in poorly maintained pirate spacesuits. But eventually I started to get into another undamaged suit. And it stunk with sweaty pirate body odour. Oh, joy.

Finally, we had ourselves all kitted up and stood yet again in front of the airlock door. I was off on another little stroll in space, one of my all-time favourite past-times. And me without a drink.

As we were getting fitted out, I asked Wallace how he happened to be in the group. He told me he had arranged to meet Thorl and go over some charcoal drawing techniques with him. H'nuth was a mutual friend and it seemed Tharls liked to paint and draw. Artistic killers, oh dearie me.

We exited in two groups having learned our lesson about being in confined spaces with a Tharl. Wallace and his new art buddy went first and then Lydia came through with me. Once outside Wallace took us to the large sled the pirates had used; it looked the same as the smaller one-man sleds just a little larger with a long, flat deck for cargo behind the main saddle area. Our small sled sat to one side with bits torn off it; it seems the pirates had engaged in some light vandalism before opening the airlock door. Of course, then they found out what real vandals can do.

Without communications there wasn't a lot of point in talking so I just shut up until Lydia touched her helmet against mine. "These big sleds are dangerous. I've heard about people using them to go from space to the planet's surface but I never really believed the stories."

"Why's that?" I asked. As I spoke little lights flickered inside my helmet. When I stopped speaking so did the lights.

"It's very dangerous. The sleds are essentially an in-atmosphere small cargo hauler; you have to be wearing a spacesuit to use them up here. Riding one down to a planet's surface is not their prime function. Lots of potential problems – they can burn up on re-entry; the engine could flame out as it goes from space to atmosphere; the controls would barely handle the buffeting and finally the rider risks being plucked off the seat. No straps to keep you there, just a small stasis field for protection. Their major benefit is they are undetectable – any smuggler would have free passage."

"I know smugglers," I replied, again watching the lights cavort in my helmet. "I've seen them ride a small open boat in a storm, trying to land cargo onto a rocky beach. If there's big enough money in it then a smuggler wouldn't think twice." I took a few moments to relish the fact this lovely woman was choosing me to talk to. "What are these little lights for in my helmet?" I asked her.

"What lights?"

"Every time I speak a little bunch of lights go on and off."

She pulled back and then bumped my head again, "Where are they?"

"Down near my jaw, just to the right. There's a little stick next to them, feels like a lever or something."

"They only come on when you talk?"

"Yeah, like now. As I speak, they're flashing." I could tell this was not a good thing. Lydia's body language, even inside the suit, was giving off worry waves.

"I think that's their communication gear."

"What gear?"

"The suits have devices fitted for short range communication between people on the same team."

"People like pirates?"

"Yes."

"Can I turn it off?"

"Push the little lever with your chin."

I did so and said, "I'm speaking now and the lights are off."

Pause.

"Have the pirates been listening to me all this time?" I asked.

"Probably." She leaned back and looked over my shoulder, "We might have a few moments but I bet someone's on the way to check us out."

"Stay here." I patted her on the shoulder and ran/slid over to Wallace and his mate. I pulled them both into a hug, touched helmets and filled them in.

"So don't say a word until that little lever thingy has been pushed," I instructed.

"I turned mine off as soon as I put the helmet on," I could hear a certain note of superiority in the Tharl's voice but then these helmets do tend to distort.

"What about you, Wallace, is yours turned off?" Wallace was just a refugee like me so I felt at least he would be a buddy and be grateful for the tip.

"Sure," the vile man replied, "I did a course with these suits when we boarded, thought it would be a good idea to know how things work. Especially things to keep me alive." It seemed like I was the only one out of the loop.

"We'd better find some cover before the rest of the gang shows up." Thorl finished speaking and leaned away and looked over my shoulder, after a moment he touched helmets again, "Too late, couple of sleds on the way. What'll we do, Val?"

I turned and saw nothing, no pirates, no spaceship, just a bunch of lights all over the hull. Then I noticed some of the lights moving. Bugger.

Leaning in again I thought for a moment but not too long – thinking's not my strong suit. "Thorl, start this sled up and send it off out into space, you and Wallace fire a couple of blasts after it then you both fall down as if hit by return fire."

"What about Lydia, Val?"

Without replying I turned and moved as fast as I could towards Lydia, she was where I had left here looking very small and lost by herself. Just a small, lonely figure trapped on the shiny skin of a giant metal beast. She could have been a mosquito about to be squashed. Over her head I could see a pair of large sleds moving towards us.

Time for a cunning plan. Pity I didn't have one.

I reached Lydia and punched her in the stomach as the first of two sleds loomed nearby; my sweetie-pie looked very astonished and then just folded up and went all limp. Poor love, she's having a big day.

The newly arrived pirate sled started to settle and I turned my back on it to look at what my pals were up to. Now I have to say this was a tense moment for me; I was pretty sure the correct behaviour towards pirates did not include turning your back on them. Not unless you wanted something sharp and pointy inserted into said back.

But my plan relied on these dropkicks considering me as one of their own; hence the punch to Lydia who was dressed in an obviously non-pirate suit. I hoped we lived long enough for her to get good and angry with me.

Wallace and Thorl were firing blasts at our rapidly disappearing sled. As I watched, they both reacted as if hit and floated all limp and dead-like. I was hoping it was all pretend but it is hard to know where blasts are coming from in space.

On Earth there was powder smoke and a big bang, lots of clues to where the nasty man with the gun was standing. But out here in space there wasn't any noise, just the rasping of your own breath inside the helmet. As I had discovered, the only way of knowing you were being fired upon was when bits of the nearby terrain – or bits of you – started to disappear under the energy blasts. If you happened to be looking at the shooter it was possible you could see the light of the blast as it left the barrel of the weapon but it's not much of a clue. You could return fire to the blinking lights thinking it was a blast gun only to take out a radio transmitter or someone's emergency suit light.

When Wallace and Thorl collapsed I was hoping they were just pretending and not quietly dying.

The second sled must have believed the miscreants were fleeing in the scene of the crime; they accelerated over the bodies of my two pals and took off in pursuit of our runaway sled. These pirates had a big gun mounted on the front of the sled and, as it glided past, I could see flashes of light which I guessed meant it was firing a few shots its quarry. Pursuer and pursued hammered onwards, disappearing into the great darkness of space.

No way would I be leaving a perfectly good spaceship on a little sled and heading into the big dark. Not this guardsman.

The second sled had dropped a lone guy off with me before sailing past to check on Wallace and Thorl. We had moments before all the tricks were discovered.

I gave the villain approaching me a quick look before bending down to Lydia and roughly pulling her to her feet. The poor lamb swayed a little in my grip as I gave her another belt which caused her to sail majestically into my oncoming pirate. This guy suddenly found his hands full of a floppy spacesuit containing a comatose Lydia. He did the natural thing and grabbed her.

I did my natural thing and stepped into him while he was otherwise engaged and pushed a knife into his helmet. It was about eye level and he stiffened before giving a small shudder and going limp. I grabbed Lydia and made sure her feet were anchored before heading back to Wallace and Thorl, they were going to need some help.

Silly me, I forgot this was Wallace. When the remaining two pirates got off the sled to check on their buddies my favourite hit man rolled to one side and shot them both with a blaster. In a matter of moments, they had grabbed the empty sled and rode over and picked me up. I jumped on board and we grabbed the lovely Lydia before roaring away.

The whole scene – from me talking to Lydia to us fleeing in the captured sled - had taken less than thirty seconds according to my helmet clock which I naturally assumed to be completely wrong. We must have been there for a week at least.

Thorl weaved in and out of things sticking out of the spaceship, a bit like riding a horse through a forest. Except it's not a horse and we weren't in a forest, but you get my drift.

He found a nice dark shadow and we slid into it, touching down onto the deck and shutting off all lights. Silence descended on our little group as we sat in a blackness I have only ever experienced in cave. I couldn't even see my companions, such was the degree of dark.

Someone touched my helmet, "Val?"

"Lydia, is that you?" I leaned in a little and opened my mouth to speak, "Look, I want to explain..."

I stopped talking because she had taken a good hold on my helmet and was hitting it repeatedly onto the nearest surface. As my brain rattled around, I reflected on my ability to really get on with women.

Chapter 20

Thorl and Wallace pulled my true love off me before she had a chance to do some real damage. I now have a deeper sympathy for those who choose to wear full armour including the totally enclosed helmet. I could never afford that sort of stuff and always felt it was a little bit unfair to go into a fight with someone covered in plate. Especially when yours truly had to defend with a grubby jerkin and fast footwork. Bloody Spaniards. Still, a musket ball tended to go through most armour so I always liked to keep an equaliser within close reach.

But now I was experiencing what it felt like wearing a full helmet as one of the great unwashed thumped you with a stick. It's noisy and your head tends to rattle around and bounce of the walls.

Not nice.

After I gathered what was left of my wits, we made a huddle and I got the chance to put my side of the story to Lydia.

"I don't want to hear about it, you thug, you bully!" My girl has a way with words.

"How'd you know it would work out that way, Val?" A sensible question from Wallace. Unfortunately, I was all out of sensible answers.

"I thought they might take off after the runaway sled, especially if it looked like you two had been hit by return fire. It just left us with the three on the second sled to deal with."

"Why did you hit me?" wailed my girl.

"Lydia, you were the only one of us not dressed like a pirate, I had to gain some time and get then to land near me without shooting first. I figured if I attacked you, it might look like I was one of them.

"But how did you know these three would split up?" asked Wallace.

"I didn't."

"Then you threw me into the pirate!" I could see Lydia wasn't going to let this go.

"He was too far away from me, all I had was a knife, for goodness' sake! Wallace and Thorl had the blasters!" I sounded a touch desperate. "I had to give him something to deal with before he realised I wasn't one of the gang. As it was, he was probably using his radio on me and wondering why I wasn't answering."

"Let me get this straight," said Wallace. "You had no idea the three would split up, you hoped Thorl and me could handle them – dead as we were."

"And you hoped by using me as a bludgeon you could have a chance at taking out the third pirate!" Come on, Lydia, I thought, move on.

"Well, when you put it like that it all sounds so risky." I could see I was on the losing side here; a sulk seemed called for.

Wallace wanted to have the last word, "I don't know how you've lived so long, Val."

You and me both, pal, I thought.

"We still need to get to the engine room," Thorl joined the conversation and brought us back on track. "How are we going to do it?"

"We can get in through the Main Hanger doors. Part of my job is repairing all the shuttles which means I'm authorised to have the codes for the main doors. If we get back on the sled, I can drive us to them and we should be fine."

"What if the pirates are there already?" I asked.

"I'm sure you'll come up with a brilliant plan," said my sweetheart. Even through the layers of helmets I could hear the sarcasm.

Thorl sat behind Lydia while Wallace and I found places in the rear of the sled. It was just a big, flat surface with various holes and studs for securing cargo. I watched Wallace open a small compartment and take out a bit of cord with funny metal bits on each end. He pressed one end onto his suit where it matched up with another metal bit, they must have clicked together because he was soon wandering around with the bit of cord hanging off his suit. He attached this with another click to an eyehole on the sled.

Pretty clever, I thought. Not wanting to look like a complete novice I took out another piece of cord and pressed it to my suit several times in several places. Not a thing. Then I tried to get it to attach to another eyehole on the sled – more raging unsuccess.

I looked up in exasperation to find the other three all staring at me. Just watching and waiting. Yes, ma'am, I am a twit.

Wallace leaned over and bumped helmets, "Want some help, sergeant?"

I mumbled something vague; he took the cord and I watched him attach both ends - I was now tethered to the sled, oh, goodie. As soon as I was attached Lydia moved us off; the initial thrust was slight but enough to knock my magnetic boots free from the deck of the sled. I watched it move slowly past my feet as I practised running on the spot – must have looked hilarious but I didn't get the joke. Eventually the slack in my tether cord was taken up and the sled towed me off into places unknown.

We travelled this way for a while, I could see Lydia and Thorl were very used to this method of transportation and Wallace just seemed to know how to handle himself in strange situations. He didn't float off the sled and get towed along like a bit of flotsam; no, he had braced himself very gracefully and was leaning back comfortably as we moved along.

I was bouncing and twisting behind the sled, every small course change sent me off into another little spin. My helmet reflected a wonderful vista of stars rotating in the sky, just the sort of thing I love about space.

We pulled up somewhere but I continued floating forward until Wallace grabbed me and pulled me back onto the sled.

"Stop farting about, Val," he said. "We've stopped, let's go and see what's going on."

By this stage I was seriously considering being sick inside the suit. All the spinning and turning was not doing my gentle nature any good, it was all I could do to manage a confused grunt in response.

Lydia and Thorl came back and joined us in another helmet touch meeting.

I didn't contribute much to the conversation, most of my concentration was being used to keep my insides from getting outside so I missed a bit. I gather we had reached the Main Hanger doors but they were open which meant the pirates were already there. Thorl seemed keen on doing something heroic about those pirates but my head was still spinning too much to pick up on details. At this point I couldn't have cared less so I did not have anything to add when asked my opinion aside from a noisy belch. I fought hard to keep it at just a belch.

I did catch Thorl saying, "That's settled; you three get off here and wait. Lydia and Wallace stepped on to the deck while Thorl took the controls. I was wondering how Wallace undid the cord holding him to the sled when I felt myself tugged gently back into movement.

Thorl was taking the sled somewhere and I guess I was going along for the ride. Part of my spins allowed me to see Wallace and Lydia shrinking behind me as they stood on the hull. Her stance seemed a bit pensive but I lost sight off her on the next spin, Wallace had a hand raised towards me. Not sure if meant he wanted to help or was just waving goodbye.

What I did see was the view over Thorl's shoulder as he piloted the sled directly towards the open Main Hanger doors.

The hanger bay had a small crowd of pirates all pointing at us and running around. It didn't take much imagination to work out Thorl's plan, he was using the sled to charge at the pirates – very elegant. Very terminal. While I don't object to someone sacrificing themself for the team, I do take umbrage at being included in said sacrifice. On my next spin I saw the pirates raise their arms and little sparks of light blossomed from their hands.

We were being fired upon.

Blaster fire is really, really hard to see in space – yet another reason for me to not love the environment. I was hoping our distance and wild gyrations would help to make us a harder target; as I was thinking this through Thorl started firing the gun mounted on the front of the sled. All I had was the knife, not a lot of help in current circumstances; big shooty things seemed to be the order of the day so I left in my belt. We're all having fun here, everyone except poor old me.

As a child one of our pastimes –when we could skive off from chores and lessons – was to tie a piece of string on to a cork and throw it into our nearby stream. Someone then ran along the bank pulling the string while the rest of us threw rocks at the cork. It bounced and plunged along until we got bored and started throwing rocks at whoever was pulling the string. Way more fun.

I spent a few moments apologising to all those corks because I now had a deep understanding of how they felt. Absolutely powerless.

Thorl dodged and weaved, throwing the sled in all manner of extraordinary gyrations to avoid incoming fire. I twirled and turned, sometimes seeing the landing bay, sometimes the eternal night and on one memorable occasion I smacked into the side of our loyal craft. I tried to grab on to something but it's hard to coordinate a quick response when all your energies are given over to yelling obscenities. My head rattled around inside the helmet which nudged the little radio lever back on so my wild yells could be shared with a wider audience. I hope they were having as much fun as I was. Golly gee, yes.

When another one of my twirls threw me against the side of the sled and I managed to grab a convenient bar to steady myself. Now we were getting somewhere; with a death grip on the bar, I started waving my other hand towards the cable linking me to the bloody machine.

A bit of the front cowling disappeared, I guessed someone scored a lucky hit. When the jerking subsided for a moment, I was able to grab the treacherous cord attaching me to the sled. I released my death grip on the side bar, drew my knife and decided to part company with the horrible machine. At this point, I did not care what happened to me.

I cut the cord and became my own little projectile.

The sled accelerated ahead of me, Thorl was going in hard. I just maintained my previous speed and direction; probably some science in there which could explain it, not that I care. The big takeaway was the fact the sled moved away from me and I got to fly through space like a damn fool.

About the same time as I cut the cord with my knife, I noticed Thorl's right arm glow and disappear. A little blast of air and other bits and pieces of Thorl jetted out from the hole in the suit. The sled thundered towards one end of the landing bay while I sped off on a tangent aimed at the other end of the bay. 'Aimed' may be too strong a word.

I watched the sled hit a large clump of pirates, squashing many of them before sliding around the landing bay causing more mayhem. My own journey had a choice of finishing points - would I crash somewhere in the landing bay or miss the landing bay but smack into the hull of the ship or miss everything and sail off into space.

Did I mention I was still slowly rotating? Must have slipped my mind. Each spin gave me a moment or two where I could see the ship growing larger, so much larger. And so, I re-entered the ship - waving a knife while yelling and flailing about in a wonderful example of out-of-control flight.

And I was screaming. Add some stomach-churning terror and you will have a good idea of the situation as my journey's end resolved itself. No, I did not sail off into space. No, I did not squash against the hull like an insect ending it all. I did, in fact, come into the landing bay with my terminal point being the back wall. The huge, giant, impenetrable back wall. I may have lost a little bladder control.

Before I hit the wall of the landing bay, I managed to collect two pirates who were just standing around watching the fun. I suspect they had been so enthralled with Thorl's epic assault they never noticed little old me until I hit. I smacked into both of them with a lot of pent-up momentum, so much that I pushed them ahead of me towards the back wall of the landing bay. They did look surprised as we sailed merrily along.

My eventual crash was therefore broken by the wall and the two very unlucky pirates. I hit them both about mid-section and we all became a flailing mass of arms and legs as we careened into the far wall of the landing bay. Let me tell you, they build these walls tough, I imagine they have the occasional crash as someone mis-times their entry – a bit like me, except I didn't have the luxury of sitting in a padded pilot seat with nice, comfy restraining straps and other sundry safety gear.

What I did have were two nice soft pirate bodies, I grabbed one by his suit and used my fear-driven muscles to hold him in front of me as we hit the wall. We squelched together with him doing most of the squelching after which he seemed to lose all interest in the proceedings. I lay there doing my usual self-inspection to see if I was dead when his companion lurched into my view. He must have only taken a bit of the thump from me because now he seemed perfectly fine.

Perfectly fine and leaning over poor, helpless me; our helmets touched. he was asking if I needed assistance. You bet, I thought. I lunged upward with my knife and he became an ex-pirate. I couldn't pull the knife out, it seemed to be jammed into his ribs.

This gave me time to catch my breath and wonder how I get into these situations; after a few moments my well-honed survival instinct chimed in and I staggered to my feet. The landing bay was quite a sight, the sled had squished most of the pirates before crashing into the rear wall, Thorl was slumped over the controls and should have been dead but it's hard to tell with Tharls, they're a bit hard to kill.

My recent victim had a blaster on his belt so I pulled it free and lurched over to the wreck. On closer examination all the pirates except one were either dead or pinned under the sled. While Thorl was a great pilot, I'm sure he could have been a cannon ball in another life. The one remaining pirate still on his feet was moving gently towards the sled, blaster in hand; we saw each other and he stood stock still for a moment looking at me. I dropped my pistol at my feet and held my hands to my head hoping he would think I was one of the home team injured in the crash. This wasn't so hard to do as the hammers of Hades seemed to be still playing their clarion call in my skull. I may have hurt myself in all the excitement.

The floor was looking better and better, very soft and inviting. Thinking I could maybe just lie down for a minute, I sank to my knees and slumped my poor, battered skull onto my chest. My hands brushed the floor. This brought the pirate closer, no doubt coming over to check on a pal.

When he was right on top of me, I pulled up the pistol and shot him full in the visor – I had made sure my injured slump put me right next to the blaster. Dead sneaky, I am.

As he sank down, I stood up and checked on Thorl, which is hard to do when they're in a spacesuit. His right arm was missing and I could see into the suit at the big guy; it wasn't pretty. The shot had taken his arm off quite cleanly and even cauterised the stump – it sure beats hot tar over an open wound. Unfortunately, there remained the problem of the hole in his spacesuit, I guess the jets of gas I saw when he was shot was his air making a break for it. I poked him again a few more times and finally his body just slid off the saddle and slumped to the floor.

I was guessing he was dead.

My reflexes were a bit shot - thus, when Lydia finally made it over to me and put her arm on my shoulder, I didn't automatically attack her. Perhaps a part of my brain recognised the crazy emergency suit she was wearing or maybe I was at the end of my resources. After performing this herculean task of mental analysis, the rational part of my mind decided to call it a day and turned itself off.

The rest of me soon followed and I sank to the floor, the lovely, soft and comfortable floor.

Chapter 21

My rest was short-lived. Lydia clashed helmets with me and encouraged me to keep going; actually, what she said was, "Get up, you idiot!"

I pulled myself up with a little help from my girl; since I'm a fairly large and heavy man she struggled and I wasn't feeling like making it any easier for her. Finally, I lurched erect and peered over her shoulder at the chaos Thorl had caused. He sure was a tough guy, even as he was dying, he had managed to jink the sled a few more times and finally land in a very surprised bunch of pirates.

Most of them were dead and my mate Wallace was quietly walking around with his blaster finishing off the wounded and helpless. Not a lot of heart in our boy.

Lydia touched helmets again and said, "We have to get to the engine room quickly. If those codes are typed in the doors will open and the ship will lose all air. Everybody not in a suit dies!" She tugged my arm and dragged my stumbling form towards an exit door. I stepped over a few of Wallace's victims and had to admire his technique – his blaster was on a thin beam and he had neatly shot every pirate through the right eye. I was beginning to suspect Wallace was a neat freak.

Lydia did strange things to the door seal and we entered another airlock room. It was much larger than the one near the Chief Trader's quarters, about the size of an inn back home - probably because it had to be able to cope with large and bulky bits of broken spaceship as well as greasy mechanics. Speaking of which I looked around for my best girl, not only did I like to see her but at the moment I was in real need of some help standing up. She was at a control panel doing more magic, I stood in thought for a bit and then leaned back against a wall for a bit of a rest. Wallace poked about on some large tables against one wall, he was a very curious man. Personally, I think

172

curiosity is overrated; I was leaning more and more to the quiet life with a mug of ale, a warm fire and...

Lydia hit me on the helmet. Again.

This broke my cosy train of thought and I was feeling I needed to express my objections to her thumping me all the time when I noticed she had her helmet off. So did Wallace.

I may be slow but I'm not stupid. No, wait, I may be a little wrong there. Anyway, I realised Lydia had somehow put air into the big room so I unlatched my helmet and breathed in some lovely fresh air. After a few breathes of sweetness I began to notice a foul and stinky smell mixed in with the ambrosia – it was coming from inside my suit. There was a delicious mix of sweat, lots and lots of sweat, and the tangy aroma of some bodily fluids. Umm, boy, was I Mr Stinko.

Wallace was still over by the tables; I moved over to him hoping a bit of circulation would diminish my own excruciating smell. No such luck, he looked over his shoulder and saw me coming after smelling my imminent arrival. His face was a picture of someone who had just stepped into a steaming mass of horse dung with me being the dung. But I have a robust self-esteem, I continued to walk up to him with my cheery smile.

"How you doin', Wallace, my old friend?"

"You stink, Val."

"Thanks for asking. No, I'm fine, how about you, pal? You've been in a suit as long as I have; I bet you smell a bit ripe, too."

"Not as much as you. Did you also lose control of your bladder?"

"Maybe."

"Do me a favour, Val, keep a bit of distance. Make it a lot of distance." He walked off leaving me feeling all alone and unloved.

But not for long because there on the workbench was a hammer. A lovely, big hammer, probably used for hitting dents out of something metal. I didn't care because now it was my new best friend.

"Come on, Val!" called my sweetie pie from the far side of the
room. "We have to keep going. The engine room is through this door
and down a few corridors, it's not far." She punched more buttons on
a control panel and then looked back again. "Before I open the door,
I suggest we put our helmets back on. If the ship becomes open to
atmosphere, we will need them to keep going. She matched actions
to words and pulled her helmet back over her pretty face. Wallace
gave me a smirk and did the same. Body odour wafted out of my suit;
I left the helmet off. How bad could it be to breath vacuum?

I kept walking until I was next to them and then waited. Waited
for a reprieve, for the angel of good smells to come down and tap
me on the head. Frankly, I was having trouble not being sick with
the odour and now Lydia wanted me to lock myself away inside the
suit to keep it company. By this time, I was thinking of the smell
as something alive, it had its own mind and was enjoying spreading
itself around.

They both stood waiting and looking at me. I think Lydia tapped
her foot a few times. I put on the helmet.

Oh, dear, sweet heaven's above! I almost died.

When we opened the door there was only one of the Undead
on the other side. I'd almost forgotten about them in all the pirate
excitement; my brain was a little slow, but my body had not
forgotten. I automatically stepped forward and raised the hammer.
Before I could complete the blow, Wallace shot Undead guy in the
face with his blaster on a wide setting. Its head sort of unravelled or
melted or evaporated or something. Whatever it was, in the space of
a few moments we were facing – if that's the right word – a headless
body which sank to its knees and then fell over. That Wallace sure
can shoot.

There wasn't anyone or anything behind the first guy, off we
marched with Wallace in front followed by Lydia and then me

staggering along at the rear trying not to throw up from my own smell.

I have to hand it to Wallace, he's not a man who hesitates. We met about twenty of the Undead, some Tharls but most humans. Wallace shot every human as soon as he saw one. The Tharls he left alone.

I'm not even sure he broke stride during the jaunt down the first corridor. He just walked at a brisk pace and shot anything he didn't like. I walked through a small honour guard of really dead Undead.

We stopped at the end of the corridor before another door. Lydia started to open it, I felt I had better pull my weight so I stood next to Wallace and made the hammer ready. The door opened and a few steps down the corridor we saw only one of the Undead, my old pal, Wilks. Sometimes things just fall into place.

I didn't want Wallace shooting him, I held up a hand and signalled to the big guy I would take this one out. As I walked towards Wilks, I reviewed all the petty tyrannies he had inflicted on us, especially me. Not through any sort of malice but through his absolute devotion to some book of rules and regulations. I didn't like him a great deal.

But he had saved my life on Gamma 5, this merited some concessions to my normal method of operation. When I hit him with the hammer there wasn't a lot of force behind the blow, just a little tap. He fell down, I hoped he was unconscious and not dead; I might not like the guy but he grew on you. Like mould.

We didn't stay to check on him because Lydia was becoming more and more agitated as she walked along. She even trotted up to the last door which is not an easy feat in her spacesuit. When we were all gathered around, she touched helmets again and said, "Behind this door is the control room. Are you ready to go in?"

"Hold on a moment," I said. "You mean when we open this door, we'll see Magic and a whole bunch of twitchy guardsmen. What are the chances of them shooting first – we are dressed like pirates, you know."

"Can we signal them somehow, let them know we're friends?" she asked.

I pulled back from the huddle and pulled off my helmet. I was becoming accustomed to my odour which meant the fresh air made the smell take on its full, rich texture. Still, I knew if the door opened and the guys saw a fully suited figure they would probably go all aggressive before considering other options. Remember, these guys used to walk through the Thieves' Quarter on a regular basis and usually walked out again. Usually.

I had an idea. Gesturing Lydia to wait before opening the door I raised my hammer and to hit the door a few taps. A brief spasm of inspiration hit me and I did my best to tap out the beat to a drinking song we used to, well, drink with.

Lydia didn't have to open the door, someone on the other side did. It slid back to reveal Right Honourable and Teddy Boy, both sporting humongous blasters and pointing them at my face.

"Gidday, fellas, what's new with you?" I asked, in my best cheery voice.

"Why aren't you dead yet, Val?" asked a perfectly reasonable Right Honourable.

"He sure smells dead," said Teddy Boy.

Before I could think of any more witty repartee Lydia pushed herself past me into the room. Magic was sitting at another control panel and I watched with great interest as my girl pushed him out of the way. He was on one of those funny chairs with wheels on legs, he slid along the floor a few paces which allowed Lydia to access the control panel. As she started hitting buttons the lights dimmed and a siren began to howl. Off on one wall a bright glowing bulb began flashing red bursts of colour into the room.

All in all, it seemed like a pretty good party. The guys and I were looking around, not too concerned. The lights and noise were a nice thought by the welcoming committee. I was very touched.

Ted said, "Uh-oh," and all the doors opened at once. Every door in the ship, the pirates had entered their codes and the atmosphere was rushing out through every opening. The gale swept by me with enough force to snatch the helmet out of my hands and make me rock back a few steps. The rest of the gang staggered about and I thought we were all about to die. Again.

Life is never dull in the NightWatch.

All over the ship people would be dying as the atmosphere vented into space. Anyone near a door would be sucked out – I knew the majority of people dying this way would be the Undead but it still seemed somehow, I don't know, wholesale for my taste. And the rest of us would follow quite soon as the last scrap of air left us; my helmet and smelly suit didn't seem so bad now. Pity I'd lost the helmet.

I staggered a few more steps until I came up against a wall from where I could see my mates as they realised we only had a few more moments to live. Lydia was still doing things on the console as the wind howled through the room like an uncaged beast. I exchanged looks of astonishment and fear with my fellow guardsmen, lots of wide eyes and open mouths.

The doors started to close again. We watched with the detached interest one acquires when great things happen over which you have no control. With a final blurt of disgust the doors shut and the wind died away to the gentle zephyr of air conditioning.

We all looked at each other in mild amazement, grills in the ceiling began pumping air back into the room as Lydia stood up and stretched, a little smile on her magnificent face.

"Did you just do something clever?" I asked.

She nodded, "I managed to get the system back under control, and this desk is now the sole means of accessing any door or room. Plus a lot of other neat goodies." She punched a few other bits of machinery, "Watch."

A bank of monitors lit up and we could see various sections of the ship. Some rooms were empty while others had the usual complement of the Undead. And then there were the pirates. Several rooms and corridors contained our unwelcome visitors, all wearing spacesuits similar to the ones we had taken off the recently deceased.

"These screens let us go to any part of the ship, I can also command the space drives, life support, you name it."

"You're the man, Lydia," I proclaimed. She gave me a funny look.

Magic was right back on task. "Let me get this straight," he asked, "you could open and close doors from here?" She nodded. He smiled his nasty smile.

"Time to go hunting, boys," he turned and gathered us all into his gaze. "I want us to break up into groups and hunt those bastards down.

"I may be able to help a bit more," my girl said. She moved to a wall of storage units and opened up a long sliding drawer. From inside the drawer, she pulled a small headset, "If everyone wears one of these we can communicate, you can tell me which door you need and when you are ready to open it."

We all beamed at each other and Lydia handed out the headsets. I noticed a few of the lads had edged away from me until I was standing in quite a large personal space. I looked at the nearest shuffler who happened to be Teddy Boy, "Was it something I said?"

"Val, stay out of my group. You stink like a week old corpse."

I really wanted to give him a sharp response but he was right.

"You can't go with any group, Val," ordered Magic. "Stay here and do something to clean yourself up."

"Can I get a headset?" I asked.

Lydia gave me one after taking a deep breath. I wasn't feeling the love in the room.

"How am I going to clean up, I need a river."

Lydia chimed in again with the perfect solution, "There's a small room just past that far door; we often get into a bit of a mess pulling down engines so there has to be someplace to wash off the grease." A vison of Lydia in soiled attire and grease marks flitted in and out of my libido..

"Lydia can watch from here," continued our fearless leader. "We'll keep the pirates trapped inside whatever room they are in until we get there. Then we'll open the door and show them the error of their ways."

"What about the Undead?" asked Smiley, "Remember them? The reason we all hid in here in the first place."

Magic looked at Lydia, "What about it, Lydia? Can you guide us through rooms that are empty or nearly so?"

She thought for about a heartbeat and said, "I can try, but what about their shuttle?" she asked the room.

"What shuttle?" asked Magic.

"The one they came up in from the surface. Those sleds can't escape atmosphere, they can re-enter if you have a death wish but there is no way they came up here by themselves. I just bet they have a small transport shuttle nearby."

"Any idea where?"

"I could probably find it, now I have access to the scanners and so on."

"How are we going to get to a shuttle. No suits," said Right Honourable. "Wallace has a suit; Lydia's garb looks far too fragile and there is no way in seven hells I am putting on Val's suit. This last comment caused all and sundry to cast another glance in my direction and then, as one, they took another step away from me.

"Not a problem," said our fabulous technician. Behind Val there is a storage locker for suits, we use them when we have to go out and do maintenance.

I looked behind me and saw a handle so I pulled it, the door swung open and revealed a long narrow storage space. Hanging on a rail was a spacesuit, behind it I could make out the shape of several more hanging neatly off the same rail.

"Push that lever, Val and the rail will slide out," said Lydia.

I dutifully pushed said lever and the rack of suits smoothly slid out of their home to hang before us in all their splendour.

"They're red!" I blurted. "Bright red!" Indeed, the suits were a radiant shade of crimson, so bright it hurt the eyes to look at them.

"To make sure we are easy to see outside the ship." Lydia made a good point but I could see the downside of wearing bright red while fighting pirates. This situation would not arise for me, of course, since I was determined not to exit the ship again unless I was getting into a bigger ship.

Magic issued orders and a few of the braver lads came over to pick up their suits. Others were detailed to move off into the bowls of the ship and bring a little law and order to the chaos. I was quite aware of the looks of disgust coming my way so I moved off to have my clean. Just to be petty and spiteful I walked through the centre of the room making sure I passed in the midst of all my buddies as they discussed tactics. Small moans and cries filtered behind my back.

I rather hoped someone could become ill. Over someone else.

Chapter 22

The room I found had running water, I peeled off my many layers of soiled and odiferous garments and climbed into the most wonderful cleaning experience ever devised – a hot shower. Having been brought up using river water and the occasional frozen pond in which to bathe this latest example of space technology made me think there may even be a heaven right here.

I found some clean overalls in another locker and soon returned to the engine room feeling like a new man. The room had thinned out a bit, Lydia was on the control panel directing a few groups to and fro; I saw Right Honourable and Teddy Boy walking down a deserted corridor with a bunch of other NightWatch. Lydia was concentrating on a series of screens showing rooms over the ship, I guess she could tell where each room was because she spoke short commands to each group from time to time; things like, "Don't open the door on the right, use the door on the left," and, "around the next turn in the corridor are three Undead, one Tharl and two humans. You'll have to deal with them – they've scented you. Get ready."

On the screen the two human Undead lurched around the corner and were quickly hit on the side of their unthinking skulls by members of the NightWatch. The gang was becoming well versed in rendering a human being unconscious. To stop the Undead from getting up too quickly, they secured them to various wall studs by means of those little restraints we all carried.

I caught the last few words of Magic as he repeated instructions, "Do not kill any more of our people unless absolutely necessary. Restrain them. At some point we are going to have to answer for our actions"

This wasn't the team becoming all soft and caring about their victims; I mean we couldn't just kill everyone on the ship. Back in the Days of the City we preferred to just cold cock the miscreants rather than shuffle of their mortal coil. It wasn't a case of being soft and sentimental, just practical. Too many dead guys on our evening patrols could cause us a lot of embarrassing questions. It also made the next time we patrolled the area more dangerous than normal as the rest of the dead villain's family sought to get a little payback.

Some bit of the old life I don't miss at all.

Magic was still in the main room with Wallace and Smiley plus a handful of the guys; they were busy climbing into the bright red spacesuits. I was determined to avoid any more out-of-spaceship activity, I even broke into a little limp to emphasise how truly weak and pathetic I was, small cough.

"What's up, boss?" I croaked. Maybe I could volunteer for a little light guard duty on Lydia, someone should stay and keep her safe. You know, someone reliable and handsome and strong and...well...me. But I couldn't bring myself to mouth these arguments since I suspected they would not carry much weight with my leader. I was racking the old brain for some good solid reasons to stay back when Magic started issuing orders again.

"We're going over to their shuttle, Val. Lydia will guide us in. We're going to use the jetpacks to get there."

I wondered what a "jetpack" was but since everyone else was not asking questions I decided to keep the old mouth shut.

"You stay here and keep contact with the Man in Black, give him a report on what's happening. Lydia's going to guide one of the groups up there to get him out. Any questions?"

"Sounds perfect to me, boss. I'll make sure Lydia is safe," I felt I sounded quite chivalrous.

"What makes you think Lydia needs guarding?" asked Magic.

"Well, er, the pirates and ....all... Undead coming in... bad guys....er...stuff," even I could hear how weak I sounded.

"The squads are moving out from this room and making each room safe. Any space with a lot of the Undead in it will remain sealed. Any space with a lot of pirates in it will be very quickly filled with dead pirates." He picked up his helmet, "You're staying here because you are my sergeant and I feel the need to have someone with authority here. Plus no-one wanted you on the team for a while, you seem to be more of a bad luck magnet than normal at the moment. I'll leave a few of the lads with you; Santini seems to know a bit about this gear, he might even be able to help." He shrugged, "Sorry, Val." He didn't seem too sorry to me.

I stood up bravely under the pressure of leadership thrust upon me even if it was coupled with strong feelings of rejection. I'm the bigger man here, I felt a scathing and biting comment was called for to demonstrate my insouciance.

"Whatever," I said.

"Look after him, Lydia," was his parting comment as they all filed out the exit door, leaving my sweetie-pie and me alone.

I turned to her thinking we might exchange a small, shy grin, a little smirk of fellow conspirators. Followed by a little gentle touching, a few kisses and .... I was beginning to feel all hot and bothered.

"Are you alright, Val?" She asked. "You don't look well."

"No, I'm fine." Long pause. Long, long pause.

I cleared my throat and made other vague sounds. This casual conversation with a pretty girl was not in my skill set. "Umm..."

"Have you got a sore throat?" she asked. It was then I noticed she wasn't really paying me any attention; all her focus was on the screens and guiding the gang through the Undead maze. Maybe this wasn't the best time for a little bit of woo; she plainly was not going to be distracted from her task. Very commendable. Keep it up, soldier.

I sat on the deck and debated falling asleep, bits of my anatomy were beginning to remind me I had been abusing my body quite a bit recently. My head started to throb, my shoulder ached and my left elbow was giving me a right old turn. What had I done to my left elbow? Of course, my brain decided now would be a good time to grab my attention and run through a few of my recent actions in an attempt to educate me about stupid, harebrained actions.

Let's see - stepping a guy's head to mush, walking though bundles of creatures who may want to eat you, fighting off Undead with a stick, crashing a broomstick INSIDE the ship, walking OUTSIDE the ship, head butting a pirate and breaking the seal on my helmet, punching Lydia, being tugged around like a cork behind a wildly careening sled, smashing into the side of the ship, stabbing another pirate, almost dying over and over again while becoming really, really stinky.

I felt all overcome, and decided lying down on the floor and shivering for a while was the best course of action.

"Val!" cried my sweetie, "Val, get up!"

"Harrumph...." Low moans from me.

"Stop messing about and get up here!"

"But... but I'm all....sore and....you know...."

"Stop being such a baby. Get up here and keep briefing the boss like Magic said."

"Get up here and keep briefing the boss like Magic said," I mimicked. "Yes, Miss, and what did your last slave die of?" And when did she start referring to the Man in Black as 'boss.'

"Now open the door, there are three pirates about twenty steps in and to your right."

I sat up quickly, "What pirates? Where pirates?" Then I saw one of the screens; Teddy Boy walked into a room and shoot three guys in the head. The dead guys were all wearing spacesuits so I assumed they were the pirates Lydia was warning me about. Actually, probably not me. She must have been talking to Teddy Boy and the crew. Maybe the universe doesn't revolve around me.

Since I was sitting up, I decided to wander over and maybe stand next to my girl, a bit of close proximity might just get her thinking along my line of thought. I know, I'm tragic.

"How do I talk to the Chief Trader's quarters?" I asked.

She handed me a small stick and pushed a button. One of the screens lit up to show a very surprised Meataxe.

"Captain Franz!" he turned his head and bellowed, "I've got someone!" He turned back to face the screen, "Val! You made it! I thought you'd be dead!" I didn't know whether to be pleased he was pleased or miffed he doubted my ability to get through.

"Not really a problem" I answered, stoic but casual. "We've got help coming to you. How's things up there?"

"Val..." he leaned in and almost whispered, "The Man in Black got a lot of information out of Don'elk. Way more than you ever could." Yeah, thanks, mate, makes me feel really valued.

"What sort of stuff?" I asked, "And how did he do it?"

The big guy's eyes bulged a little as he leaned into the screen, "I dunno," he said. "He just seemed to.... reason with them." He drew a breath before continuing, "He's really, really good at this stuff, Val. I think he's even scarier than you."

What did he mean by the comment? I felt deeply offended; I am not a scary guy, I'm a nice man.

Before I could utter any strong rebuttal, Meataxe jumped out of his chair and the Man in Black slid casually in. "Got some news, Val. Might have an answer to the Undead problem. But you first, bring me up to speed on what's doing down there."

I told him about the plan to hunt down the pirates on board, plus the news Magic had taken a crew out to the shuttle. "That's good, Val, we can use it to get down to the planet."

This seemed a bit enthusiastic to me, "And why would we want to do that, boss?"

"Because Don'elk tells me the language nanobots had been infected with a virus."

"What, like they've got a fever or something?" I must be learning stuff despite my best efforts. "Do our little beasties need a cuppa and a good lie down?"

"No, Val, it means they were adjusted to do more than just help translate. They were made to incapacitate the crew so the pirates could board easily."

"You mean they wanted a ship full of Undead lurching around?"

"I think not. The whole thing sounds a bit hotch-potch; from what Don'elk says the pirates were approached by one of the scientific community with the idea. This guy agreed to slip a little something into our mix once he'd seen the original test results. The ones from you and the forward landing party."

I did remember that many of the group on our first jaunt had to go back for a second shot, we were told the occasional poor sod needed a top up of the nanobots. "Does this do us any good?" I asked.

"It might." I saw him mull a few things over, I just stood patiently looking into the screen while those far above me worked out the plan; that's what they get paid for. He gave a grunt, looked off-screen for a moment and said, "There's no way out of it, we have to get down to the planet and find this scientist. Where's Magic now?"

"Still off looking for the pirates' shuttle. Lydia's guiding him there as well as helping our teams on the ship find the bad guys. Speaking of which, I was hoping I could have a chance at doing a little get-even myself; I've gone right off the idea of pirates."

He ignored my question, "Ask Lydia if she can spare me a few moments." I did so and shortly listened in on how a planner works, "Lydia, we need to get down to the planet, any suggestions?"

I thought this seemed a bit lightweight in the planning department. Surely there should have been a series of terse instructions and then people running to and fro. Or hither and thither. Anyway, there should be running about involved – if it came down to it, I could have asked these simple questions.

My girl just rode over my querulous looks, probably because she didn't notice them. Her eyes were darting from screen to screen over a bank of them mounted on the far wall. Looking up I could see several squads of the NightWatch moving through the ship, opening doors and killing pirates. And here was me stuck in a boring old conversation about flying, my least favourite topic. As I watched I saw Teddy Boy enter a room behind two pirates, he shot them in the back before they could even move. Some people get all the fun.

We don't mind shooting people in the back, or hitting them from behind, or any other sneaky trick which lets us stay breathing a little longer.

"There are several of our shuttles we could use but they are inaccessible now. All Landing Bays have either a group of pirates guarding the shuttles or else the corridors leading to them are swarming with Undead. In some cases, it's both at once. Some of the pirates seem to have gotten themselves pinned down in the landing bays by the hordes of Undead in the next few rooms. When all the doors opened it seemed to have drawn them all out of wherever they were lurking and left them in the public corridors. It's getting harder and harder to guide our men around these crowds to get at the pirates.

"Val," barked the boss. "Any thoughts?"

This took me by complete surprise, I wasn't planning on doing any, well, planning. I just stood there like a doofus opening and closing my mouth a few times. I think I grunted once.

My girl saved me. Again. "If we can acquire their shuttle, we can fly it down to the planet."

"We don't have any pilots," I said. I may not be able to come up with clever plans but I can sure shoot them down when they arise.

"I can fly one," said Lydia. Why was I not surprised. "They're pretty basic, we often have to make runs back and forth. Once Magic has taken the shuttle I could jet over and take them all down to the planet."

I liked this plan. Magic and the boys could play hero, fly through space in a fragile tin cup and then plod over the local dust ball looking for a bad guy on a planet full of weirdos. I could stay up here where I was comfortable and never have to see the outside of a spaceship again. I might even have the chance to off a few pirates if the fates were kind. I beamed my approval.

"Are you alright, Val?" asked the Man in Black, "You look a little ill."

Lydia rode over any comment I was going to make –which was a good thing because I was all prepared to dribble threateningly. "I'll have to get to the shuttle, most of our teams here are in a good position. Santini's been doing a good job with the comms, I'm sure he could finish things up without me."

Santini looked far too pleased with himself, I felt he could do with some close supervision so I sidled over and stood looking over his shoulder in my most non-threatening, scary way.

"Val," commanded Lydia, "Leave Santini alone and come and help me into this suit." I crossed over and took great delight in helping my lissom wench into a tight-fitting suit. Much fun was had by all, but mostly by me.

"You sure have a lot of hands, Sergeant Valentine!" she said after slapping away a repeat offender; I grinned at her and reached for a little goodbye kiss.

She pulled another helmet in between us as I puckered up which meant I formed close and personal relationship with a bit of unfeeling apparel. Probably not for the last time.

"Suit up, cutie," she cooed. "You're coming with me."

Chapter 23

I think not.

My implacable will was met with total disregard by my girlfriend, a state of affairs we would have to discuss if I ever survived these early steps in our relationship.

"But I don't want to go outside the ship again. Ever." I pleaded.

"That's nice, dear." She zipped me up and handed me my helmet.

"But I don't wanna go..."

"Of course you do, sweetie. And I need a big strong man to protect me."

I snorted at this. Lydia is not a wilting flower.

"But why have I gotta do it....Why can't I stay here... Take Santini, he'd love a bit of exercise."

Before she passed me my helmet, she reached inside it and did something twirly with her fingers. "I've changed the frequency of your suit radio."

"What's a frequency?"

"Our suits can change frequency by moving the small dial inside the helmet, or you can use the external controls on your left sleeve. Frequency is the modulation of the signal through the ether.'"

"What's a modulation?"

She looked at me a moment before smiling and saying, "It's the little bit of magic that lets us talk on the radios."

"Right, got it. And the bad guys can't hear our frequent sea?"

"It's frequency. No, our suits randomly change it to make tracking the signal impossible without the key algorithm."

"Algorithm? I'm going to stop now, my head hurts."

"Don't worry, Val, we can all talk to each other, even the men inside the ship who have the headsets." She patted my arm and placed the helmet on my anxious head. "I need you to be with me over at the pirates' shuttle; I can fly it but I'm not a fighter. I want the biggest, meanest man with me when I go into a scary place, just in case we meet someone unpleasant. And you, my sweetums, are the scariest man I have ever known."

Not a lot of blokes get the girl by being Mr Nasty, but I would take what I could get. Backing out now didn't seem to be an option, my girl needed me so I guess I was just going to have to suck it up. "What about the rest of the crew, who's going to guide them through the corridors and such like?"

"Santini has been working with me so far, haven't you noticed?" I turned and looked at my fellow guardsman. Ever since Gamma 5 Santini had become our unofficial priest or pastor. I suppose it made some sort of sense to have him be the one who guided the lads from above. I gave him a little wave and he smiled back; he had walked his own treasonous road, poor guy, and I had no doubt he would do his best to get our guys through this mess safely.

I followed Lydia out the doors and down a corridor until we hit an airlock. This one had more storage bins built into it, my girl opened a large one and pulled out two backpacks; they weren't for carrying stuff, each pack had rods and straps and strange handles attached to it. After checking our helmets and suits were all sealed she helped me climb into one of the strange rigs and left me standing there feeling the weight pulling me backwards About waist height were two handles, each handle carrying a range of buttons. This was looking a bit complex for my poor old thug's brain, I felt I needed to give out some warnings. "Lydia, what's all this stuff for? I mean, it looks a bit tricky and I have trouble with tricky. Come to that, how are we going to get across to the shuttle? Say, how did Magic and the team get there? Did they take a sled? Could we take a sled? Lydia, why are you pushing that button? Lydia? The exterior doors are opening? Lydia?...."

For some reason she seemed to be ignoring me. She opened the external doors until I was again confronted by the vastness of space. Maybe my radio wasn't working, "Lydia!! Can you hear me? LYDIA!!"

"Do shut up, dear boy," Right Honourable's voice blossomed in my left ear, "you're scaring the fish."

"Right Honourable?" I turned around. "Where are you?"

"No idea, lad, somewhere in the bowels of our hearth and home. We have all enjoyed your little bleat but could you possibly shut up, Santini is trying to keep us alive."

During all this confusion, well, for me it was confusion, Lydia had been attaching a set of cords between her suit and mine. As I realised this I had a shudder memory of being dragged behind the sled, but this time I was attached to my girl and not an almost out of control lump of metal. I desperately wanted to ask her what was going on but now I was aware of other voices in my left ear, voices from the rest of the NightWatch as they walked their violent and cleansing route.

Lydia's voice boomed into my right ear, "Just relax, Val, I'll tow you over, using my jetpack." Tow me over? What did she mean by that?

"What's a jetpack?" I pleaded.

She turned away to face the great outdoors and said, "You won't have to use yours."

What was she talking about?

My question was answered by her actions, she grasped the two handles next to her suit and did strange things with buttons, and a small flame erupted from a small vent in her backpack. Other flames came and went in seemingly random bursts until I watched my girl gently glide out of the open airlock door. I stood gawping at her slowly receding figure, my brain vaguely registering the gradual tension on the cables joining us together until I felt a gentle tug and my own true love pulled me unwillingly out into the great nothingness. Again.

If I didn't have bad luck, I'd have no luck at all.

I'd like to say I was getting used to this outside of ship experience. I'd like to say I was rich and handsome, too, but some things just aren't going to happen. I was able to contain the old heebie jeebies and keep my bowels from contracting. My iron self-discipline helped, of course.

Who am I kidding? I was terrified of making a sound in case the lads heard and reminded me of any momentary panic for the rest of my life. It's good to have mates.

I lay like a wet rag, slowly drifting out into nothing at all, I couldn't see any destination, no ship, no shuttle. I couldn't even turn to see the craft we were departing. I tried to look around but Lydia told me to stop wriggling which brought a burst of ribald laughter from my left ear as well as several pleas from various husky male voices beseeching me to wriggle some more.

Right, I had this figured this out now. My left ear brought comments from the NightWatch team while my right ear came from Lydia. Cool.

The ride was remarkably gentle, no swerves or madcap jaunts, just a nice, steady pull. I lay there and tried to keep a lid on my terror, I don't know how the regular space team did it, going outside like this and just floating in ...nothing. I tried to think of other things, the layout of the city, the various steps in loading and firing a musket; how to skin a rabbit, and bit by bit I kept the quivers at bay as we floated along. Very soon I could make out an area of space which had no stars, this shadow grew and grew until I could see the outline of a shuttle craft – it had no exterior lights on at all. I have no idea how Lydia found it. More magic, no doubt.

I know it's not really magic but my brain hasn't caught up with all the technology yet so, in order to maintain my slender grip on sanity, I invent little mental shortcuts to help me understand the big, mean world.

We drifted into another landing bay, this one still had a couple of the pirate sleds on board and Lydia gently touched down before turning to watch me ghost past her. I was wondering how she was going to bring me to a halt, I had begun to work out things kept moving in space unless you stopped them so I was curious to see what she did to reduce my momentum. I sailed past her and gave a little wave before smashing into the rear wall of the landing bay. My feelings were hurt so I yelped a little.

"Why did you do that, Val?" she asked, her voice coming from my right ear. She unlatched the cable linking us together.

My ears were ringing, I checked the suit for little jets of air – see, I was learning some things – and queried her braking procedures. "Why didn't you stop me? I just kept going!" Laughter from the left ear.

"I just assumed you would stop yourself. You have to practice safe procedures, Val." More laughter.

"But you had to stop me, I was out of control!"

"Typical!" She sounded a bit put out. "Men always assume the girl will stop them in time."

My left ear was being battered by numerous insults; I replayed the last few bits of our conversation and muttered. "Grow up, guys, show a bit of maturity."

Lydia unclipped me and helped me find my feet, I felt the reassuring pull of some force holding my boots on the deck. Safe at last.

The explosion took me quite by surprise.

The deck erupted under my feet, Lydia was thrown against the rear wall and I landed face down in the saddle of one of the sleds. What the hell had happened?

Magic's voice came out of my left ear, "We're under attack!" More explosions shook the ship but no more in the landing bay, even so I could feel the shuttle shake as some heavy duty blasts landed somewhere.

"Control room breached!" Magic sounded under a bit of pressure. "We have two men down here, a lot of damage to the control room, and we are open to space."

I turned to check on Lydia, she was getting to her feet and seemed unhurt. "What's going on?" I asked.

"This shuttle's under attack," she replied. "I would guess one or more of the pirate sleds have come back to try and retake their vessel."

"Can we fight back?" I asked.

"I don't know, Val," she sounded a little exasperated. "I'm just a technician, I have no idea what we should do. You're the fighter."

Oh, great, just the time to remind me of my role. Now let me see, what does a City Watchman do when faced with a space battle? ... umm ...doesn't seem to be in the Manual for Musketry.

Standing very still while some idiot roars past shooting bolts of energy may not have been my wisest move. Lydia must have taken in my utter lack of action – truth to tell, I was well and truly out of my element – because she hit me on the arm and yelled, "Val! Do something!"

Great.

I moved to the sled still in the landing bay, the controls looked similar to the ones on the smaller version I had piloted around the planet so long ago. I thought I could probably manage to fly the machine. The question was, what on earth was I going to do with it? Still, my girl was looking for action so I climbed aboard and started the engine with no real plan. Situation normal.

"Val!" said my girl, and I think there was a little tremor in her voice but it could have been my own shaking as I sat on that blasted sled contemplating taking off and riding out into the great unknown. "Val! What are you doing?"

I mumbled some sort of response, not sure what I said.

"But you can't go out there," she said, "you might get hurt, it's too dangerous!"

You think I don't know that, I wanted to say. But nerves and fear kept my mouth shut, I think I did manage a grunt. Into the silence came Magic's voice, "We have some casualties here, Val. Whatever you plan on doing better be real soon, we've had two passes at us so far and each one is doing more damage to both the control room and us. We're trying to retreat into the rest of the shuttle but the door controls won't respond."

"They shut as a safety protocol when the control room was breached and became open to space." Lydia sounded remarkably calm. "I can open them once I get into the body of the shuttle."

"Better hurry," said Magic. "We think there are only two sleds attacking us but they're getting bolder and bolder. I think the next pass might see them pause and just shoot directly in at us."

"Val, we need you," he finished.

Bugger.

I twisted the right handgrip to increase the power from the engines while at the same time changed thrust direction with my feet, the sled rose and moved out into the dark of forever night. A thought crossed my mind, "Does this thing have a weapon?" I asked. "Or will I just be ramming him out of spite?"

Lydia was already moving off to a door which I presumed would lead her to my embattled companions. She turned and spoke to my slowly moving form, "If there is a weapon, its controls will be a large red button near your right thumb, press it to fire." I looked down and saw the button, mild relief passed through me.

"I've got a red button," I said. "Can I aim it or do I just point the sled and shoot?"

"Under your left thumb is a small lever, a little joystick," said Lydia.

I wondered what a 'joystick' was but sure enough there was a little lever near my thumb. I gave it a wiggle but didn't see or feel any response from the sled."Yes, it's there. Okay, I have a weapon, time to go shooting."

"Uh, Val," said my girl, "sometimes the controls are on a sled but the armament isn't fitted. You'll have to test fire it to make sure there is something fitted to the machine." Great, I thought. I shoot off a test shot and the bad guy could spot it and know I'm nearby. Or I shoot and pray there was something going bang. Pretty sure anyone I faced was going to be more experienced at this sort of fighting than me. Saints above, I had no idea how to go about flying and fighting in space. Hey, how lucky am I?

"I can see them outside, they're coming back to the control room," said Magic. "Yep, one of them is slowing down and swivelling to point directly at us. The other one seems to be hovering off to one side, probably making sure we don't fire back." I looked around and turned the sled so I was following the curve of the shuttle's hull as I slowly made my way forward. I was far enough out to miss the protrusions; I kept fiddling with the little lever near my left thumb and hoped it was attached to something deep and sinister.

Gradually the curve of the hull swept off to the right, any moment now I would see the pirate's sled as it lined up a clear shot on magic and the lads inside the control room.

"Here it comes, boys. May the Lord make us grateful for what we are about to receive," I heard Magic say. A burst of light reflected from around the edge of the hull, just out of my vision. It was followed by some snarls of pain and horror, some of which were cut off as the suit radio disintegrated in the blast.

I think one of the screams was Magic.

The hull tapered off to a stubby point and I found myself looking at a sled with one pirate hunched over the controls; my imagination populated his face with looks of malicious glee as he kept firing burst after burst of energy into the control room.

I hit the red button and then, because I still didn't know if there was anything more fearsome than bad intentions attached to this button, I twisted the speed grip to full and aimed the sled at the pirate. At the same time, I was moving the little aiming lever around and around because I had no idea how to point the hoped-for blaster. I was running on possibilities, I might possibly have a blaster, I might possibly shoot the sled and I might possibly ram it. I might possibly miss and kill us all.

It's the same way I play cards, and I'm really lousy at cards.

There must have been a blaster attached to my sled. I missed the guy I was aiming at but one of my wild sweeps caught the back-up sled. It exploded in a very decorative display of metal and bits of ex-pirate. I guess I hit something very important and dangerous. Goody.

Of course, the guy in the sled closest to me was totally unharmed except for a fairly large dose of utter surprise. I hoped the bastard had a weak heart, especially since my sled was very close to ramming him and thus taking us both out of any further plans.

He was a good pilot, I'll give him that. Somehow, he managed to accelerate and turn at the same time so the front of my machine only caught him a glancing blow. It was enough, however, to send him and his sled twisting and tumbling out into space. I saw him roll off to my right, still hanging on to his out of control machine. Most of my attention was focussed on keeping in the saddle as my own sled took off for the wide open spaces. Behind me was the shuttle and in front was a whole lot of nothing.

And I was accelerating.

Chapter 24

In front of me was a vast expanse of black, speckled with one of the most beautiful sights the good Lord has given to His creatures – the immensity and glittering panoply of stars, stars large and small, stars of yellow and blue, of white and gold, stars in numbers beyond imagining.

And the sight took my breath away, it stilled my fear and replaced it with a soft wonder and amazement at the beauty of creation.

"Val!" A voice in my ear insisted on disturbing my reverie; I had given myself up for lost and was feeling the beginnings of a deep peace settle into my bones. This was a not a bad spot to spend eternity, up with these jewels.

"Val! Val! Can you hear me?"

"Is that an angel I hear?" I murmured.

"Don't be a wus, Valentine," came Right Honourable's voice in my left ear.

Trust my friends to sully a tender moment. "Leave me alone, boys, I'm heading off on that last great journey." I was feeling quite poetic, perhaps the lads would benefit from some thoughtful phrases from me as I confronted the last great adventure.

"Turn on your autopilot, Val," said Lydia.

"I'm already on autopilot, sweetheart. Don't worry about me, it's quite beautiful here. Remember me fondly, I think we could have made a go of it..." A deep sigh escaped my poetic lips.

"Give it a rest, Valentine." Magic didn't seem too interested in my last few heartfelt words. "Listen to what Lydia is saying, you moron."

"Val," said my girl, "the autopilot will bring you back to us, it's the large green button in the centre of the control yoke. Can you see it?"

I looked and sure enough there was a big green button. I pushed it.

"Don't push it," said Lydia.

"Er..." I started but was interrupted by the sled swerving wildly to the right, most of my attention was focussed on hanging on really, really tightly.

"If you push it once it will fall into the default destination, and we have no idea what that could be, it could be a place, it could be this shuttle of theirs or even another sled. You have to call up the set of destinations in the Co-ordinate Tracker and choose the set which corresponds to this shuttle.

Great, I thought, a bit of technical dexterity would be no trouble to a man of my many talents. "There could be a problem with that plan."

I could feel the tension across the radio, folks hanging on my every word. "So, uh, how are things with you guys? All well?"

"You pushed the button, didn't you, muttonhead?"

"Possibly," I tried to inject a little bit of insouciance into my voice, it may have sounded like suppressed panic to the uninitiated.

Even over the radio I could detect Magic's deep sigh, "We're fine here, Lydia got us out. We lost Guido and Francesco, Right Honourable had his suit torn but we're in a pressurised compartment now." At least most of the lads seemed to have survived, pity about Guido and Francesco, two more original NightWatch down, two we could ill afford. "You did a good job there, Val. Pretty fancy flying and shooting, taking out both sleds at once. Good plan."

Should I tell him it was all a fluke and I missed the guy I was aiming at? Best not, the gang needs its heroes. My sled had settled down and moved forward at a leisurely pace. My attention was drawn to a new piece on the landscape. "Uh, guys," I said, "I think the default destination may have been, um, a little more identifiable than we thought."

"What do you mean, Val?"

"I'm heading for the planet."

My immediate front view was taken up by the huge planet, I could see the masses of blue of the oceans and the gentle orange of the land. Let me tell you, seeing a planet up close makes it HUGE! Forget big, this thing just hung in front of me like a giant ball. I felt like an insect about to be swatted.

"That's a bit strange" grunted Magic. I was pleased to hear he was taking it so well. "Why would they program in a spot on the planet? It couldn't be a rendezvous point, what criminal in his right mind would put their location onto a machine? If the local constabulary found one of the sleds all they would need to do would be to sit and wait for the bad guys to arrive. Surely, they can't have been that stupid?"

Right Honourable chipped in his opinion, "They could have a temporary location programmed in just for this heist; after they filled the shuttle up here, they could probably take an extra load down on each sled. Still, programming the gang's location on the planet does seem a trifle stupid. Also, I imagine flying one of these things down through the atmosphere takes a bit of skill."

"You think?" My voice dripped with sarcasm. "What are the chances of someone unskilled and inexperienced being able to fly a sled down to a planet and land safely. Someone like me." Something flashed ahead of me. "Hold on, I see something.... it's the other sled! That's why I'm heading towards the planet, the autopilot must be locked on to that sled! He's making a break for it. How do I turn the blasted autopilot off or change its headings or some other damn thing. Get me out of this, Magic! Lydia! Help me!" I'd like to say begging doesn't come easily to me but unfortunately it flows like the summer rain, regular and plentiful.

"You can turn off the autopilot easily enough, Val," my girl was right there for me, "you just..."

Magic barged in, "Hold on a minute, Lydia, let's not rush into this."

"No," I said, "Let's rush really quickly. Magic, do you have any idea how big this planet is?"

"Man up, Val," said my boss. "If you follow the other sled down you might be able to catch this guy. If he gets away, we lose a lot of time and maybe our best hope of finding whoever caused this mess in the first place. I know we still have pirates inside and we could end up with other prisoners - but I doubt it. The lads are dealing with their own terror, the undead, the pirates and the chance that the ship might kill them somehow. Asking for prisoners might be a step too far."

Okay, I thought, that makes sense. I didn't like it, but it made sense. I tried another clever stratagem, "But Magic, I don't wanna go."

"Stop whining, mate," he replied. "If he takes you to a rendezvous point there might be some clues which will help us find the cure Don'elk was telling the Man in Black about. We can't use this shuttle, it's out of commission, that means we have to get back to the main ship, fight our way through pirates and Undead and hope to find one of our shuttles still working and only then can Lydia fly down a squad. By that time the trail will have run cold. Especially if the guy you scared off lands first. Lydia, is there any way of ensuring Val stays locked on to the other sled?"

"Not from here, but Val's sled would have a locater and tracker. Val, listen to me but DON'T DO ANYTHING UNTIL I TELL YOU!"

I think she was implying something here so I treated the comment with a dignified silence. She explained which buttons and knobs I needed to twist, turn and pull to get a small screen in the front panel up and functioning. She finished with the instruction to do the deed and shortly after I was treated to a soft glow coming from the screen and on the screen was a blip.

"I see a flashing light on one side of the screen and another, smaller light glowing constantly in the centre." Big deal, I thought.

"The flashing light is other sled. You are the small light" said Lydia.

"How very consistent," put in Right Honourable.

"Oh, yeah...," I seemed to be out of quick retorts, "and so are you!" Pathetic, I know.

"Shut up, Right Honourable," commanded Magic, "Val, what's the other sled doing?"

I watched for a few beats, "It's moving away from me, going towards the top of the screen. Hang on, the top of the screen is now a full bank of light."

"That's the planet, Val, "said Lydia, "'He's definitely heading down there. Your autopilot will not be reliable enough to follow another sled as it enters the plant's atmosphere. You will have to go manual. When you are ready, press the green button again and take back control. You can use the tracker to follow him."

"Up to you, Val," put in Magic. "What do you want to do? Come back here and play it safe or have a go at following him down?"

"I want to come back where it's safe, of course!" I said. "But I understand what's needed. I'll try to follow him down. Lydia, any help here? Any magic buttons to fly the sled for me? Please?"

"Taking a sled from space down to a planet is tricky," she said. "And dangerous. There are no options other than using the manual controls. It will be like sliding down a snowy hill on a piece of wood. You'll have some control but not a lot."

I have done this; I have rolled down snow covered hills and even enjoyed it. Except for the times I crashed into trees and hidden rocks. Probably best not to mention that to Lydia. "Any safety tips?" I asked.

"Let me think," she said. "They must use the sled's stasis field to get through the atmosphere...Val, have you used a stasis field before?"

Thoughts of Gamma 5 flashed through my poor brain, "I've had some experience."

"Under the screen are a set of three buttons, the one on the left will activate the stasis field. But..."

"I don't want to hear any 'buts', Lydia."

She took a breath, "But...these sleds have a limited capacity to power a stasis field at full capacity. Usually it functions as added protection during travel, half power is more than enough – a stasis field at half power will protect the occupants from a sudden crash at any speed. It draws full power automatically on impact which prevents any real damage. The thing is, this surge of power is only needed for a brief moment of impact, even the longest accident is over in less than a minute. Going through atmosphere is another story."

"I'm sure I going to love this story," I said. Sarcasm again.

"Surviving atmosphere means having the field at high power for a long and sustained amount of time, possibly up to seven or eight minutes. No stasis field on a sled that size could cope with that sort of power drain. The Drop Markets on the ship have stasis fields on their couches which could probably handle it. Actually....weren't you the security squad that had to land on a planet in a malfunctioning Drop Market..." She broke off, probably remembering some of the stories circulating after our little adventure, "oh...."

Magic stepped into the social awkwardness, "Val knows all about riding a stasis field through atmosphere."

"Good thing we have an experienced man out there," put in Right Honourable.

"Drop dead, Right Honourable," I replied. Pithy, but to the point.

"You will have to ride through atmosphere with just the suit as protection for as long as possible," instructed Lydia. "Only use the stasis field when you have to. And then for as short a time as possible because you will probably need it again when you land. Or crash land"

"No 'or' about it," said right Honourable.

"Right Honourable, I am going to drop you." I threatened.

"Look forward to it, dear boy. Just make sure you come back so you can administer a jolly good thrashing to moi."

"How will I know when I have to turn the stasis field on?" I asked Lydia.

"Your suit will heat up and begin to glow."

"Excellent," I replied. "I wait until I start to cook."

"Something like that, but don't wait too long. When you activate the stasis field the built up heat will stay inside the field and you will continue to cook inside your suit."

Great. The sled started to bounce a little as I hit the outer stretches of atmosphere, I tightened my grip on the control handles and keyed in my communications again, "It's getting hard to control this thing. Any riding tips?"

Lydia came back with a small voice, "It will get very bumpy, Val, you'll have to keep a strong grip on the control handles and not just to keep you on the sled. You also must keep the sled at the appropriate angle as you re-enter. Go in too shallow and you will skip off it like a stone on a pond."

I didn't like the sound of this, "Where will I go?"

"Back into space and heading away from us. No coming back, sweetie."

"Terrific, so I hang on for dear life at the same time as holding the yoke down. I can do that" like hell I could but I could give it a good try. I intended on keeping the handles pushed down as far as they would go – no skipping for me, pal.

"But you can't hold the angle down too much."

A sinking feeling was trying to find space in all of my emotional reactions but fear, terror and panic weren't giving it any room. "Why shouldn't I hold the handles down too much? Tell me, do." The sled was bouncing a lot now, I wasn't even sure if I could hold the controls anywhere I wanted at all. Just hanging on was taking all my grip and concentration.

"If you enter at too steep an angle then you'll burn up. Nothing will stop it; no stasis field could cope with that amount of sustained pressure."

"Peachy," I jammed the toes of my boots under the foot controls, I needed to anchor them somehow or I would fly through the atmosphere hanging on by just the handles. I didn't fancy the visual image of me strung out behind it like washing on a line in high wind. "Any more good news? How do I know what's the correct angle?"

"I don't know, there must be some extra tech on the sled installed by the pirates for just this event, probably some automatic mechanism for piloting the sled down so the pilot isn't put under stress."

"Fabulous," I replied, this was some long awaited good news. "How do I turn it on?"

"I don't know, Val. It's not a normal piece of gear for our sleds, it could be a button, a lever, it could even be hidden somewhere."

"What do I do? How do I fly this thing down given I have no experience, knowledge or desire to do so." If it was a horse, I'd shoot it.

"Keep the other sled in view and follow it as closely as you can, that's the best path of re-entry. Move away from it too far and you'll either bounce or burn."

"'Bounce or burn'? This is the sort of language you use to a man trying to ride a hunk of metal onto a planet. A few words to give hope, please, sweetie?"

"Let's keep your personal life out of this, Val," said Right Honourable.

"Val...," started my girl.

My sinking feeling finally got a bit of space, "There's more?"

"We're going to lose communication when you hit thick atmosphere, the suit radios can't punch through the ozone layer."

"Have I got an ozone layer?" I asked. "Sounds like something Meataxe might have. Not me, I have good personal hygiene."

"We've all smelt your personal hygiene," said Right Honourable. "Quite recently, in fact."

"Your days are numbered, sport."

"The planet has an ozone layer, Val. Not you." My girl was at least sounding a little choked up. "Come back to me, sweetie," she whispered.

Not that I needed any more incentive but her last words gave me a warm mushy feeling inside. I hoped it stayed inside, too, I didn't want to wreck another suit.

"That's it, Val," came in Magic, bringing us all back to the here and now. "All you have to do is fly the sled through the atmosphere without getting yourself killed, find the rendezvous point, capture the pirate, interrogate him to find out who's responsible for the mess on the ship and track down the big boss. Shouldn't be a problem for someone with guts and talent."

He paused before continuing, "Since we haven't got someone like that, it'll have to be you."

I didn't say anything. My concentration was being interrupted by hammer blows of wind trying to pluck me from the sled. A gentle warmth was beginning to spread on the front surfaces of my suit.

"Getting hard to control......"

"You're breaking up, Val," came the lovely Lydia's voice.

"Good luck, sergeant," said the Man in Black. He must have listening to everything.

My response was to repeat as many curse words as I could, a nice steady monotone, one word after another.

It's amazing how a bit of good old cussin' can help you through a tough spot.

And I was definitely in a tough spot. My suit was beginning to glow, the sled twisted and turned under my arms. Over and over again the handle would leap up and strike me in the chest then dive away from my hands before lurching off to one side. My arms began to ache, sweat ran down my forehead in waves and dropped off the tip of my nose. Very uncomfortable inside an enclosed helmet. The wind smashed and bashed the vehicle; my arms and the front of my torso began to get hotter and hotter.

"Anyone still there?" I croaked into the radio.

No answer was the stern reply.

And down I went, riding the sled towards a giant lump of rock through a hurricane of wind and force, through heat and pain.

Some guys get all the fun.

Chapter 25

Up ahead I could still see my quarry, his sled was jerking about, I could only hope he was as miserable as I was. If these pirates planned to do this descent with a sled full of cargo, then I say let 'em have it. Poor sods deserved the rewards of their ill gotten raids and suicidal travel methods.

Except, of course, when they picked a ship under the protection of the NightWatch.

I was becoming distinctly warm now and thoughts of cooking inside my armour began to frequent the thinking part of my brain. I had heard stories of the Crusade, of knights dying from heat exhaustion as they wore full plate in the desert. I found I had a renewed and deeper sense of sympathy for their plights.

The decision was when to turn on the stasis field. I could put up with the heat a bit longer but then it would remain trapped inside with me and I would continue to cook. It's all in the timing.

And blind luck.

I needed to get closer to the other sled. Deciding more loss of control couldn't really hurt, I twisted the power grip under my right hand to ramp up the speed. I got hotter but I also got closer – the thought flashed through my mind that only a true imbecile would actually accelerate into a planet.

As I came closer, I could see a blue shimmer around his sled, his stasis field was already on! This was good news because I really needed to get some relief from the pounding I was taking; the bad news was I would need to take one hand off the control yoke to be able to activate my own field. Not that I had a lot of choice, at this speed the wind was almost visible, the pounding immense, my time was short and I started to believe I was a dead man.

I clenched my right hand even harder and willed my arm to become a rigid bar. Slowly I slid my left hand along the control bar and moved gradually to the central console. Then I stopped and waited – for what? I have no idea, a break in the weather, perhaps? The button to active the field was a hand's breadth below my left glove but I had to take my hand off the control stick if I was going to depress it. There's not a lot of choice in these situations - either you do it or you don't. I took a breath, clenched my teeth and buttocks and dragged my left hand through the pounding. I had to lean forward with my whole body to force my hand to stay in front of me, with a snarl I hit the control and the stasis field snapped into being around me.

Marvellously, the buffeting stopped and I found myself in a small island of calm, I could see the edge of the field as bits of dust and muck impacted it. I realised all those little pieces of sediment were until recently hitting me. I looked down and saw my suit, it was covered in a fine collation of tiny impact marks but most noticeable was the soft red glow – the heat.

The heat which was trapped inside the field with me.

Bit by bit I cooked, sweat continued to run down my face and I could feel my feet starting to squelch as my toes became sodden with various bodily fluids; I was a particularly noxious piece of space junk. How things change, a year ago I was happy sitting on a midden heap drinking myself senseless; ah, the good old days. Sometimes we just don't know how good things are until we lose them.

We sped on like this for a few more minutes, the heat inside the suit had started to dissipate, something to do with clever bits of construction and cooling technology, no doubt. I couldn't relax, Lydia had said the stasis field would only be able to stay powered on for a few minutes before failing and when it failed my body would suddenly be confronted by the buffeting of the atmosphere again. The stasis field still allowed me to control the sled, it seemed to cover the saddle I was on, down to my boots and over my hands. My hands, of course, were clenched firmly on both ends of the control yoke. At the moment no part of me was being hit by the wind but how long that would last, I had no idea.

I descended through the cloud cover and erupted into the magnificent clarity of a golden day. The panorama of a planet lay before me, I felt an honest to goodness awe. Below me was a lot of ocean, a beautiful blue, much like earth. Off to the left was the beginnings of a land mass and slowly we edged towards it. The forward part of the stasis field had been glowing for a few minutes; this surprised me because I thought the stasis field was an invisible barrier yet somehow it was heating up. As we burrowed through the last few wisps of cloud I saw bits of atmosphere hit the field and burn away, at one stage I even fell through hail. This was one crazy ride.

But I had to keep the tension on the control yoke- there was probably some countdown timer on the sled to show me how long I had until the stasis field failed but I wouldn't know it if it bit me. I hung on, clenching all parts of anatomy. I'm sure my quarry was having a more relaxed time of it but I was becoming quite exhausted; I knew the moment I relaxed and sat back the field would fail and the wind would pluck me from the saddle. Therefore, I hung on., I did manage to look down at my feet and find a set of straps and plates into which I could fit my boots for added security. I clicked them into place, looked up at the evil sod who had put me through all this and began planning our next conversation – it was going to be painful for him.

The stasis field died. I went from a gentle island of calm and peace back into a roaring wind and a bucking sled. A bit more harsh language seemed to be called for.

We were well and truly over land by now, screaming through the sky at an altitude which brought its own set of accident scenarios. While I was in space, and even during the first part of the descent, all I wanted to do was get down to land. Now that it was a very real possibility, I was having second thoughts. For a start, my idea of landing included a gentle kiss with the soil as I stepped lightly on to the planet. But now I saw the error of my ways, I was going faster than I have ever gone before. I know in the various space vehicles I had endured I had probably gone faster but this time I was right out in the open. Life in the raw. Valentine the bullet.

I could still see the pirate ahead of me but strangely I had lost my desire to speed up after him. My concentration was now taken up with slowing the sled down. I pulled the power back down to a less than maniacal setting and started to give some serious thought to how I was going to bring this big lump of metal to a stop; I still needed to get rid of a lot of speed if I wanted to be able to manoeuvre.

Try as I might, I couldn't get the speed down to what I considered to be a sensible number. My sled continued to bullet after the pirate – so long as he went straight, or reasonably so, I had a chance of having enough time to bleed off more velocity. Naturally, he chose that moment to change direction; he dipped his nose, rolled to the right and started a gentle descent to the countryside. I was still some distance behind him and wondered how he had managed to be able to bring his machine under control so quickly – I daresay skill and experience had a lot to do with it.

He was landing near a small cabin next to a lake. I could see a city in the distance and networks of roads joining up all manner of little farms and snugly places. The lake had small stands of trees nearby, some cosily nudging up to the shore. My quarry's building had a tiny jetty thrusting out into the placid waters and I even saw a cute little sailboat moored ready for some easy pottering about.

I was going to overshoot the whole thing unless I did something clever and skilful. With this thought uppermost, I wrenched the yoke to the right and dragged the sled slowly around until it was aimed at the pirate. I was now even more bullet-like and with about as much control. For some reason my violent twist made the machine even more unstable and it went into a complete spin and I, of course, spun with it. More swearing.

The saving grace of the whole operation was the sled's guidance system. Some safety protocols must have been in place to prevent idiot pilots from plummeting straight down. The sled would not allow me to nosedive directly into the ground. It did, however, allow me to screw up any chance of a gentle landing. The spin, you know. My attempt at reefing the machine around and altering course had the combined effect of changing the final destination of the landing. Now I was merrily spinning out of control in a vicious twirl aimed at the cabin and still fanging at great speed.

This seemed a good time for me to part company with my metallic steed.

I pulled my boots out of the restraints and let go of the control yokes. Part of my brain was asking what on earth I was doing; the rest of it was trying to find a small space to crawl into down near my boots.

When I leaped off, I could watch the sled drop away beneath me. It was a real treat to see it crash through the roof of the cabin, taking out the front wall at the same time. The pirate was very surprised. He may have been unaware of my presence and my pursuit until he turned around and saw my sled destroy his holiday home.

He had cleverly landed his sled on the jetty and casually disembarked when I contacted terra firma. That's not quite correct, I contacted pirate firma. Slammed right into him.

I caught a glimpse of his face – he had removed his helmet – just before my trajectory punched into his abdomen. His face went from mildly curious, skipped past totally surprised and finally settled on bloody painful as, together, we shot off the jetty into the lake. Big splash.

He did, however, drop his helmet, the clumsy sod.

Chapter 26

We hit the water and down we went, sinking merrily. I instinctively took a deep breath and watched my companion try to do the same thing. He struggled because when I hit him, I knocked all the air out of his lungs. His deep inhale consisted of some air and a lot of lake water.

I realised my deep breath wasn't necessary because I was still encased in my spacesuit. Safety first, that's my motto.

As we sank, the pirate tried to wriggle out of my grip. Obviously, he wanted a bit of air but my meaner side was uppermost so I grabbed him around the waist and looked into his eyes as we fell to the bottom. I didn't have a plan, I just don't like pirates. We hit the bottom with him prostrate underneath me, I was able to look into his face and watch the various shades of panic and terror rush across it. His face had a vague familiarity to it but covered as we were in silt and goo, I couldn't see more than his eyes. He finally gave a little gurgle as the last of his air escaped and he went limp, I let him go and struck out for the surface, hoping it was possible to swim in a spacesuit.

It isn't.

But the news wasn't all bad, I could still walk. As I raised myself up to strike out for the surface my helmeted head popped out into the clear sky; we were only submerged because we were both prone. I was able to clamber to my feet and reach down to pull the now unconscious pirate up into the life giving air. I dragged his unconscious body back up on to land and plopped him down on the bank; I sank down beside him and took my helmet off, sucking in huge breathes. I'd had a big day.

My companion was either dead or unconscious; I had plenty of time to get out of my spacesuit. The front was full of little holes and much of the exterior was burned away as a result of my descent.

Finally, I stretched out on the ground and closed my eyes for a few moments. I just needed a small space of quiet, a little bit of time in which the universe was not trying to kill me.

The pirate groaned and threw up some lake water; I sighed and rolled him onto his front so he wouldn't drown in his own liquids. Now that I had a chance to get a decent look at my victim I recognised Jenks, the man who set up deals with Don'elk before fading away into the night. Goody.

While I was there, I decided to get him out of his suit and check him for damage. After a short time interspersed by much frustration due to pulling an unconscious body out of a pair of pants, I finally had him lying on his side in his standard issue, pirate overalls.

With a little time on my hands, I decided to go through his pockets to see what I could find; there wasn't a lot – I took his blaster and what looked like a radio and then decided to take everything. No telling what little widget would be a weapon, or something else to cause me pain.

I looked through his odds and ends hoping for a map or a sign. The big clue which would lead me effortlessly to my goal with minimum of effort and thought on my part. No such luck. He had some emergency food and water – which I consumed – but his coveralls had very little. A very serviceable clasp knife, which I pocketed, and a small pouch containing two of the cylinders they used to inject the nanobots into us. Nothing else.

A rumbling sound drew my attention back to the little cabin in which my sled had taken up residence. Another wall fell away as the vehicle groaned its way further into the cabin. Flames emerged from part of the wreckage.

I dragged his sorry carcass further back up the little slope between the cabin and the lake. Since he was making some retching noises and started to shudder, I decided to hang around before investigating the remnants of the cabin. He rolled on to his stomach and threw up a belly full of lake water, it's amazing how much the stomach can hold. As he lay there groaning, I felt it was time to introduce myself. I walked into his line of vision and squatted down so he could have a good look at me, the long arm of the law. He sure looked a mess, one hand kept clutching his stomach. I guess my arrival had done a bit of damage.

I poked him on the shoulder and introduced myself, "Hello, Jenks. You're nicked, me old mate."

"Who...," he threw up a bit more, fortunately missing my boots. "Who the hell are you?"

"Can it be that you don't remember me? I'm Sergeant Valentine of the Watch, you may recall my handsome visage from our recent discussion in the Chief Trader's quarters. The Chief Trader whom you shot, you horrible little man. We haven't been formally introduced - I work security on the ship you tried to hijack, and you are steaming pile of excrement." I found a dry piece of grass and sat down to make myself a bit more comfortable for the interrogation, we may be spending a bit of time here.

"Bugger off...," I'm just a peaceful fisherman you've assaulted." He clenched his teeth and grimaced in pain, "God, my stomach hurts. What did you hit me with?"

"What, when you were peacefully fishing?"

"What's that burning smell?" He rolled his head back to see his cabin in all its remodelled glory. "Oh, no, what have you done?"

"Why do you assume I was responsible?"

One eye rolled back to give me a jaundiced look – I know that look well, seen it many times. "Oh, all right," I admitted. "It was me. Want me to go and rescue the family jewels or anything? Top fisherman like yourself must have boxes of special lures and hooks and....whatever else you use to catch fish. Can't see the sense in it myself, just sitting with a bit of twine in the water, pretty boring really."

"What are you talking about?" He hauled himself into a sitting position and I noted the way one hand crept towards the pocket which once held his clasp knife.

"Fishing, of course. I thought all you old salts could sit and yarn for hours over technique and tales of the ones that got away. Say, want to see what I caught?" I pulled out his clasp knife and opened it out, "Check this out, what a little beauty. Bet you wish you had one just like it."

"That's mine, you....you..."

"Thief? Is thief the word you're looking for? Bet it is, just bet you want to call me a thief, don't you? Go on, get it out, make yourself feel better." I opened and closed the knife a few times, looked around the area taking in the ambience, "You can feel the serenity here, can't you. Ahh, the serenity." I drifted off into a little reverie.

"What do you want!" he spluttered. "I need help, I need medical attention! Something inside me is broken!" A small moan escaped his lips.

I pulled the injection kit out of my pocket, opened it up and withdrew one of the cylinders, "You know, it's a brave new world where a poor old fisherman, out in the woods, can have a conversation with me, the nasty man from the stars. I know what you're saying because I have lots of little monsters running around inside me – I wonder if you have also had an injection of nanobots? Now why would some poor isolated dweller in the wilds get himself filled with these little things?' I stood up and pointed at our two spacesuits lying near the water's edge. "And what about those things? Do you often go fishing in deep space gear? Hmmm, maybe it depends on what you were fishing for?"

"You've got nothing on me, pal. I can just wait."

He probably could. I was the one running out of time- the cabin was sending up a nice smoke plume and I anticipated the equivalent of a bucket brigade turning up any time. I needed to get something out of this guy; I put the loose cylinder and the pouch back into different pockets, just too lazy to tidy up and put things away neatly.

Time for the old tried and tested interrogation techniques.

"Which finger do you want to lose, Jenks?" I opened the clasp knife out and reached for his hand.

He sensibly pulled it back, "What do you mean? What are you going to do?" His hands were now cowering in front of his damaged midriff, some more possibilities there, I thought.

I yanked his hand back hard, causing him to fall forward onto his face. Now he was lying supine, belly down with me pulling one hand at full stretch out to one side. "I'm going to cut a finger off unless you tell me who's behind the raid on my ship. You remember the ship, big Trading number way up high? You and a few of your dopey mates thought you could just take the whole thing." I spread out his fingers – this all seemed horribly familiar to me – and held the knife blade over the pinkie.

"Now you get one chance to answer and then I cut off this finger. I then ask again and cut off another finger and so on and so forth. Get the idea?"

"Who are you?" his voice had the beginnings of a scream tucked away inside it.

"Now pay attention, fish breath. I've already told you I am Sergeant Valentine of the Watch. Last chance, who sent you up there? Who put the nasty stuff in our injections? Who's behind it all?" I raised the knife in what I hoped was a threatening manner.

It must have worked because he yelled, "I don't know! You can't do this to me!"

I cut off the finger. He screamed.

That's when the local law enforcement arrived.

"PUT. THE WEAPON. DOWN!" boomed an amplified voice. The air was full of machine, some great big airborne beast blasting air and noise over our quiet little lake district. I dropped the

knife and slowly stood up. Using deliberate movements I placed my
hands behind my neck and stood very still. It didn't take a whole lot
of imagination for me to picture nasty, horrible men pointing lots of
big shooty things at me, after all they had just witnessed me chopping
a man's finger off and probably formed the wrong idea about my
character.

The craft landed and several large men in scary helmets and
evil looking guns leaped out to bring law and order to the scene.
One pulled my hands behind my back and tied them together with
something metallic and hurtful. My pirate friend was examined by
another uniformed official, this one had a bag full of bandages and
other medic related tools. He wrapped up the chopped finger and
placed it into a little bag – I assumed he just like to collect body
parts. He also waved something over my recent companion's torso
and seemed surprised when he read the little screen on the device.
He spoke into one of those neat helmet microphones and in a couple
of shakes they had placed my poor injured pirate on a stretcher and
whisked him away.

Maybe Jenks really was badly hurt, just as he claimed. That'll
teach him to have a dishonest face.

"Who are you, ugly?" asked a uniformed thug.

"I think you mean, 'Why are you ugly?' to which I could reply..."
I stopped talking because he hit me in the stomach and I fell down,
after which kicked me. I groaned, it seemed only polite after the
effort he had gone to.

"Pick him up, boys," old gnarly said, "We'll take Mr Bigmouth
back with us and have a little chat about the poor career choice that
is piracy."

Great, mum always told me I should be careful who I hang
around with. I could just see my next conversations with the local law
were going to be riveting and unpleasant.

Hey-ho, it's a man's life in the modern NightWatch.

Chapter 27

I was bundled into their machine with several beefy and smelly types. I felt fairly comfortable because I am reasonably beefy and smelly myself, especially after my wild ride down to the planet. All the strain and tension started clamouring to be dealt with so my brain does what it does best, it turned itself off and I fell asleep.

A finger poking me in the ribs woke me up, the machine didn't have any more feeling of movement so I assumed we had arrived back at base. A large door slid open on the side of the machine and I was tossed out onto the cold, sterile floor where I came to rest facing a pair of large boots.

"Pirate, eh?" said the boots. "I hate pirates."

I rolled over and looked up at some cavernous nostrils several feet above my head, "Me, too. Let's start a club – I get to be president." The boots kicked me hard so I decided to play nice and shut up.

"Throw him in the Confinement Cells!"

My arms were used as handles by a pair of uniformed beefcakes, they hauled me to my feet and dragged me off into a series of corridors. I let my feet drag even though the strain on my arms was considerable; it meant these two space cadets were forced to really put some effort into moving me along and the narrowness of the passageways added to their struggle. I rolled my head to the right and gave the guy a big smile, "How you doin'?" I asked his puffing and reddening face.

No answer. I did the same to the other side and was rewarded with a half-hearted punch to the ribs. "Excellent! Good work, that man." I had nothing else to do so a bit of mild torment seemed called for, "Now try for the upper body, bit of muscle this time."

"Sharrup," he said.

"Aww, you guys..." We entered a room containing doors which I recognise; they were the sort of doors behind which you throw felons or people you wish to be able to put your hands on at a later date. The other giveaway was the iron bars which made up each cell wall and door. Some of these cells were occupied by the normal sorry collection of layabouts who were either too stupid or too slow to make good their escape after performing their crime of choice. I put myself in the 'too slow' category because I was way over my ration of stupid.

They threw me into a cell and locked the door, I knew it was locked because I kicked the front bars and only hurt my foot, this seemed to me to be a good time to come up with a cunning escape plan. Instead, I rolled onto the little cot they had against one wall and fell asleep. I struggle with procrastination.

When I awoke, I hurt more than when I went to sleep, a lot more. Sleep is not the great healer it's made out to be. I swung my legs over the side of the bunk, held my head and groaned. This helped a little, I felt I could make it to my feet and survey my little kingdom as well as check on my peers. The room held six cells, three on each wall; these coppers didn't get a lot of out and out villainy - six cells would only be good for a slow Sunday in a country village back on Earth.

The cell on my right was empty, the one on my left held a figure swaddled in soiled clothes; not filthy enough to be called rags but certainly not their finest hour. He was sitting on the floor with his back against the wall, he raised his head to look at me when I leaned against the bars.

"What are you lookin' at?" he snarled.

"I would have thought that was obvious, sport."

"Go 'way."

"Quite the charmer, aren't you? What are in for, possessing a sparkling personality?"

"H'rumph..."

I gave up on this character, he was no fun. The door to the cell complex opened and we had a new visitor, he was thrust into the cell opposite me with what passed for tender care in these parts; meaning the guards didn't kick him when he was down. Or maybe they kept that sort of treatment for special guests like me.

When the warders left, I had a good look at our new companion, it was my old friend, Jenks. The man I had met so recently, the man whose finger I had cut off as well as breaking a few ribs.

"Good to see you again, Jenksie old pal," I called. "How's that finger?"

He gave me such a look. "I got nothing to say to you."

"Of course, you do. Remember all those questions I was asking? They still need answers. How about we keep going from where we left off? Who hired you guys? Who put the little extra zing into our nanobots? What's your favourite flower?

"What?" he seemed a bit confused, "My favourite flower? What are you talking about?"

"I want to know what to send to your grave if you don't start giving me some answers."

"And how are you going to make me talk? Have you noticed we are a bit locked away, smartarse?"

He had a point. For the life of me I couldn't work out how get my hands around his scrawny neck. If he was in the cell next to me, I might have been able to grab him but across the corridor – no chance. His irrefutable logic forced me into silence.

"Not so chatty now are you, you big lug," he stepped up to the front of his cell and held the bars, one hand had a rather neat bandage around the fingers. "See this," he held up his paw, "Got it sewn right back on. That's how good we are on this planet. Anything you need, we got someone who can do it. Sew back on a finger or hand? No problem!" He threw his chest out a little more, "You spacers think you're just it, moving from place to place in your great big ship! Well, let me tell you you're nothing! Do you hear me? Nothing!"

Some small part of my brain kept my mouth shut.

"Yeah, I might have known," he went on. "You've got nothing to say because you have no idea what's going on. We own you, pal, Grenchkar owns you. We own your ship, your cargo and whatever else we want. You think I'm scared of you? Of you? Don't make me laugh!"

I grabbed my own door bars and rattled them as hard as I could while letting out a loud and positively aggressive yell, "HAR!!"

Jenks leaped back so quickly he hit the back wall of his cell and smacked his head. He yelped in pain and slid down the wall to end up sitting with his legs pulled up to his chest while he glared at me. "You don't scare me," he muttered in a small voice.

No-one really believed him.

He had said the name 'Grenchkar', I now had a clue. My normal practice at this stage of an investigation was to find someone further up the food chain and tell them all I knew. Generally Magic or someone else would then go away and think clever thoughts, I would be brought in again when there was a head to be hit or a door kicked in. I know my strengths.

What do I do now? I had no idea.

We spent the next few hours pacing our cells or snarling the odd threat at each other. My odiferous next-door cellmate finally rose to his feet and began taking a few tentative steps around his small room. Now I recognised his struggle, he was recovering from drug use. He didn't smell of alcohol but there are some drinks with no odour. He could be coming down off something he smoked or injected. He was certainly replete with pong; his body odour could kill a brown dog at thirty paces. Sentient beings have many and varied methods for altering their appreciation of the world. I've been known to have a drink myself.

At one point he leaned against the bars separating his cell from mine and groaned, this is what gave me my clue to his condition. 'Feeling a bit crook, mate?" I asked in a companionable way.

"Hrumph...shut up....," followed by a groan.

Yep, hung-over and feeling bad.

"Stick it out, mate, the day can only get better," I could feel his pain.

The main door to the cell area opened and in walked one of the long-limbed creatures I had first met way back when we were first injected with the nanobots. He came complete with garish colours and long flowing robes; behind him strode my old friend, Policeman Boots, the wonderful man who had shown me such compassion during my arrest.

"Looking good, officer," I beamed, a little bit of ingratiating never hurt. Probably wouldn't help with this character but it cost me nothing, he gave me the look I associate with nightsoil collectors.

"Ahh, Technician Jenks," smarmed Stretch as he greeted the pirate. "I have come to inspect your condition – I believe you lodged a complaint of cruel treatment against the police."

"No, I never did," said Jenks the pirate. "I said this thug," he pointed his bandaged appendage at little old me and I gave them all a shy smile. "This one cut off my finger! He should be arrested!"

We all looked at Jenks for a moment, each of us probably wondering what his mother saw in him. I made the obvious comment, "I am under arrest, you dropkick."

This observation caused him to splutter a few words about prisoner safety, loss of liberty, high handed treatment and other stuff I had heard a thousand times before in my capacity as law enforcement thug.

"Yes, indeed," said Stretch. "Do I understand you have no complaint about your treatment by the authorities?"

I cleared my throat, this seemed to me to be an appropriate time to join the main conversation. "I do," I claimed, pointing at the copper with the big boots. "I'd like to make a complaint against the authorities!" No sense of professional courtesy from me, buddy.

They continued to ignore me although Boots did glare at me over his shoulder. I winked at him, he turned his head back to face pirate, "Last chance, Jenks. Do you want to make a statement to Counsellor Hret'cken here about your treatment?"

"I do!" I tried again. "I want to make a statement."

"No, of course not," stated Jenks. "I just want to go home, back to my quiet fishing cabin and my writings. I am a poet, you know."

I may have gagged a little. Even Boots seemed a little nonplussed by this claim but he came back like a good 'un. "A poet?" he asked.

Jenks tried to look all deeply contemplative as he replied "Yes, a poor, lonely poet. Struggling to get by in a world full of harshness and cruelty." This last phrase was reinforced by a long and meaningful look at me. I could not care less.

Stretch turned to the guard and said, "There being no complaint I now turn the prisoner back over to your authority, captain." I may have to promote Boots from standard issue thug to Officer-grade Thug.

"Prisoner Jenks is now in my custody," replied Captain Boots in a formal voice.

"Are you going to let me go now?" asked Jenks. "I'm just an innocent bystander; I was attacked by this thug!" More pointed fingers at me. A man could get a complex hanging around Jenks.

"Keep it up, buddy," I said, "keep talking that way and I'll come over there and put your finger in a better place. A darker place." I leaned casually against the bars, wondering where this was all going,

I can spot a bit of jail theatre when I see it and Captain Boots was putting on a fine old show.

"Shut up, Valentine," he said. Again, I kept my mouth shut, he knew my name which probably meant he knew a few more things. His next comments confirmed my opinion of his state of knowledge, "Jenks, I am holding you while we examine the contents of your cabin and the sleds found in their proximity. A search of the sled's flight logs reveals their use off-world in the same location as the recently arrived Trading Ship, a vessel with which we have lost contact and suspect foul play. There are also allegations of piracy to be investigated."

Jenks's face was a picture, I blew him a kiss.

"Valentine," continued the captain, "you're coming with me. We need to have a little talk."

I knew this phrasing; it generally meant the one being talked to was encouraged to be full and forthright in all answers or else lose a few body parts. At least, that's my version of a little talk, maybe Captain Boots was full of the milk of human kindness.

Somehow, I doubted it.

Chapter 28

"Okay, Valentine, what's your story?" We were sitting in the captain's office, not a blunt instrument in sight, nary even a hot poker. I can't get used to modern policing methods.

"What do you mean, captain....er..whoever you are?"

"I'm Captain Boaths, I deal with off-world security issues. You're Sergeant Valentine from something called the NightWatch, sounds like a musical act."

"How do you know who I am?"

"Grow a brain, Valentine, we recorded your DNA when you first landed. After picking you up with that worm Jenks we naturally checked your DNA against our records and there you were. Not that hard, really."

"What's DNA?"

He gave me the look I have grown to know and love. "Stop being funny. Now tell me what's going on up in your ship, why we can't raise it and how you came to ride a damned sled down through the atmosphere in one of the most stupid, harebrained, dangerous and risky acts it has been my poor lot to witness? Have I mentioned I think you're an idiot?"

"I'm picking up the subtle vibes, captain. Don't worry, you're not alone. Now, sit back and relax – something hot to drink would be nice – for I have a tale to tell."

We sat there drinking a hot herbal concoction, eating little yummy things wrapped up in pastry while I told him the whole thing – the injections with nanobots, people dying and rising again, Don'elk and the revelations about the pirates, our retaking of the ship and my pursuit of Jenks back down to the planet.

"You're putting me on," he stated as I wrapped up the story. "Dead people rising again? Come on, pull the other one, it's got bells on it."

"I have no idea what you just said but I am telling you the truth. I need to find out who's behind the attempt to hijack our ship."

"What have you got to go on?"

"Not a thing."

He looked at me for a beat. "You're not real good at this, are you?"

There didn't seem to be a lot I could say to refute the allegation, "Any suggestions?" I asked.

He sighed and held up three fingers, "For a crime to be committed there need to be three things – Means, Method and Motive. We must ask ourselves who had the Means to make these nanobots with the Undead twist."

"Sure," I said. "That makes sense. Right......'Means'.... Good." My brain was running on empty.

More sighs from the captain, "Some information about this planet, Valentine; we are very, very good at medical technology. Even so, not everyone in the street is capable of producing nanobots, let alone making the Undead strain. We could probably find out who has that level of skill and the ability to produce it. With some investigating, I think we can do 'means'."

"Terrific!" I said. "Okay, now we need to think about....um.... what was the next one?"

"Try to keep up, Valentine. Once the stuff had been designed and manufactured – the 'means' – we must ask ourselves who could bring it to you in the clinic. Injections like that are strictly controlled, not just anyone has access to off-worlders in a medical institution and certainly not if it is an experimental procedure. This is our 'method'. How are you going to find out who could do that, Valentine?"

"Well," I began, eager to please teacher, "I would, um, go to the clinic and, um, possibly, ask around."

He looked at me slowly, one eyebrow raised, "Just go and ask did anyone slip the illegal injections into your batch. Hands up all those who are guilty – that's your plan?"

"When you put it like that it sounds so tawdry and cheap. Maybe I could be all subtle and clever, ask incisive questions and tease out responses."

We stared at each other for a beat and then both burst out laughing.

"Yeah, righto," I said, wiping an eye, "What's your plan?"

He sat back and smiled a genuine smile at me, "No, your idea's not bad. But we might give you a hand with the questions, maybe work together on it. Okay, we now have Means and Method, let's talk about 'Motive.'"

I leaned forward, "Pretty obvious, I would have thought. Money." I mean, I have known a few psychopaths who kill for fun or fanaticism – memories of Dominic caused me to rub my stomach as I flashed back to his efforts to skin me alive – but generally a killer doesn't wipe out all and sundry unless there is a profit in it. I continued, "Probably doesn't help us a great deal, we are talking about a whole lot of money from the trade goods on board the ship. And the ship itself, it must be worth a fair bit. That sort of temptation would be hard for anyone to resist."

"You make a good point, Val," he said. I noted the chumminess we were building, "But a Trading Ship full of goods would not be an easy thing to get rid of. That's a lot of goods, it would require storage facilities, transport nodes and so on. A big enterprise. I might narrow the search parameters - but we need more information otherwise all we have is blundering around. Do you have any leads at all, any clues?"

Blundering around was my modus operandi but I suspected the captain required a more balanced approach.

"I'm clueless, captain."

He opened a drawer in his desk and took out a box. "These are yours, let's go and have another talk with Jenks see what we can find out."

I opened the box and saw my weapons, the pouch, the loose cylinder and assorted bits of debris from my pockets.

We walked back to the cell area. As we wandered along, I broke the companionable silence by saying, "You were pretty thorough when you picked us up at the fishing cabin."

"What do you mean?"

"I'm talking about you punching and kicking me during the arrest."

"What's your point?"

"Nothing, but you need to lean into a punch if you really want it to do damage. And your footwork was pretty soft."

He opened the door to the room containing the cells and stepped back to let me enter first, "I'll bear it in mind, thanks for the tip."

"No problem. Professional interaction, cross-fertilisation of ideas. I'm keen to learn."

"How have you lived so long, Valentine?"

"Lot of people seem to be asking me that."

We approached Jenks's cell, he was lying on his cot, sound asleep. "Wakey, wakey, Jenks," I said, "I've come to discuss the placement of your finger. Pick an orifice."

He rolled over and fell off the cot, white froth came from his mouth, "Open the door, captain!" I yelled, "He's in trouble!"

The captain punched a big red button on the wall and lots of things happened. Men rushed in, I was pushed against the wall out of the way and watched some medics examine Jenks. He wasn't dead but he wouldn't be answering questions anytime soon; I decided to give them all more room so I moved back into my recently vacated cell next to the hung-over character. He was standing watching all the excitement, I figured he must have seen what happened.

"What happened?" I asked, keen questioner that I am.

"Didn't see nuthin,'" he replied.

"How'd you like it if I came in there and gave you a good belting?" I asked.

"Probably be an improvement on how I feel now."

"You must have seen something, some visitor who gave him.... something?" A certain sameness was creeping into my vocabulary; maybe I could just hit him.

"You're really crap at interrogation," he said. "No-one came in, you two were the last visitors we had in our happy little hide-away."

I knew I hadn't given Jenks anything. Did Captain Boaths? Maybe he was part of the whole scheme? But then why would he release me? My head was hurting.

"Did you slip him something, captain?" I asked Boaths. Might as well try, I thought.

"Sure, I did, Valentine. I cleverly passed him a nasty poison in my last visit while the councilman stood beside me and took note of all that occurred – but wait, that means he's in on it too! Looks like you've discovered our secret plan, the whole planet is one giant conspiracy against you.

I looked at him blankly for a moment. Was he having me on or was there something to what he said. Had he just outlined the whole plan or...? My head was still hurting.

"Oh, grow up, dimwit," The captain sounded peeved, we were still in our little huddle next to the recovering drunk, Boaths put one hand on the bars and rested his head on his arm. The three of us leaned in to each other. "No, I didn't give him anything," said Boaths. "He could have been carrying it in his bloodstream on a time release, maybe he wasn't searched thoroughly, there's a host of reasons to explain how he got this way."

"He might be just sick."

The captain and I both turned to the speaker, the third member of our little huddle. The little guy smiled and nodded a greeting to captain Boaths.

"Mister Greenash, back with again, I see," said the captain. "Who cares what you think?"

"I'm just saying, that's all," said the prisoner. "He might have any number of sicknesses. Or he could have a few clever nanobots in his system."

My ears pricked up, "Clever Nanobots?" Fiendishly incisive questioning, that's me all over.

"Yeah," said our new consultant. "Nanobots. You know what nanobots are, don't you, Valentine?"

"How do you know my name, smelly?"

"Because I heard old fartface here say it, of course." He leaned in and gave us a whiff of his breath. "And you can leave off calling me 'smelly', it's a side effect of my drug of choice."

I reeled back a little, "What would that be, dead cat puree?"

The captain was made of strong stuff or had no olfactory sense, he stayed where he was and explained, "Greenash here is one of the many recreational drug users we have on the planet. Unfortunately, his 'drug of choice', as he so eloquently puts it, is illegal. It's on the list of minor offences. To balance off the nastiness of its use it does have one saving grace, a peculiar side-effect – the users sweat out the substance over a period of weeks, it is not metabolised in any other way. The downside for Greenash and his chums is the rank odour of their sweat; makes the user stink like week old fish. It also makes them so very easy to find, we just walk through the local haunts and arrest anyone with a peculiar odour; most users have now woken up to themselves and given up or switched drugs. Greenash here, however, is a die hard, stubborn man of the old school. Never give an inch, eh, Greenash?"

"Give us a kiss, captain darling," said Greenash. "You've quite turned my head with your pretty words.

The captain turned his back on Greenash and flicked his eyes up and down my sorry state before saying, "He's right. The guy could have any number of little goodies inside him just waiting for the right trigger to be released; it's expensive and illegal but if you want to ensure your employee's silence and loyalty it's a winner." He crossed his arms and looked into the cell previously occupied by the pirate. "The medics will run a few tests and we might be able to turn them off, our lab people come across this all the time. We just have to hope they can get them all. But Jenks won't be answering questions anytime soon, and this little episode will have told him he is on thin ice if he talks. Looks like you have another dead-end, Valentine. Pity you couldn't get him to say anything."

"What about 'Grenchkar'?" asked Greenash.

"Leave your love life out of this, Greenash," said the captain.

I thought back and mentally replayed my pirate, "Greenash is right, there was mention of something called 'Grenchkar'. Mean anything to you, captain?"

"No, it does not, Valentine, but it might mean something to someone else. We in the trade call that a 'clue', you sorry excuse for a copper. Did he drop any other little phrases that might be of use? His real name? The address of his boss? A full confession?" The captain stood erect and turned to leave, "Come on, let's go and ask around, we'll run 'Grenchkar' through our computers and see what pops up."

Greenash got a word in before we left, "It's a small manufacturing firm out near the harbour."

We turned and looked at him, "Say again, Greenash?" asked the captain.

The smelly man sat back down on the floor and leaned against the wall of his cell, "Sorry, were you talking to me?" he asked, gazing wistfully into space.

"Ha. Ha. Very funny, Greenash," said the captain. He went back to the cell door. "Tell us what you know."

"What's in it for me?" asked Greenash.

This conversation was getting tedious. "Open the door, captain, I'll get some answers out of him," I snarled. "What's in it for you, Greenash? How about the ability to keep walking,"

Chapter 29

Greenash looked at me, swallowed and stood up; he approached the cell door and stood close to the captain for protection, "He can't talk to me that way, Captain, can he?"

The captain remained relaxed, "Whatever do you mean, Greenash?"

I stayed where I was, a little towards the centre of the corridor and about one pace away from Greenash's cell door- I was saving that pace for a sudden rush if needed. I smiled my best smile.

"Here, now just hold on a minute," said Greenash. "There's no need to get like that." He shuffled his feet and breathed visible fumes over the captain; the policeman stood his ground. Very impressive. "What do you want to know?"

"Tell us about 'Grenchkar,'" said the captain.

"Like I said, it's a small business out near the harbour; they make engineering nanobots," said Greenash.

"Nanobots!" I stepped forward, this was the big break! "That's them! They made the little thingies to go into the injections! Case solved, captain – let's get out there and ..." I stopped because the captain and Greenash were giving me the old stare, the one I know so well, the one which means I am the only person in the room not in the loop.

"Every second business on the planet makes nanobots, Val," said the captain. "Nothing special there. How do you know about them, Greenash?"

"I'm a nanobot technician," said Greenash with a touch of pride. Then he slumped, "When I have a job, that is."

"You ever work for these Grenchkar?" I asked.

"No, I was an outsource worker; the agency sent me to fill gaps when there was an absence or sudden increase in workflow for a particular job. Saw lots of companies but never Grenchkar, they seemed a small outfit. I did a short stint at one of their neighbours, that's how I know where they are."

The captain touched a keypad on the wall near the door, a small screen lit up with Greenash's photograph and some markings which could have been writing. "Says here you were found unconscious in an alley last night, still to be formally charged." He typed in some bits and pieces and the cell door opened. "Out you come."

"You mean I can go?"

"Fair's fair," said Boaths. "You gave us some good info, I can take that into consideration and release you for 'information exchanged'."

"You can do that?" asked the newly released prisoner.

"I am the captain of this station, Greenash, and I am sort of a Big deal." He smiled and nodded at the door, "Go through there and have a shower, you stink. I'll arrange some coveralls for you before we burn those rags you're wearing."

Greenash stepped quickly through the door, probably a bit surprised at his good fortune. I wasn't so readily impressed by the milk of human kindness, "What else do you want him to do, you devious man, you?" I asked Boaths.

"I just think Greenash might take us to Grenchkar, our own private guide. Of course, we could find out where they are and send lots of police but maybe we can have a little look at them all quiet like first."

"Why? I asked. "Aren't you a little busy with being Captain Big Deal and doing all leadership stuff? Reading reports and kicking helpless prisoners? Must keep you on the go all the time, how come you can just skive off and go sightseeing?"

We moved out of the cell block room and went back to his office, en route he instructed some uniformed flunky to get Greenash into the shower and then dress him before delivering one clean and fresh smelling prisoner to his office. "Are you going to hang on to a little thing like a kick in the stomach warp your viewpoint on life,

Valentine? Let it go, son, be the bigger man." He looked at me as we entered his office, "I am doing this for two reasons – one, pirates attacking any ship in orbit around my planet upsets my planetary masters. Make that a Trade ship and we have a major problem, in fact you're lucky it's just me coming along and not the Speaker of the Assembly and the entire Cabinet. We can't afford to let word get out that we are a security risk, interstellar trade will evaporate in a heartbeat.

Second, I am bored out of my tiny mind sitting at this desk and third, you are possibly the worst investigator I have ever come across. Finally, letting you loose out there would mean I have to double the size of the security teams just to keep up with the carnage you leave behind."

"That's three things," I pointed out.

"That sort of attitude is just what I mean; I spoke to the Head of Security on your ship after we dumped you in the cell – and after my sub-par kicking performance – and he gave me the highlights of your work in the case so far. How many dead bodies do you think you have left in your wake up to this point? Rough numbers will do."

"You spoke to the Man in Black?"

"No, his aide, Peter something or other. Franz was still interrogating a prisoner."

Bloody Meataxe. "Peter, eh? His aide?" Seems our boy had given himself a promotion. I thought back to our journey through the ship – it could be viewed, in a certain light, as one littered with bodies. I shut up.

The door opened and a clean and pressed Greenash came in, the captain picked up some gear from his desk and gathered us both up, "Come on, Greenash, I'll give you a ride home. Val here can keep us company and tell us stories of lands far away."

Greenash wasn't a dummy, he smelled a rat and looked very nervous but the captain was not a man you argued with. Maybe all captains were like this, must be part of the training.

We climbed aboard a large vehicle driven by a uniformed monster. "This is Sergeant Freznek" introduced the captain, "my personal driver."

Freznek grunted without turning his back - and it was some back. Big and broad – why can't I come across henchmen who are small and weedy? The vehicle moved off using some form of propulsion, I'm not even sure if it had wheels; my life was so different now from the City I just accepted everything around me as normal. Flying dragons would barely get a raised eyebrow.

We moved through the streets and thoroughfares in silence. Greenash fidgeted, I looked out windows at the passing parade while Captain Boaths just gazed ahead. We left the main roads and started weaving in and out of various lanes and alleys; I caught occasional glimpses of water so I assumed we were in the harbour area.

Freznek stopped us in a large parking area near the front entrance of one of the buildings. It had a front door of glass and shiny metal with a small path leading from the parking area to the doors. "Drive us around a bit, sergeant, let's see if we can find a likely candidate," instructed the captain.

There was another grunt before we tootled off around the parking area; we drove past lots of other vehicles – all neatly sitting between markings on the ground which I assumed delineated where one could stop. We stopped near a row of parked vehicles in bays close to the front door, these bays all had solid roof coverings and the vehicles in them looked pretty fancy, even to my uneducated eye. A small post held a metal plate in front of each bay, these plates had scrawls on them which I have come to learn is probably writing.

"What about that one?" asked the captain.

I had no idea what he was talking about so I said, "What?"

"Not you, Val, I'm talking to the sergeant. What do you think, Freznek?" asked Boaths. Our driver grunted again.

"Excellent," said Boaths. "Now to you, Valentine. In the back of the seat in front of you is a small panel, would you open it, please?" I did so, this door revealed a small storage area. He kept talking, "Place your weapons – the blaster and the knife into the locker, please."

"I think not, Captain," I said. "I might need them inside when we start asking questions."

"No, you will not. I will ask the questions and you will be there merely as an observer. Val, the last thing I want is for you to go all violent on me – we are a civilised society on this planet."

"Except for the pirates, you mean."

He sighed, "Yes, except for the pirates."

"And the mad scientists who inject people with infected nanobots."

"Shut up, Val, and put your weapons in the locker or stay here in the vehicle with the Sergeant. I'm going in, come on, Greenash." The captain opened the door and stepped out, Greenash slid across the seat and got out after him. I sulked for a few moments before putting my blaster and the knife into the storage compartment and closing it with a tantrum like 'thunk'. No one took any notice. I gave a deep sigh and stepped out into the warm sunshine.

"Feels a bit strange, walking around without a weapon," I muttered to anyone interested.

"Do you the world of good, Val," said Boaths. "This is how civilised people behave." He strode ahead of us and we trailed along, Greenash nervous and me sulky. Our vehicle moved off on its own mission.

"Where's Freznek going?" I asked.

"We have a little plan for situations like this," Boaths opened the door and gestured for us to enter first. "Trust me, Val." When someone asks me to trust them, it usually means I am going to die.

I became even more depressed. "And trust Freznek, he's been by my side forever," he said.

The front doors opened on to a big, uncluttered area. Off to one side were a set of large glass windows which gave a spectacular view of the harbour. The water looked clean and an array of small sail boats dotted the water. I didn't know whether to admire the boats or the sheer amount of clear glass in the windows; how do they get it so clean and clear? This was not an environment in which I felt at ease.

Comfortable chairs sat next to the windows for those idle moments in life when one wants to sit and gaze at the view. The only other piece of furniture in the room was a bench or desk behind which sat one of the tall, colourful aliens – just like my old pal, Slynkor.

"Good afternoon, sirs, how may I help you?" tall, lean and lanky asked us.

"I am Captain Boaths, these two men are assisting the police in their enquiries." I knew that phrase from both sides of the fence. The captain showed some sort of badge and the cadaverous alien glanced at it briefly.

"I shall summon one of our Media Liaison Team, Captain, I'm sure they can help you. Please have a seat."

"I don't want Media Liaison; I want to speak to the president of the company." Boaths leaned on the desk and showed a touch of his aggressive characteristics.

"Out of the question, captain, and I do not appreciate your attitude. I have called for our own security and legal people – kindly have the good manners to wait."

This seemed to me to be a good time for a hammer, unfortunately I was all out of weapons so I would have to make do. I leaned across the bench and grabbed old scrawny by his robe and dragged him across the desk until he could get a good look at my eyes. We were nose to nose and I was about to launch into some undoubtedly clever and incisive questioning when my hands were grabbed roughly and I was pulled off my target.

Chapter 30

"What do you think you're doing, Valentine?" demanded Boaths. He had my arms twisted behind my back and held by my fingers only. He used one hand to do something very, very painful on these fingers; the pain made my eyes water. This guy had mad skills.

"I was...," I squeaked, "...I was just going to get some answers. What's the problem?"

"You don't treat a member of the public that way!" said the captain. "We are the police, we have laws. We are not a bunch of bully boys!"

Since when, I thought. But I wasn't sure if he was serious or not - he certainly had no qualms about kicking a helpless prisoner when I was arrested. This probably wasn't the time to mention these little nuggets of information.

"We may be laying charges of assault," said a new voice. I looked up and saw we had company – two obvious human thugs in uniform and another tall, skinny alien had entered the fray. The alien had his arms folded and was giving us the old evil eye as he observed our little scene. "You have no right to physically manhandle one of our staff in such a fashion. Please identify yourselves."

Normally at this point, in a standard NightWatch interrogation, we would be heavily into exchanging blows, not ID. As a result of this I was a little out of my depth, if I couldn't hit someone what was I going to do?

The captain let go of me and held up his own hands in a peaceful gesture, "I apologise for my colleague, he is recovering from an injury sustained while fighting off an attempt by pirates to capture a vessel in close orbit. May I ask your name, sir?"

"I am Mr. Sleth, one of the legal representatives of this firm – and I am still waiting on your own identification." He stood and smiled his toothy smile, a smile which would have been improved by a large fist in the face but what do I know? Boaths pulled out his ID again and showed it to Sleth who took it and examined it with great care.

The alien handed back Boaths' ID and turned to me with an outstretched hand. "Do you have any identification, sir? Are you also a member of the police?"

"Well, yeah," I said, "er, that is, no. I work for spaceship security. Um," I pointed to the roof, "up there."

"Can you prove your claim?" he asked.

This guy was good, I was getting all nervous and patting my pockets looking for something which would link me to the ship. My uniform was way back in the past and the spacesuit - the one I had worn in my descent to the planet was still at the crash site. Little beads of sweat broke out on my brow, I'm not good at personal interactions, and pretty sure my idea of conflict resolution differs quite a lot from these guys in legal.

My hand found a bulge in a pocket and I pulled out the object, "I've got this!" I stated, in a clear, rising tone of voice.

We all looked at my hand, in it was the injection pouch I had taken off the downed pirate. Not really much good at all.

I looked up weakly into my interrogator's eyes and found him gazing at the pouch, "Where did you get that? May I see it?" he asked.

I gave him the pouch and turned the brain off – it had given up on the day so I just stood there and waited for what next would happen. Sleth opened the pouch and touched the single cylinder with a thin, bony finger before gesturing over at the waiting chairs and said, "Please have a seat, gentlemen. I'll just be a moment." He turned and left the room.

We sat in the chairs, the two thugs stayed near the reception desk so we were all alone in the waiting area. Captain Boaths leaned towards me and asked, "What's so special about the pouch?"

"No idea," I answered. "I picked it up off the pirate I, er, was talking to when you arrested me at the crash site." Greenash was fidgeting more than normal, squirming in his chair, twisting his fingers in and out so I asked him, "What is it, Greenash?"

"Well, the pouch...it's used to hold the cylinders containing nanobots before an injection. You just press the nozzle of the cylinder against the person's neck and the cylinder does the injection automatically."

"So what?" I said.

Boaths groaned, "If the cylinders still contained nanobots they could be traced back to the place of manufacture. We do it all the time, Val." He leaned back in the chair and gave me a look I was long familiar with. "Do you mean to say you've had this clue with you all this time? I emphasise the word 'clue'."

"Maybe," I said, then confessed, "I guess so."

"I don't know what to make of you, Valentine, you are either the luckiest copper I have ever met or the stupidest. That's two clues you've had – the word 'Grenchkar' which led us here, and now the pouch for the nanobots. If we had known about it back at the station, we could have run tests on it and sewed this case up quickly."

"We can still do that, can't we?" I asked.

"We could," replied Boaths, "except you've just handed the clue over to a complete stranger. We certainly couldn't trust whatever he gives back to us."

At that point Sleth re-entered the room and walked over to us, we stood to meet his toothy grin, "Sorry to keep you waiting, here is your pouch, sir." He gave me back the pouch, now useless as a clue thanks to my dim-witted actions. "I thought it might be one of ours so I gave it to our test centre, a brief examination of the contents shows the nanobots came from another company, perhaps you would like me to supply you with their address?" His smarmy routine was getting on my nerves. "We will be in touch with your superiors, Captain Boaths, when we lodge our formal complaint against this young man and your department. Now, is there anything else I can help you with?"

Maybe you could have a heart attack, I thought. I put the pouch back in my pocket and came up with an idea. I felt quite clever - me, having an idea about the investigation.

"Thank you, Mr Sleth, but we are quite finished here," said the captain. "We will await your communications." He gestured to Greenash and me, "Come along, gentlemen."

I stayed where I was, "Are you sure the nanobots in that pouch didn't come from this company?"

"Very sure, sir. Thank you for coming, have a nice day." He turned to leave.

"To whom did you give the pouch?" I asked. My speech had become very formal, using appropriate syntax and grammar. I was, after all, talking to a lawyer. I thought I sounded all grown up.

"I beg your pardon," asked Sleth, in a voice redolent of ice and cold. He was almost at the door leading to the back of the building, a few more steps and he would be gone.

"I asked you who ran the tests," I took a pace towards him. "When I gave you this pouch it held only one cylinder." I opened the pouch to show its solitary occupant. From my pocket, I withdrew the second cylinder and showed it to all those around me. Sleth looked surprised but recovered well. "What do you think is in this one?"

Sleth looked at the new cylinder, and then shrugged, "I have no idea, and frankly I see no point in continuing this conversation. If you will excuse, me gentlemen, I shall be about my business. Good day to you." And he left the room.

"Come on, boys," said the captain, "time to go." He spoke into his sleeve, "Freznek, bring the car around."

He caught my querying look, why was he talking to his sleeve? I'm not used to someone giving orders to their wardrobe. "Police radio, Val," he explained. "Standard kit."

We left the building and bundled into our waiting police vehicle. As we pulled away, Boaths asked, "Any luck, Sergeant?"

"Just checking now, sir," said Freznek. His gaze flicked from the front window to a little monitor set in the control panel. I was keen for him to keep looking where we were going and not crash into something. "Got one," he said.

"Who is it?" asked Boaths.

There was a pause while he did things with buttons, plus a brief heart stopping moment when he accelerated to overtake a slow, lumbering vehicle. My mouth went a little dry.

"Head of Security," he replied.

"Looks like we're in business," said Boaths.

"Want to tell me what's going on?" I asked.

"The sergeant and I play this little game. I go in and rattle cages and he places a tracker on some likely vehicles. I do my best to be confrontational and unpleasant while upsetting everyone. If we get a good, strong emotional response we find someone will generally leave our interviews and go to make a report to their boss."

"You didn't seem unpleasant at all in that discussion," I said. "Is that your version of being the nasty copper?"

"Ahh," replied Boaths, "but I soon realised I was in the presence of a master of the craft. When you grabbed the receptionist and threatened physical violence, I was able to play another role. I could be Mr Reasonable."

"I'm generally not at home to Mr Reasonable," I said. "I rarely hear him knocking."

He smiled at me like a proud parent, "Who's a good boy, then?" he said. "Thanks to your superior interrogation techniques, we will be able to use the tracker and follow their Head of Security. My bet is he will go straight to some high mucky-muck and tell on you."

"Why wouldn't they just contact their bosses by radio or communicator? Why go to all the trouble of a face-to-face visit?" I asked.

"They could, but then we could be listening in on their conversation, us being a sneaky police state. A personal visit is the most secure way of getting the point across." He had a big smile on his face, clever dick he was. "Your turn, Valentine, where did the extra cylinder come from?"

"It was in the pouch originally, I had taken it out at the crash site and just put it in my pocket while I, er, asked some more questions of the pirate."

"I may have to hit you again Val. Quite hard," he said. "You are very casual when it comes to evidence. That second cylinder could have given us a good lead, especially if it leads back to Grenchkar. Unfortunately, the chain of evidence has been hopelessly compromised, even if it had a big sign saying, 'we did it', it would be inadmissible in a court of law."

"What do you mean 'chain of evidence'?" I asked. The captain explained there had to be a neat and tidy link between evidence and the culprit, able to withstand scrutiny by their legal system.

"Don't you just go before a magistrate and tell them what happened? That's what we did in the City, our courts of law believed the Watch – not a lot of point having someone guard you if you don't trust them."

"What if the guard is corrupt?"

"Of course, we're corrupt!" I said, mildly surprised at his naivete. "One of the perks of being in the Watch."

Greenash joined in, "You mean you took bribes?"

"Well, duh, yes. You don't think we got by on the few coppers we were paid."

"But that's dishonest!" Greenash was struggling with the concept of relative morality.

"But not as dishonest as the ones we arrested. They were the real crooks; plus, we kept the crime rate down to a dull roar. The City survived, and those who were weak and powerless got a fair shake from us."

Boaths mused a moment, "Why didn't you join the pirates, Val. I'm sure you could have got a good share – especially if you helped take out the rest of the NightWatch."

"That'd be wrong, you stick by your mates, Captain. Besides, the pirates I came across were hopeless. I've got standards."

Boaths seemed to see me for the first time. "Just when I think I have you figured out, Sergeant Valentine, you go and say something like that. Amazing." It seemed to shut everyone up, finally the captain broke the silence by saying, "But let's see where their Head of Security is going."

We travelled on for about 30 minutes before Sergeant Freznek said, "We've lost the signal, captain. Their vehicle turned the corner up ahead and then disappeared."

"Think they found the tracker?" asked Boaths.

"Could be," said the sergeant. He turned the corner and stopped speaking because his attention was taken up in avoiding the vehicle parked across the road ahead. We slammed to a halt just missing the other machine. The sergeant and the captain both leaped from the car like startled goats – I suspected this was a bit of police procedure I would have to learn; when you hit a roadblock, get out quick.

Because it was a roadblock, fortunately it wasn't an ambush – there is a difference. A roadblock just blocks the road, an ambush kills you. Got it? Good, let's move on.

Greenash and I emerged from the car and stood beside our two companions in time to hear a voice say, "We'll just add to the complaint I intend to lodge with the police department, this one will be harassment." Sleth moved from the side of the road accompanied by another alien, a Tharl; oh, goodie. "Allow me to introduce our Head of Security, Mr Porthalk. As you may realise now, he is a very good Head of Security – we thought you might enjoy a little tour of the city while my legal team draws up the required papers. They should be arriving at your headquarters about the same time you do."

The captain was seething, I think even the sergeant was doing a slow burn but I didn't know him well enough to predict his moods. Still, if he was any sort of copper, he didn't relish the thought of being made a fool of by criminals like Seth and Porthalk.

"Hey, Porthalk!" I called.

The Tharl turned to me, "Valentine, right?" He held my gaze for a moment before continuing, "Been hoping to catch up with you, I've got a message from Chayla."

I moved in closer to him, "Chayla....Chayla....," I repeated. Name doesn't ring a bell. Did he have any distinguishing marks?" I asked. "Any tattoos?" I was close enough to touch him now, "What about large holes in his stomach – did he have one of those?"

"You....," he snarled. I avoided the stab kick easily enough but missed his follow up punch, it spun me around. I used the momentum to continue the spin and gave him a return slap on the cheek.

He stepped back and laughed, "That's it. A slap? How did Chayla let a tiny insect like you get the better of him? He deserves to be dead."

"Dead like you, smiley. I give you about an hour with that body weight." I opened my hand and showed him a cylinder. "I just injected you with the Undead nanobots. On the ship, the Tharls died first, usually in a lot of pain – you know, thrashing about, biting tongues off and so forth.

Sleth said, "He's bluffing. Leave them, Porthalk. Let's go."

Sergeant Freznek said, "I'm afraid not, gentlemen, your vehicle is unsafe and may not be driven. I've made a call to traffic control and they'll have a unit here within the hour. You're in no hurry, are you, Mr. Porthalk? No pressing deadlines like a medical emergency?" I had to hand it to the sergeant, he was a man of few words but when he said them, they were certainly worth listening to.

"Don't be ridiculous," said Sleth. "The vehicle is fine – you missed us completely. Come, on Porthalk, get in."

The sergeant drew his blaster, "Step away from the vehicle, sir, or I shall arrest you for attempting to leave the scene of an accident."

"What accident?" demanded Sleth. I noticed Porthalk hadn't moved, he just stood there rubbing his neck.

The sound of breaking glass caught my attention, Captain Boaths was walking around Sleth's vehicle smashing everything he could. "This accident," he said.

"You are in so much trouble, captain. This will end your career!" He turned to Porthalk. "Don't be fooled by them, the police are not in the habit of killing civilians."

I smiled at Porthalk, "But I am. Say hello to Chayla for me." I nodded at my companions, "You might want to wait in the vehicle; up on the ship the Tharls died hard." I looked at my watch "You've got about 20 minutes, Porthalk; can we give you a lift somewhere? Somewhere with a cure? Perhaps the place that made these nanobots?"

The tableau held for a few moments before Porthalk snarled at me and moved to our vehicle, "Come on, I'll show you what you need to know – just get this stuff out of me."

"Sergeant Freznek," said the captain, "perhaps you'd be kind enough to remain at the crash site with Mr. Sleth until the Traffic team arrives. I'll drive Valentine and Mr Porthalk to a place of their choosing. Greenash, you come with us, we might need a nanobot technician to help save Porthalk's life."

"Porthalk!" screamed Sleth. "Think! The Syndicate will never forget a betrayal! You'll be a dead man."

"I'm a dead man already with these things inside me!" growled the big Tharl. "This is you're doing, Sleth, you and Slynkor! Well, I'm not dying for you, I can run, I have places to hide."

"Hide!" yelled Seth, "You can never hide from the...," his tirade was cut off by Jencks smacking him in the front teeth with his blaster. I was right, he did look better that way.

"Mr Sleth, sir, are you all right" asked Sergeant Jencks. "I think you've been injured in the accident." He turned to us, "Off you go, captain, I'll take care of this."

Chapter 30

The captain drove while I sat in the back seat with Greenash and Porthalk. The big Tharl had been placed in restraints to stop him from taking over the car in case he suddenly found loyalty to his old firm. We careened around roads with lights flashing and a big siren making enough noise to wake the dead. I said as much to Porthalk but he didn't seem to appreciate the reference to waking the dead. No sense of humour, these Tharls.

"We're not going back through the front door, Porthalk," said the captain. Show us another way in, you're Head of Security, you must have a way in and out for the odd emergency or bit of private nastiness."

Porthalk gave directions and we moved back into the harbour area as the afternoon faded and sunset sparkled across the bay. We pulled up next to a small shop front. "We go in here," said the Tharl. "In the back room is a hidden door which leads to a storeroom inside Grenchkar."

"Will Slynkor be in the building?" I asked.

"Sure to be, he's always tinkering with his nanobots," said Porthalk.

"What's this 'Syndicate' Sleth mentioned?" I asked.

This question shut the Tharl up, finally he said, "Forget that. If I live through this, I'll need some leverage to keep going but if I tell you guys about the Syndicate, I'll have no chance."

"Val," said the captain, "in the centre console are some restraints, take them out. We'll need them once we get inside."

I took out a handful of twisty loops made from some sort of tough yet flexible material. I knew how to use them; we had something similar on the ship. "And, Val," went on Boaths, "better get your goodies out of the storage compartment." The night was looking up already.

The captain wasn't finished with instructions, "Greenash, you wait here in the car. See this?" he pointed to a red button in the middle of the console, "If we run into trouble, we're going to need help. You, my friend, you get to come to our rescue – if I give you the signal, push this button."

"What's it do?" asked Greenash.

"It sends an 'Officer in Distress' message out on all bands; you'll be swamped by helpful coppers. Just tell them where we are and they'll come in and get us." I liked the idea of this button; I liked it a lot.

"What's the signal?" asked Greenash. Good thing he was on the ball, I had neglected this bit of information.

The captain just smiled and said, "You'll know." We got out and moved to the door of the shopfront, it was opened by an electronic code entered by a set of buttons on a small panel. "Key code?" asked the captain. The Tharl told him and we were soon inside the store and moving into the back room.

I was walking beside the Tharl and decided to pass the time by annoying him – I am very shallow. "Throat getting dry yet?" I asked.

"Drop dead," he snarled.

"You first," I replied. "It's not a pretty sight, you know. I saw things on the ship which will keep me awake at night." I tried to put a little shiver in my voice.

"Must have been your girlfriend".

This guy was a winner, "Have it your way; just trying to pass the time."

The captain entered the back room, he signalled for Porthalk and me to wait in the main area while he checked things out. After a few moments of silence my Tharl companion broke down, "What's it really like?"

"What's what really like?" I repeated. The shop was some sort of ship's chandlery, all ropes and nautical gewgaws. Lots of technical things showing screens and buttons were mixed up with richly carved pieces of timber. Something here for every sailor. I wandered over and looked at some lumps of metal and wood – presumably for tying bits of rope onto the boat.

"When we die, I mean," he went on. "What happens when the nanobots finally, you know, take over?"

"Yeah, it's not pretty. I locked one Tharl in a cell, he was so scared of turning. He's probably up there now trying to chew his arm off." I picked up a few pieces of wood, moved some displays around to cause confusion for the staff the next day, I'm easily bored.

The captain called us through and we both began to move off into the inner room but the Tharl wasn't quite finished with his line of questioning, "Why didn't you die? Did you get the injections of nanobots?"

I indicated for Porthalk to go through the door first, "I sure did, but it seems they don't kill someone who's spent a lot of time on a planet recently."

The big Tharl stiffened and began to turn back to me, "Hey, wait a minute..."

I hit him in the head with a solid piece of electronic equipment. The gear broke and lots of little components fell over the floor mixed up with pieces of Tharl hair and skin. The big guy looked a bit surprised so I hit him again and his eyes glazed over. As he started to fold at the waist, I figured the piece of gear I was holding had one more kick in it so I smashed it over his descending skull – now about waist height - he was well and truly out of contention now.

Boaths poked his head around the corner, "What's going on..." He stopped when he saw me standing over Porthalk and looked me a question.

I gave him a smile. "Boring conversation."

He sighed; people seem to do a lot of that around me, "Had he finally realised he wasn't going to die?"

"Yep, it took a while and eventually I had to give hints."

"Drag him in here. Tie him up and stuff something in his mouth so he doesn't yell the place down. This is the way into Grenchkar," he pointed at a door at the end of the room. "I'll go through the connecting door and see if I can locate Slynkor's office. You wait for me here and try not to break anything or anyone else."

A few more ties and some rags in the mouth took care of the Tharl. I could see his chest rising and falling so I knew he wasn't dead - Tharls are a bit hard to kill. And I got bored.

I cracked the connecting door in time to see Boaths creeping back towards me along an adjoining corridor. He waved me in and we stood skulking together while he gave me a brief report, "Nothing down there." He pointed the way he had just come from, some elevators and a storeroom. Let's try down this other way."

I followed him and we set off to explore the building. We were in the body of the beast, I tingled with excitement. Or nerves, much the same thing.

We opened a few doors to large rooms and offices but saw no-one else. We began to get a bit more casual and unconcerned as we strode through the building so it was something of a shock to open a door and see Slynkor sitting behind a workbench with an array of tools and instruments in front of him. He didn't seem too interested in anything, however. I was guessing the large hole in his head had caused him to rethink his life goals.

"He's dead," I whispered.

Boaths gave me a pitying look and said, "Really, what was your first clue?" He carefully entered the room. I followed, shutting the door softly behind me.

"Someone beat us to it, Val. But were they stopping us from asking questions or just tying up loose ends as a matter of principle."

I joined the think fest, "What?" I muttered.

The captain began going through the papers on the workbench, riffling through draws and so on – so I started taking the rings of Slynkor's hands. "What are you doing?" he asked.

I stopped, mentally reviewing my actions, "Aren't we robbing the dead? You know, taking what we can?"

He stopped still for a moment, his eyes flicking up and down my face as if seeing me for the first time, "You and me will have to have some long talks after this; talks about policing the citizens." He held a hand up to me, "No, Val, we don't rob victims. I was searching for clues; clues to his killer or this 'Syndicate'. Didn't you do any sort of training?"

I felt a bit embarrassed; Magic had trained us all to look at a crime scene, to smell it and taste it if possible. He had tried to get us to examine a crime, to work out what happened. It had all gone out of my mind until Captain Boaths reminded me of my duty. "Yeah, uh, sorry." I looked at the rings in my hand and thought I still had a few bad habits to get rid of.

One of the rings had a button, I pushed it and it popped open. "Have a look at this?"

We both peered into the little container within the ring, I didn't recognise it but the captain did, "It's an electronic key."

"Is that a good thing?" I asked.

"Could be. Bring it along; let's get out of here and call in the rest of the lads. We have a murder scene now; therefore, we have a reason to come back and tramp around in big boots."

"So, we're taking the rings now?"

"They're clues, dimwit!" He sounded just a teensy exasperated; I was having trouble keeping up with his modern methods. He stuffed a few more things in his pockets so I grabbed all the rings, some tools and an electronic tablet lying on the workbench. "Now what are you doing?" he asked.

"These might be more clues," I replied. I was getting the hang of this clue business.

He rolled his eyes, "Come on." He opened the door and peered into the corridor, "We can't use any of it because we have committed a crime by breaking in here without just cause."

I moved behind him and peered over his shoulder, the corridor was still empty, "What's 'just cause'?"

We ducked into the corridor and moved quickly but quietly back to the hidden door in the store, once inside we both breathed a bit easier. "If you have a good reason," he said, "a legal reason, to enter someone else's property it is called 'Just Cause.'"

"What about just 'cause I want to come in and I'm a big copper?" I asked. "That gets me into places really easily."

By this time, we had secured the secret door back into the Grenchkar facility. We headed back into the front of the shop; I thought I should check on Porthalk.

"No," said Boaths. "If you enter premises and find clues without having a good reason to be there then the other side can accuse you of harassment or of putting incriminating evidence there yourself."

"Naturally," I agreed. "Done it many times. I used to keep some incriminating evidence on me for just such an occasion. Hang on, I want to see if Porthalk's conscious yet."

He stopped. "Are you saying you have wilfully planted evidence?" There may have been a note of mild surprise in his voice.

We reached Porthalk and I bent over, a quick look showed his condition had changed for the worse. "Captain," I said, "I think someone else has been in and planted a few things of their own."

I pointed at the prone Tharl's head, it now had a large blaster hole in it.

A voice from behind the serving counter called out, "It wasn't me! Honest!"

Boaths and I spun about, both of us diving for cover as Greenash slowly stood up with his hands in the air and a worried look on his face.

"Boys," he said. "We've got trouble."

No kidding, I thought.

Chapter 31

I stood up, strode over to our erstwhile companion and grabbed him by his scrawny throat, "What's going on, Greenash?"

"I got scared waiting for you, so I snuck into the shop." He gasped a little so I let him go but kept my hand on his shoulder; all friendly-like. "I felt way to conspicuous sitting in a police vehicle – what if another copper had come along, how was I going to explain what I was doing there." He gave Boaths an accusing look. "And you never said what the signal was going to be, how would I know when to press the panic button.

He had a point, I wondered what Boaths had planned for that event so I joined Greenash in looking questions at the captain. "The button doesn't do anything, Greenash, he said. "I just told you a story to take your mind off the waiting."

"Did. Not. Work." said Greenash. "I had too many things to think about, so I came over here after you guys."

I pointed at the corpse of Porthalk, "What happened here?"

Greenash swallowed, his eyes flicked around the room. I caught some of his nervousness and only stopped myself from doing a quick scan with an effort of will – the little guy's panic was infectious. "Well," he whispered; Boaths and I leaned in, "I came in here and found the big guy all trussed up, he saw me and started grunting and groaning, thrashing around the room. I think he wanted me to untie him. Why didn't you tie him up better, or at least knock him out?"

Boaths looked at me, "Yeah, Val, why didn't you do that?" I saw the man's smirk.

"Who shot him, Greenash?" I asked, at least I could maintain a professional tone in the discussion.

"I heard a noise outside so I ducked behind this counter; someone came in and just walked up to Porthalk and shot him in the head. Just strode right in like he owned the place, took the shot and left; it was all over in a heartbeat." The little guy had managed to lower himself down so he was again behind the counter, big eyes peering over the top and flicking around the room.

"Did you get a look at the guy?" asked Boaths.

"YOU IN THE SHOP!" An amplified voice drowned out all discussion, the front windows of the shop had been showing the dark of early evening but now a strong light blazed through them. These windows were not huge and were mostly covered with shelves and ship-like things. I hadn't given the windows any attention, they hadn't registered since we had come in on dusk and they didn't really stand out.

But now they stood out now, intense bright light blazed into the shop.

"THIS IS THE POLICE. OPEN THE FRONT DOOR. RAISE YOUR HANDS AND STEP OUTSIDE."

Greenash gave a small yell of surprise and bobbed down out of sight. I turned to Boaths and asked, "Friends of yours?"

"I didn't call them," he replied. "But at least they're here; saves me the trouble of calling up support."

"How'd they get here?" I asked. "Have we been set up?"

"Of course, we have, dummy." Boaths adjusted his uniform so he looked more policeman like – not possible. "We've been left in a compromising situation. We'll have a hard time explaining the dead bodies and the fact we were conducting an illegal search. But we don't have any choice." He crossed to the front door, pulled his blaster out and placed it on the floor of the shop. "I do not intend shooting my way out or whatever crazy plan you usually devise."

He gave me a questioning look. "What do you normally do in cases like this, Val? How does the NightWatch solve these problems? A big fight, lots of stabbing and shooting?"

I stayed where I was, "No, our normal procedure is to run away real fast. People get hurt in a fight."

"Incredible," he muttered. Boaths straightened his shoulders, opened the front door and raised his hands above his head. Over his shoulder he called back to me, "I'll talk to these guys, you find Freznek. You can trust him.'"

He stepped out of the shop and a blaster shot punched into his chest, erupting out his back. He collapsed in a heap. I was pretty sure he was dead, most of his back had vaporised.

"CEASE FIRE! SAFE ALL WEAPONS!"

I could hear some mixed shouting and yelling happening outside; Greenash and I stayed behind some shelves and stores.

I was in no hurry to find out why the captain had been shot. I and had no other plan beyond keeping my head out of sight for as long as possible. The noise and confusion from outside died away a little and we heard a new voice booming at us.

"VALENTINE? THIS IS SERGEANT FREZNEK. IS THAT YOU IN THE SHOP?"

At this point I realised a few things; the shot which killed Boaths had come from outside; the police were outside. Ergo, the police may have killed the captain. On the other hand, Sergeant Freznek was also outside which meant either a dreadful mistake had been made and the captain was shot by accident or Freznek was part of the gang trying to do us harm.

Either proposal had merit. Someone coming out of a darkened building where you suspect the bad guys are hiding could certainly be shot by someone who was a bit eager or green. Seen it happen in the City many times, probably done it myself once or twice. A bit of careful talking and gentle behaviour would see us come out of this safe and sound. I could be careful when the need arises.

Then again maybe Freznek was part of the whole plot and we would be gunned down in here or the moment we stuck our heads outside. But Boaths said I could trust Freznek.

Any other options? We could go back into the main building and try to find a way to escape. It might be possible to find an unguarded window and sneak out but then what? I had no contacts, no resources and no friends here on the planet; all my mates were back on the ship – I was alone. Lucky me.

"THE CAPTAIN WAS SHOT BY MISTAKE. I AM COMING IN ALONE, VALENTINE. HOLD YOUR FIRE."

If Freznek was willing to come in here alone it would seem maybe Boaths was shot by mistake. This result helped us but certainly wouldn't do Boaths a lot of good.

"I WANT TO SEE YOUR HANDS, FREZNEK," I yelled. "KEEP THEM HIGH AND KEEP THEM EMPTY. I'M A GUARDSMAN ON THE EDGE!"

I wasn't coming out from behind my boxes for anything, that includes holding a weapon aimed outside door. My head was staying well and truly down. Still, it wouldn't hurt for them to think old eagle eye Valentine was squinting down the sights of a blaster and ready to shoot into the massed ranks of coppers outside.

"Sergeant Valentine...Hey....Sergeant...," I became aware a little voice had been tugging at my ear. Greenash had been trying to get my attention but I guess I had been a trifle distracted. I looked around the room and could make out his darkened huddle behind the next set of shelves.

"What do you want, Greenash?" Outside I could hear a heavy tread on gravel as someone approached the open doorway and the captain's body.

"The one that shot Porthalk?" Greenash was slapping the floor with his hand trying to get my attention, "I've been trying to tell you..."

A figure appeared around the doorway, hands held high and empty, "Valentine? It's me, Freznek."

"It was a policeman!" said Greenash.

"I'm coming in, Valentine" said Freznek.

Freznek stepped over the body of his previous captain and looked down to where I was crouched. He knew I was there because, at Greenash's last statement, I had finally pulled out a blaster and aimed it at the door. Freznek was on his best behaviour.

"You want to put the weapon down, Valentine?" he asked.

"Not particularly," I replied. "How about you keep your hands up and step over here. I may have to shoot you and I want a better chance at your head."

It wasn't hard to spot his nervousness but I give him full credit for ice cold veins. He stepped fully into the shop and moved towards me, "There's no need for this, Valentine, the captain was shot by accident – a rookie outside. He's going through all sorts of misery now and will get more back at the station. Captain Boaths was a popular man.

"Not all that popular," I said. "What happens now?"

"I tell them all is well here, you come out safe." He looked around the room, Porthalk's feet were just visible in the doorway to the next room. "How's the prisoner?" asked Freznek.

"Been better, he's dead," I replied. "You want to give the all clear now, this gun's getting heavy."

He lowered his hands and spoke into his sleeve, "Freznek here. Stand down, send a medical team in."

We were soon joined by crowds of men in angry boots, a team grabbed the captain's body and took it off to a place where all bodies go. While this was happening, Freznek was inspecting the reclining form of Porthalk.

"Did you do this, Valentine?" he asked.

"No, he was like that when Boaths and I came back from seeing Slynkor." I gave Greenash a shut up look.

"Who's Slynkor?" Freznek asked.

"He's another dead body. You'll find him in his work lab next door at Grenchkar."

A new voice joined us, "Dead people seem to gather around you, Sergeant Valentine."

I looked back at the door to the shop and saw another human entering, the rank and file were stepping smartly out of his way. Freznek pulled himself into attention and clenched his fist to his chest in salute. "Commandant!" he said, "We were not expecting you."

The Commandant sauntered over to where we had gathered around Porthalk's corpse. "It has come to my ears we have a rather strange investigation running within the police department. Captain Boaths seems to have taken it upon himself to break and enter various buildings without due process under the law, the complaints are already coming in from very respected members of the legal community. I understand there is also talk of a massive pirate attack on an in-orbit Trader but I have yet to receive a briefing on this matter. I find the concept of pirates, in this day and age, quite unbelievable."

He turned to me and continued, "Now I see an armed alien – that's you, Sergeant Valentine – that has been given extraordinary freedom to run amok within our society. Quite frankly, Sergeant Freznek, if Captain Boaths wasn't dead, he'd probably wish he was."

This guy was a real charmer, I wasn't going to stand for Boaths being spoken about by such a prig. "Boaths was doing his job," I said, "catching bad guys. And who are you, anyway, to be bad mouthing the captain?"

Freznek slammed out a response, "This is Commandant Bras'an, he is the Chief of Police."

"How-de-do, Commandant," I said, my well-developed sense of respect for authority chose this moment to evaporate; maybe I never had it, anyway. "There has, indeed, been a bit of crime on your patch.

Us 'armed aliens' have been fighting off pirates and other murderous types since we first arrived in your fair city. If you are the guy in charge then I guess it's all your responsibility, so how about you stop trying to pass the blame onto the poor dead copper at your feet. How's your day been so far?"

"Sergeant Freznek," said the commandant, his voice had acquired the quiver one gets when speaking while gripped by rage. "Please take Sergeant Valentine and ... he vaguely indicated Greenash, "this person back to your station. It might be best to relieve him of his weapon in case we lose any more of our citizenry.

"Sir!" Freznek thrust a hand in my direction. I gave up the blaster. I kept the clasp knife since it was only for personal hygiene and not really a weapon. To be on the safe side, I neglected to mention it.

"Am I under arrest? Again?" I asked and then added, "Or is it 'still'?"

"No, you're not under arrest. Not yet, but that may change," said the commandant. "I have had a long conversation with your Head of Security on the Trading Ship. He has much to say about you. And your little ways. No charges will be laid but I feel my city will be better served by having you under close supervision to prevent the rest of us from moving through a sea of dead bodies." He glanced around the room, I followed his gaze, took in the body of Porthalk and Boaths. "How many is it now, Sergeant Valentine? How many corpses have you brought to my planet?"

"Listen, pal," I was getting fed up with my day and this officious git. "You want to talk about bodies? Fine, let's do that. Let's talk about your lousy planet sending up pirates to my ship. Let's talk about your planet infecting the people on my ship with something that not only kills them, but then brings them back to life. Let's talk about watching these things eating your fellow crew members. Let's talk about your planet and how it just shot and killed a police officer, the only one so far showing any interest in getting to the reason we are waist deep in bodies! This is your mess, Commandant! Your planet made it! You want to talk! Talk away!"

The room now had several police doing police things, this meant my little tirade had an audience. When I finished my spiel, they were all standing quiet and still, a few eyes flicking between me and the commandant. Freznek was rooted to the spot, I noted his hand had drifted to his holster ready for a quick draw in case I was looking to up the body count. His action caused the last bits of my self-control to go on holiday.

"Back off, Freznek" I snarled, "I'm not about to run amok. But you," I leaned forward and tapped the commandant on the chest with a stiff finger, "have got some serious problems in your department. You want bodies? Fine, next door in a lab you'll find another one, a scientist called Slynkor. He's the sweetheart who gave us all the dud nanobots. I don't see how that could have happened to a sanctioned delegation from a respected Trading Ship without someone inside the police running interference. Factor in the ability to turn a blind eye to a bunch of pirates attacking the ship and you have a major cock-up in your department."

The room was decidedly still now, everyone frozen in tableau as I poked their boss like he was a raw recruit. Part of my brain finally bundled my anger back into its box and locked it away. When reason finally gained the driver's seat, it was taken aback at my effrontery, I held my finger hard against the commandant's chest and contemplated my future in the land of the living, or at least the land of the free. More jail time beckoned.

"Perhaps it was wise to relinquish your weapon, Sergeant Valentine; you seem a little overwrought." The commandant's suggestion was accompanied by Freznek stepping quietly beside me to be an ominous hulk.

"Am I under arrest?" I asked.

"No. As I said, not yet." the commandant replied. He gave me some reflective looks and before continuing, "Your Captain Franz speaks highly of you and your ability to get to the bottom of problems. He does admit your methods can be a trifle...confrontational." He waved the others in the room to keep on at their tasks.

"What now?" I asked.

"You will go with Sergeant Freznek back to the station; we will meet there when we have had a chance to investigate what has happened here. You will stay in the station as our guest and refrain from carrying out your own inquiries. Your methods of policing are somewhat primitive for a civilised society."

Freznek must have sensed a resurgence of my anger, he grabbed my arm and suggested, "Come along, Sergeant Valentine, how about you come with me, sir?" His question was accompanied by the gentle pressure a copper knows how to put on someone's arm, pressure which signals that there will, indeed, be some movement happening. My first reaction was to pull away and break his arm – old habits die hard – but I let him guide me out to a vehicle with Greenash tagging along for the ride.

The journey passed in a fog of anger and frustration as I came to terms with losing Boaths. I had begun to like his style and he seemed to tolerate my own methods. I realised we had been in the early stages of a good, long friendship. And some mongrel had taken that away.

Freznek settled us back in Boaths office; I sat in a chair, leaned back against the wall and closed my eyes. I was emotionally done in – sleep claimed me.

I was brought out of my fug by Greenash tugging my sleeve, we were all alone except for what might have beens.

"Are you alright, Sergeant Valentine? Valentine! Snap out of it, I need to talk to you."

"Shut up, Greenash, I've had a big day."

"I've read Slynkor's case notes. I know how to do it!" He stood up, grabbed me by the hair and shook my head vigorously. The little guy sure liked to live dangerously.

I batted his hand away and let my head fall back to rest on the wall behind my chair, "You know how to do what?"

"I can fix the nanobots, I know how to adjust their programming!"

He said it like it meant something important. "What's 'programming'?" I asked.

His eyes gleamed with excitement - or drug withdrawal. "Your crew! I can bring them back to life!"

Chapter 32

I stood up, knocking over my chair, and grabbed the little guy's shirt. "What are you talking about, Greenash? They're dead!"

"Well, yes," he replied, "and no." Neither of us seemed to notice my tight grip in his shirt or the manner in which I pulled him off his feet. I was looking him in the eye with his toes dangling on the floor.

"Not your actual dead. Not your dead which ends up buried and smelly in the ground. Your guys are more 'sort of' dead," he said. "The nanobots have a subroutine – a set of instructions – which overlays the brain and supplants all controls. The nanobots have been running all the bodies!" He looked at me like this meant something.

I lowered him back to the floor and ran my fingers through my hair; for good measure I dusted the little guy down. "Greenash," I said, "I don't really have a handle on all this 'nanobot' thing. As far as I'm concerned, they are little beasties running around my body with some of them making a nest in my brain. My head hurts when I think about the nasty little things eating me from the inside. For that matter I haven't got a clue about 'subroutines', 'programming' or anything to do with all this stuff. Break it down easy for me."

He looked at me silently before asking, in a gentle voice, "Do you really think there are little monsters in your body? Eating you alive?"

I sat down, putting my head in my hands, "Sometimes. I think I feel them walking around inside me, their little legs and tiny mouths...." I brushed my arms as if I could sweep them off me.

"Oh, Val," he said. He sat beside me and put an arm around my shoulders. "Nanobots are not alive, they are not tiny animals or insects."

"Insects!" I sobbed, raising my tearful face to his. "That's what I feel they are! What happens if they have babies and thousands of them hatch inside me! And they burst out of my cheek and run across my face!"

He gazed at me with a look of total compassion and tenderness. Then he smacked me hard across the face. I think I might have a scar from the blow.

"You dipstick!" he said. "Nanobots are not like living things, they are little machines, they do the jobs we tell them to do. They do not 'nest'. They do not have babies!" He stopped, then continued in self-reflective voice, "Come to think of it, they do reproduce." He hit me again, "But they do not 'hatch'. Get a grip, for God's sake, you big baby!"

I checked my teeth and vision, no permanent damage seemed to have been done. Greenash was obviously feeling very comfortable in our relationship. Or he had a death wish. Still, the little guy was trying to help me come to grips with the concept of little things inside my body. And the slap across the face had definitely helped.

"The nanobots injected into your crew had some instructions," he caught my blank look. "Trust me, Valentine, we can tell nanobots what to do. I'm a Nanobot Technician, I know what I am talking about."

I grunted. He continued, "I read Slynkor's case notes, you had his journal from his workbench. The guy was a certifiable nutcase, but he was also brilliant. He was trying to make nanobots which could be programmed while they were in a body."

I looked at him. He took a deep breath and sighed. "God, you are a relic from the dark ages, aren't you. Look, Val, we can build the nanobots and we can give them instructions, but all this is done before they are injected. Once they go into a body, they are out of our control. Each bunch of nanobots can do one thing and that's all. The ones which regulate the heartbeat or calm brain conditions stay in the body and reproduce so that the condition is always cared for. Others can cure a disease or repair damaged tissues like burns or breakages. Once the job is done, they are flushed out of the system."

He stared at me and tapped my head with his knuckles, "Is any of this getting in there?"

"How are they," I gulped, "flushed?"

"Lots of ways," he said. "Sweat, urine, any bodily excretion."

"Gross," I said.

"Have you been seeing what you do to people who annoy you?" he asked. "I would think a little sweat pales in comparison to the guts you have opened up for inspection." He leaned back in his chair, "How about you grow a pair, Valentine?"

"Don't push it, Greenash," I said, "I'm feeling better. Keep telling me about Slynkor's journal."

He wriggled in his chair, took a deep breath and went on, "While you slept, I read through it and… well, see for yourself!" He held up the tablet thing I'd taken off Slynkor's desk; I'd seen Magic and Teddy Boy using them, it was a reading device and one of these days I would learn how to use them. When I had a spare hour or so and someone wasn't trying to kill me. I knew the guys could read stuff on the small screen but Greenash showing me one of them was about as useful as giving a fish a bicycle.

"What am I looking at, Greenash?"

"See here," he pointed at some squiggly marks. "If we infuse an infected person with this chemical it will interact with the nanobots and negate the critical subroutine."

"Greenash," I felt it was time to bring him up to speed on my abilities, "Start making sense or I will hurt you."

He looked around the room and spotted the lunch tray I had shared with Boaths earlier in the day. "Aha!" he claimed. I folded my arms.

"This stuff!" he said, grabbing a little packet from the food tray. "This stuff will fix them up."

I took the packet and tore it open; it held little white crystals. I wet my finger, stuck it into the packet and tasted the contents. "Salt!" I exclaimed.

"Exactly!" agreed my resident companion. Then he shut up and shared a knowing look with me.

I really, really wanted to hit him.

"The nanobots used by Slynkor had a back door," he said. "They can be deactivated by swamping the person's system with a specific mix of chemicals, the main ingredient of which is salt. Straight salt will cause the nanobots to initiate a shutdown of the host's body while maintaining life functions. In essence, they will fall asleep. If the NightWatch on the ship can force even a small amount of salt into one of your 'undead' – dreadful term, by the way – this will give trained personnel - ahem, me, - time to inject every infected person with a permanent nanobot inhibitor." He beamed at me, "How does that sound?"

"The wee beasties now have doors?" I asked. "Back doors?"

I have to hand it to Greenash, he didn't yell or scream too much. His face went a light red and his eyes bugged out the smallest bit but that was all. You could barely tell he was stressed. Anyway, he went through it a few more times until I got the hang of his message.

"Okay, Val, one more time," he said. "All you have to do is get some salt into the infected person, the nanobots will pick it up from the stomach where it will begin to turn off the subroutines. As the 'bots travel through the body they pass it on to others until all have been de-activated. The person will become unconscious and go into a deep sleep. After I permanently shut down the nanobots, the person will wake up about a day later. Hungry. Very, very hungry."

I understood that word, "They'll be hungry, huh?"

"Yes, the nanobots have been using the stored fats and so on to keep the body going; that's why they want to eat someone else. Given enough time the, er, undead – please get another word -would use up all the excess tissue and begin to harvest the host's critical organs. They would start to eat themselves."

What a horror story, Slynkor had really done a number on us. "What do we do now?" I asked Greenash. The little guy was doing a better job of solving our problems than anything I had done.

"I just need to get to a radio. If we can communicate with the ship I can pass on some instructions – be all over soon."

"Hey, Greenash," I said, putting my hands on his shoulders and looking into his eyes, all manly like. "You pull this off and you'll have a bunch of friends in the NightWatch. Anything you need, come to us."

He got all dewy eyed so I cuffed him on the side of the head, "Don't go all sookie on me, let's get this done."

I opened the door and found a guard there – no real surprise – he jumped a bit when I pushed him in the back. "Get Freznek" I instructed. I know how to give an order - the old hands in the Watch taught me all about tone, demeanour and personal ruthlessness when passing out commands – the trick is to communicate with the other guy's muscles and bypass the brain, it's a neat skill. This guy leaped to attention and saluted me before running off, he was probably a few steps along the corridor before his brain worked out what his body was doing.

When the sergeant arrived, we brought him up to speed on the salt thing, at least Greenash did. They both spoke using words that went over my head before Freznek said to the policeman beside him, "Take Mr Greenash to the radio room, contact the ship and let him give them instructions." He turned to me "How will those on the ship know to trust what we have to say. You were right earlier about the harm this planet has done to the crew up there, they might be a little unwilling to take our word for this cure. Could you go with Mr Greenash to vouch for him?"

"No," I said, "just get Magic on the line and tell him I gave the okay."

"Why should they believe the message came from you?" asked Freznek.

"Give Greenash something yellow to wave and tell Magic that he's a mate of mine."

"Just that?" asked Freznek. "Just wave some yellow cloth and say he is a 'mate' of yours? You think it'll be enough?"

"It'll be enough." We had used yellow scarves before when we needed to identify members of the NightWatch from other guards. Yellow worked for us. Greenash was giving me a wide –eyed look so I cuffed him again, "Make it happen, sport.

"Why don't you just go with him?" asked Freznek.

"I need to go to the sick bay; I think I damaged myself in all the day's excitement. My stomach hurts."

Freznek expressed concern, Greenash raised his eyebrows – this was the first he had heard of any complaint from me. "How did you hurt your stomach?" asked Freznek.

"Let's see," I said. "The day started with me on the ship but under arrest in a cell. I was released and had to fight the first Undead guy – stamped his head flat – then we fought our way through the ship before going outside in emergency suits and finding the Chief Trader's quarters. Fought off a couple of bands of pirates with blasters and knives, got myself dragged along behind a sled and smashed into the spaceship's landing bay when the sled crashed. Next, I piloted a small sled in a space battle against two others, shot one down and pursued the other one through atmosphere and down to the planet. Crashed on the planet, smashed into another pirate and then you guys turned up. Well, you know the rest. So, yes, I'm feeling a bit fragile."

They were looking at me with the look you see in bars when the big stories fly around. The sort of open mouth, incredulous look plus a bit of 'I don't believe you' thrown in. Can't blame them, really.

"Right......" said Freznek, he shook himself a little. "I'll take Greenash to the radio. Sergeant Valentine, you go with this officer to sick bay. And... thank you."

My guide walked quietly beside me through the various corridors, he was very silent and deeply respectful. I can be a real smart-arse sometimes.

He left me in the hands of concerned medical people before he moved off to other duties. The surgeons – or whatever they call themselves - poked and prodded me before murmuring among themselves. Finally, one detached himself from the huddle and said to me, "Sergeant Valentine, we can't find anything seriously damaged, certainly your stomach and internal organs are fine. You do carry a lot of old injuries...." He paused, "....an awful lot. You might want to consider some treatment for the various scars and other, er, odds and ends on your body."

"I'll be right. I earned those scars; I wouldn't want to go looking all pretty and clean – spoil my charm." I stood up and put my clothes back on, "Thanks, anyway. I'll find my own way back to the others."

Once outside the examining room I explored the area and finally found what I was looking for, a room with a guard outside. I strolled up and smiled a hello, "This the pirate they found out near the lake?" I asked. "You know, the one who had a bit of a turn in your cells?"

The guard looked at me the way guards do when they find something unpleasant on their shoe. "Move along, sir. You can't stay here."

"I'm Sergeant Valentine of the NightWatch, helping the police with their enquiries," I said. "Just need to ask our boy in there a couple of follow up questions. Be no time at all."

He folded his arms, sighed and said, "I do know who you are, sir. But no one is allowed in. Order of Captain Boaths."

"Boath's dead," I said.

"I know, sir." You were there, weren't you?"

My fame had spread, "Yeah, he was good man." I peered over his shoulder, trying to see through the little window into the room, "So, is that the pirate? Is he okay?"

"He's fine, sir, they're keeping him here for observations while they make sure all nanobots have been deactivated." He straightened up a little before continuing, "I'm sorry, sir, I have to ask you to leave this area."

"No worries," I replied. Then I hit him.

Chapter 33

My fist caught him square on the jaw after travelling a very short distance with all my weight behind it; he collapsed like a sack of potatoes. The door had a number key code on it and I didn't have the code. But I did have a boot.

A hospital door, even one in a police station, is no match for a man who has had to kick down solid oak doors in taverns and places of ill repute. This particular door sprang inwards and slammed back against the internal wall of the room. A very surprised pirate was lying in bed as I dragged the unconscious guard inside with me; I closed the door and leaned my most recent victim up against it, his weight should keep it shut against a casual push.

The pirate had pulled himself to a sitting position but couldn't do more due to the restraints on his arms. His mouth formed a little 'O' of surprise. I pulled out the clasp knife and ran my thumb down the edge. Giving him my most favourite evil grin, I said "Now then, Jencks, where were we...."

The little bloke fainted.

After slapping his face a few times his eyes opened, "What....what do you want?" he blubbered.

I had been giving this some thought, especially after my talks with Boaths; I needed clues. I wanted to be able to take something back to the Man in Black, an explanation for all the bad things that had happened. It might be that Slynkor had contacted the pirates and set the whole deal up – or vice versa. But someone had killed Slynkor. Someone else was in the mix, a real heavyweight.

And someone had killed Boaths. I didn't buy the "accidental discharge' theory which was coming out. A rookie cop was being set up to take the heat for that shot.

Someone on this planet had the ability to kill high a ranking policeman, coordinate the takeover of a Trading Vessel, steal its contents and then store the massive quantities of goods elsewhere. They had links to the leading members of the medical community, to pirates and to the police.

I was so out of my depth.

This scheme was too big to be just local criminals with no heavy hitters from within the establishment. Back in the City we had City Councillors, nobility and merchants taking casual venality as a matter of course. I was confident that any society, no matter how advanced or civilised, would still be subject to the same temptations for conspiracies and corruption.

It's what I would do if I were in power.

And I was all out of clues except for this poor bedraggled pirate in front of me. All out of clues and soon to be all out of time once my little foray into the secure areas of the sick bay was discovered. I held the knife in front of Jencks, he glared back at me. "Go ahead, do your worst, you don't scare me." It seems the nasty little man had developed a backbone.

I decided to use Magic's interrogation methods and kept my mouth shut. I've seen people wilt under Magic's silences and so I just looked at him. This was a big deal from me, requiring self-control and patience; I suspected my head would explode with the strain.

"Cut off another finger or toe," he said, "I can stand a bit more pain because you won't have much time, I can put up with anything until someone discovers you've done something to the guard and tortured me again. Me, a prisoner. Go on, do something!" he spat at me "I'll use it to get out of here. Police brutality!"

"There is one small flaw in your logic," I said. "I'm not the police."

"That's right," he said, "You're nothing! Just a knuckle dragger. No brains, no idea and no future. Don't you understand, you clown, I can't talk. I still have nanobots programmed to kill me if I talk too much. There you are, some info for free." He lay back down and even seemed to relax. "You lose, Valentine."

He had a point. I couldn't use any of my normal methods of interrogation. Jenks seemed to believe he still had some nanobots inside his body; perhaps the police technicians had missed a few. Perhaps he had some critical ones buried very deep for just such an occasion as this. I understood, after my talk with Greenash, that our wee beasties had instructions; and the ones still in Jencks would kill him if he blabbed. I don't understand how they would know he had blabbed, perhaps they had little nanobot ears.

Don't know, don't care.

The clasp knife folded back into itself easily, I put it away. What to do? I looked around the room. A small container held bunches of little gloves – I had seen the medics put these on when they started treating someone. This made me think of the First Aid courses I eventually took, the techniques of resuscitation and external heart massage. An idea formed inside my sick and evil mind; a nasty, nasty idea.

Sometimes, even I can't stand to be around me.

"You've convinced me, no point asking you any questions," I said as I reached over and pulled a handful of gloves free.

My response seemed to give him pause for thought, "Quite right, no point at all." He couldn't take his eyes off the gloves, "What are you going to do with those things."

"Well," I said, "because of you I spent part of my day in a spacesuit running out of air, it's not a nice way to die. Thought you might benefit from the experience." I wadded a glove up into a ball and stuffed it into his mouth and then used my hands to hold another pair of gloves over his mouth and nose effectively cutting off his breathing. He stiffened and thrashed for a bit before lying still, he fixed his eyes on mine with a pleading desperation. I returned a steady, steady gaze.

His thrashing came back with renewed vigour and I needed to lean my body weight on him to hold him down, this brought our eyes very close. I held his gaze, no smile, no expression from me at all.

Not much from him either. His body lurched against the constraints, he tossed and turned, his back arching and every one of his muscles screaming for air.

Then he died.

I stood up quickly, pulled the glove out of his mouth and slapped his face while pushing his chest. His body heaved and he sucked in some big air, finally his eyes opened and he saw me still there.

"Not good, is it." I asked.

"What do you want?" he croaked, "I can't tell you anything, it'll kill me."

"You mean the nanobots inside you that set off your sickness when you told me about Grenchkar? They're gone, the medics here have worked out a way to stop the subroutines and cancel the programming." I hoped I had some of those words right, it sounded like a believable lie to me.

"I don't believe you" he said.

"Fair enough," I changed my grip on the gloves, "I think you're right anyway, there's nothing you can say to help me. But what you can do," I put the glove back in his mouth, stuffing it in very carefully, "what you can do, is die. I'll keep bringing you back and then killing you again until one time I just leave you alone and you'll never revive."

I killed him again, his bowels emptied and the room filled with his stench.

This time when he came around, he spluttered, "Please! Please, no more! Pleeese......!"

"Lot of folks up on my ship would have liked the chance to beg for their lives, Jenks. You didn't give them that chance – and quite frankly, your begging won't change my mind at all. You're dying here, sport. Goodbye." This time he only wriggled a bit but his eyes stayed on mine until the light faded again.

I pulled the gloves away and hit his chest a few times before going into the full resuscitation process. I pumped his chest, breathed into his mouth and laboured mightily to bring him back from that dark domain. I'd known and used a primitive version of this technique in the City, but usually with a bucket of water and a bound prisoner. Drowning a man a few times can loosen his tongue wonderfully. Of course, a lot of times you get it wrong and end up with a body.

Yes, I am a truly awful man.

He came back again, "I'll tell you anything, please.... please don't do it again..." He sounded suitably weak and desperate; I contemplated giving him one more go round before asking questions but he might not stand another session. These space pirates seemed to be a weaker version compared to the monsters I've encountered on Earth. One guy we questioned lasted about two hours before dying. He didn't talk either, bit of a waste, really.

"You hired Don'elk," I stated. "Who hired you? How did Slynkor get involved? Who's protecting you from the inside? Who's behind it all?"

"I'm a dead man if I talk," he said.

"Probably," I agreed. "You must ask yourself what is certain in this crazy old word. You can be certain I will kill you, no problem there. Against that is the uncertainty you may be killed by others after you talk to me. It all depends on how much misery you want to go through. Ready to go again?" I held up the gloves and he shook his head from side to side.

"No more, please, no more. We were both hired by agencies."

"Pirates have agencies?" This was new to me, "What, like a job placement service?"

"I'm a mercenary. So was Slynkor."

"What agency? How do I find them?"

"You have to come with a recommendation. They're known as Black Hand."

"You're kidding me, right?" I chuckled. "'Black Hand'! Sounds like a bunch of kids trying to act tough." I put the bag back in his mouth. "Not enough, pal. I need more than the name of a silly society."

He gagged and struggled enough for me to think he might be wanting to say something. I took the gag out. "What?" I demanded. "Come on, Jencks, I haven't got all day, I can't hang around forever waiting for you to make up your mind, I'm a busy man. Places to go, people to intimidate."

I leaned forward with the glove and he blurted, "Elector S'eenyur! He's the one you want!"

I must have looked distinctly unimpressed because he went into full babble mode, "He has men inside the Police! I found out by accident in one of the meetings. He set up the nanobots and linked me to the pirates. He has accomplices in the police and ..."

He gurgled, his eyes rolled back and his body slumped limply onto the bed. Seems the technicians had missed a few of the nanobots, if they did any work on Jencks at all.

The door burst open; the guard's unconscious body being pushed roughly to one side as a handful of uniformed gorillas barged into the room. Behind them came the Commandant, one look showed him a dead man on the bed and me standing over him.

"Another corpse, Valentine," he observed.

"What can I say, Commandant. I'm gifted."

"Did he say anything?" asked the Commandant. he did not look pleased but nor did he look disgusted at finding me standing over yet another corpse. Was he mellowing towards me?

"Nope, the nanobots got to him before we could get started," I said. It was time for me to confront a big question about this commandant, "Who are you, sport? Where do you fit into the scheme of things? You act like your someone important, and Freznek bows and scrapes every time you break wind."

"How colourful you are, sergeant," he replied. "I am the planetary commandant of all security forces. Captain Boaths worked for me, he was my number 2. I am," he finished, "the chief copper."

"Ahh," I said. "Am I in trouble?"

"Of course, you are, sergeant. The only question is, how much trouble? You are a violent and aggressive man, but are you also corrupt? Are you, in fact, part of this criminal conspiracy? A conspiracy which has seen an unheard-of attempt of piracy against your ship, a conspiracy which has inserted itself into our medical community and finally, a conspiracy which has seen the death of one of my dearest friends, Captain Boaths. Are you more than just a mindless thug?"

I stood and looked at him, mouth slightly open. He was accusing me of the very allegations I had considered for him. "Do you think I am some sort of criminal mastermind?" I asked.

He laughed, "Good heavens, no. But your superior on the ship, Captain Franz, has impressed me with his intelligence. He is in a perfect position to plan and implement all of these deeds; he could well be the mind behind the scheme, using you as a mere pawn. I suspect you would make and admirable pawn."

This guy was getting on my wick, "Oh, yeah!" I retorted. Not a strong response, I admit, and certainly one which would consolidate his opinion of me. "Well, I'm not." There, that should do it. A telling argument to refute all charges.

"I believe you," he said, causing me some surprise. "Boaths had communicated with me over you and some of the situation, I only wish he had told me what he planned to do. He spoke highly of your decency and integrity. As well as your total lack of discernment in any social situation. He had faith in you, and if he did, then so do I."

Boaths thought I possessed decency and integrity? Since when? He knew of my casual relationship with the truth, my tendency to hit first and ask questions later, my total inability to plan any further than crashing headlong into a situation. He believed in me? I sat down, in dire need of a rest.

"He was my friend, too," I mumbled. "I liked Boaths." Recovering myself, I looked up at the commandant, "I trust Captain Franz, the Man in Black. He's not the bad guy. You," I stood up again, "I'm not so sure about."

We stood like that while Jenck's body was taken away. Freznek stayed near the door, the only other person in the room. Time passed.

Finally, the commandant spoke up, "You will have to go to jail, Valentine. At least while I think what needs to happen next." He took a deep breath, "I, too, will trust your 'Man in Black' and meet with him after the current situation on the ship is resolved."

It looked like I was heading back to the cells for a long, long time. I could see the Commandant coming to a decision. "Your ship has begun the recovery process; we've sent medical teams up to assist the process. We seem to have reached an impasse here; you may have gone too far in your recent actions. Even the high opinion of poor, dead Captain Boaths is not enough to allow you to go free. It is prison and the courts for you."

He turned to Freznek, "Sergeant, arrest Valentine."

Chapter 34

Freznek looked a question at me. "Don't worry, Freznek," I said. "I'll come quietly." He moved to stand beside me with one arm on my bicep. "But," I said, and his hand tightened on my arm, "I will still be investigating. I think the lads in a prison population may be able to give me some background on you and the Commandant here. I'll just see what they think of you both, see if they say you are regular, stand-up guys."

I allowed him to lead me to the door, I came to a stop before the Commandant and looked at him closely. "Because if I find either of you are to blame for my ship, for Boaths or for any of this mess, I will come looking for you."

The Commandant's eyes locked on mine; I stared deep into them. I could not, of course, see any hint of deception there. I could only see eyes. Obviously, I can't tell if someone is a villain or a saint by looking into their eyes! Maybe the Man in Black can, but I work on scaring the shit out of people.

He was tough, he didn't take step back or drop his gaze or any of those actions which betray nervousness. Maybe I was losing my touch. But just before I turned away, I saw his lips thin into a line and he swallowed. Okay, I'll take that. Maybe I got to him a little.

Outside in the corridor, Freznek spoke to me, "God, Valentine, you are some piece of work. Threatening the Commandant! What were you thinking?"

"I threated you too, Freznek," I said.

He made a dismissive sound, "Pfft! You call that a threat? Give me a break. My kids scare me more than you."

We walked for a while, eventually coming to a desk and a place where I would be processed into their penal system. I was almost out of time for questions and needed to know a few things, "If nothing else, what have you done to find Boaths' killer?"

"I told, you," he said, "the shot was fired by a rookie. It was an accident."

Freznek signed something and another guard stepped forward to take me on the next stage of my journey. My time was up. "I was there, Freznek, I was in the room when Boaths was killed. The shot did not come from the police." I had no idea what I was talking about, I didn't see anything but Freznek was not to know. Sometimes, you just throw stuff at the wall and see if any sticks.

At a sign from Freznek, I was stopped and turned back. "Valentine ...," he began, I could see him struggling for words. "Come in here," he opened a door to a small interview room, we both entered and sat at a small, central table. No one else was in the room. We sat in the silence, looking at each other. Finally, he said, "Ask your questions."

"Did you have anything to do with Boaths' death?" I asked. Might as well get that one out of the way.

"No," he stopped and blinked his pain and grief at me. "He was my friend as well as my superior. I didn't see where the shot came from, I was told by others on scene that a rookie policeman had overreacted."

"Did you question the rookie?"

"He was taken by other officers to a secure facility for questioning," he said.

"He's gone, then." More silence.

Decision time. "Boaths said I could trust you," I said.

"He was certainly taken with you," said Frenzek. "You were like a breath of fresh air."

"What do you think?" I asked.

"I think you're a dick," he said.

"What was your first clue?" I said.

"You're sloppy, ill-disciplined and ignorant. You have minimal social skills and a total inability to show any form of subtlety," he said. There didn't seem to be much to add to that little character summary. It was, I thought, quite accurate.

"I wish I could talk to my boss, get his opinion," I said.

"What's stopping you?" he asked. "There's a screen right there on the wall."

The wall held a rectangular picture frame showing an idyllic scene of waterfalls and flowers. Didn't interest me much so I had ignored it. "And this helps me how?" I asked.

Frenzek did things to other things and the picture changed, dissolving into a view of a very surprised Meataxe. I knew he was surprised because his mouth was open and I knew it was Meataxe because his mouth was full of food, some sort of spaghetti, I think.

"Val!" he cried, spitting meat sauce into the atmosphere. He turned his head and sprayed some more, "Hey, guys! GUYS! I've got Val on screen! Tell Magic while I get the boss!" No sooner had he left his chair than Lydia slipped into it.

"Oh, Val," she gushed, "Are you alright? And who's that mean man sitting there? Have you been looking after yourself? I hope those people on the planet are being sensible and keeping you out of trouble, you know how you get. Is that man helping you? Do I have to come down there and speak to people? Because I will. I miss you, sweetie, the place just isn't the same. When are you coming back and oh, here's Magic." She jumped out of the seat.

Weird stuff happened then, Magic slid into the recently vacated seat, leaned forward and touched something. The screen split. I now had two faces staring at me, The Man in Black took up the left-hand side while Magic gazed at me from the right. We all looked at each other in stunned surprise for a few heartbeats.

"How are you going, fellas?" I asked before adding, "... sirs."

The Man in Black came on line first, "Good to see you, Val. Been hearing interesting stories of your adventures."

"Why aren't you dead yet, Valentine?" asked Magic. "You'd better bring us up to speed."

I told them all, very conscious of Freznek sitting and listening. This meant I left the names of Elector S'eenyur and the Black Hand out of my tale. I told them of Grenchkar, the reference to a group called 'The Syndicate' and the death of Boaths. I also mentioned I had questioned Jenks until he died.

"We will miss Captain Boaths," said The Man in Black. "He was a good man, we had spent quite a bit of time communicating together and I believe he was on to something." His eyes flicked to where Frenzek was sitting, "I see you there, Sergeant Frenzek, Boaths spoke highly of you."

"That was my big question, sir," I asked. "Can I trust Frenzek? I believe someone in the police here had a hand in Boaths' death. As well as all the piracy and other assorted villainy." It was a risk, asking this question in front of Frenzek but I thought it was best to get it out in the open.

"What do you think, Charles?" The Man in Black was asking Magic.

"Sorry, Franz, I'm still adjusting to Val using words like 'assorted villainy'. We're obviously paying him too much. In answer to your question - we have to trust someone down there. I spoke to Boaths as well, he was communicating with me every hour about the latest mayhem young Valentine had caused. I believe Frenzek had his confidence."

They both looked back at me, The Man in Black said, "Sergeant Frenzek, we will ask Valentine to work with you. But hear me now, if we find you have played him false there will be consequences. Highly unpleasant consequences. We are trusting you."

At face value, these words do not rank on the Valentine Threat-o-Meter. Hearing one is in for 'Unpleasant consequences' would not cause any hardened crim to flinch for a moment. But this was The Man in Black speaking, this was the man who could face down the Inquisition without flinching, this was the man who could scare anyone in the NightWatch absolutely shitless with just a look. Heck, his words were not directed at me but even so, I felt a chill. Something about the look, the tone of voice and the angle of the forward lean. The man's a legend.

Frenzek gulped, swallowed, and whispered, "I will not let you down, sir."

Bloody hell, I thought, the boss has done it again. Recruited another person into the Man in Black fan club. He just has this way, especially when he says, "I trust you"; drives me up the bloody wall.

We finished the call, Frenzek and I looked at each other. "That's quite the Leader you have there," he said. I could hear the capital 'L'. "And that rather frenzied young lady seems to like you. She doesn't look weak in the head, is she quite well? Your girlfriend, I assume?"

"You betcha," I agreed, hysterically happy over the thought of Lydia and I being an item. "Is this where I get slung into prison, I'm ready for a bit of durance vile."

He pursed his lips, "Yes, you'll have to finish processing here and then be transferred to a proper facility. It will only take day or two at most before I can get you out. It depends on how much assistance I get from the Commandant."

"What do you think of him?" I asked.

"I've always thought he was as straight as they come. But then, I didn't think we had anyone on the force who would assassinate Captain Boaths. Are you sure you didn't get a name from Jencks before he ... before you ... before the end of the interview?"

Here it was, did I trust Frenzek enough to tell him of Elector S'eenyur and Black Hand?

"No, mate, not another word," I said. I'm a mistrustful bastard. But I'm also still alive.

He stood up, gesturing for me to also rise, "I get it, Valentine," he said. "I wouldn't go all the way on a first date, either. Tell me when you feel it's right. A word of warning about prison; we will aim to put you in the low security section. You should only be mixing with traffic offenders and those about to be released. Should be quiet. Should be. But you have upset the plans of the high and mighty, so watch your back."

No worries. They were tossing me into jail and I didn't care. Because I had some clues and a dead copper had taught me how to use clues. Plus, I now had a girlfriend.

I wasn't finished yet.

THE END

| Page

Don't miss out!

Visit the website below and you can sign up to receive emails whenever Terry Hornby publishes a new book. There's no charge and no obligation.

https://books2read.com/r/B-A-ZYBAB-KLWOC

BOOKS 2 READ

Connecting independent readers to independent writers.

Did you love *Valentine and the Undead*? Then you should read *Valentine and the Empire*[1] by Terry Hornby!

Valentine and the Night Watch were never meant for space. They're city guardsmen; men of horses, muskets, cold nights, and bad ale. Not the endless dark of the void.

Now they're stranded aboard a warship the size of a city, arguing with an artificial intelligence that calls itself *Caesar*.

Unfortunately, halberds don't help much when the enemy's wearing armour. The Watch are out of their depth, armed with borrowed guns, facing a battle they don't understand, and trying very hard not to break anything important.

They're not soldiers. They're thugs with a uniform.

Fortunately, they're *very good* thugs.

---

1. https://books2read.com/u/3GolL8

2. https://books2read.com/u/3GolL8

Their orders are simple: don't die, don't touch anything expensive, and try to look like they know what they're doing.

It's all rather busy, really.

And then the Emperor offers them a job.

If they can survive long enough to take it.

www.ingramcontent.com/pod-product-compliance
Lightning Source LLC
Chambersburg PA
CBHW071249250626

47163CB00002B/384